*Mic,*
*Thanks for...*
*we adjusted*
*to the world.*

# GOOD
# INTENTIONS
*Stories by Jeff Lacy*

*Jeff Lacy*

This book is a work of fiction. Names, characters, places, situations and incidents are the product of the author's imagination or are used factiously. Any resemblance to actual events, locals or persons, living or dead, is purely coincidental.

Author's photo taken by Toni Harrington © 2012

Contact author at:  hamletlacy@yahoo.com

For my wife, Jane and my daughter, Hanna
for their love, support, and permission
to go all in and play this hand to write.
To my boys, Noah and Jonathan
who give me great joy in watching
them grow into young men.
To Olivia, my angel baby.
And to my beautiful mother, Nell,
for the greatest gift: unconditional love.

## Acknowledgments

I never could have written these stories without the inspiration of my father, Leonard Wyatt, nor without the help and encouragement of my life coach, Angela Bean.

Nor could I have learned the writing craft without my principal writing instructors and mentors at the University of Nebraska MFA creative writing program: Patricia Henley who set me on the right track my first semester, the nurturing Karen Shoemaker, and Leigh Allison Wilson, who anneals and hones a common pocket knife and returns a shiny new Case. My writing style was influenced significantly by Tom Franklin who inculcated stronger and more specific nouns and verbs over less descriptive and less economical adjectives and adverbs. Fellow Atlanta native, Pope Brock was also helpful when it came to preparing my thesis. A wonderful reader due to his drama background, Pope, I really would like to see you in a gray seer sucker suit and bow tie reading some of your work.

I would not have been allowed to be exposed to such talented mentors without Richard Duggin who saw something in my rough writing samples when I applied for the program. Also, thanks to the MFA program's intrepid Jenna Lucas who patiently held my hand throughout the program in my confusion, misdirection, flailing, inartful inarticulateness , childishness, grumpiness, mania, and depression.

Other instructors in the MFA program were also instrumental in my learning the craft of writing: the groovy and insightful Patricia Lear; the passionate poet, Steve Langan; Charles Fort, whose compassionate and authentic poem about his father will always linger with me. Thanks also Charles for providing entertaining evenings at the Lied as we drew your imaginary dog in laughable situations. Additionally, thanks to the dry humorist and poet, William Trowbridge, known for his *Ship of Fools* collection of poems. His evening readings were better than a stand up comic's. Thanks Bill for the rides in your lime green Volkswagon Bug with the snazzy jazz playing.

Lastly, I would like to thank my friends, the charter students, the first class that went through the MFA program. Also, thanks to the other students that followed us each subsequent semester – the ones I ate meals with at the Lied, participated in workshops, and shared a glass of wine or a beer in the evenings at the Lied lounge. It was a pleasure and privilege working and getting to know each one of you. I am in awe of your talent and accomplishments. The MFA program grows with new students every semester who will, I know, bring increasing notoriety to the program. I count myself fortunate to have attended and graduated.

Willie B. Polite" appeared in *Conte*, "Kylle" appeared in *Sex and Murder Magazine,* "Good Intentions" appeared in *Storyglossia* (recommended reading by *DarkSkyMagazine.com's Dark Sky* blog from March 2011: http://darkskymagazine.com/recommended-reading/), "An Unaccompanied Surviving Rock Star," appeared under the title, "No Unaccompanied Surviving Rock Star," in *Unheard Magazine*, "Riptide" appeared under the title, "Shine On You Crazy Diamond," in *Fiction Collective,* "The Fire Ceremony," appeared in *SNReview*, "A Free Dog Ain't Free," appeared in *The Wrong Tree Review*, "The Probationer," appeared in *Mary Magazine,* and "Looking for Portia," appeared under the title, "Indigo," in *The Legendary*.

# TABLE OF CONTENTS

*The road to hell is paved with good intentions.*
                                    —John Ray (1670)

# LOOKING FOR PORTIA

Poss and I took in the scene through a windshield splattered with bugs and dusted with red clay. He slumped his forearms and hands over the steering wheel and puckered his lips round his toothpick. "All right. You go on up to the front door. I'll be with the car."

I sneezed and blew my nose into a couple of fast food napkins and cut my eyes at him.

"Go on," he said.

Steel cables anchored the trailer home to cinder blocks. Two scavenged cars squatted amongst broken glass, car batteries, rusted gas tanks, drive shafts, axles, busted starters and water pumps, brake pads, and other assorted car parts. Infested about were water-filled tires, mosquito egg hatcheries. A third scavenged car sat on the other side of the trailer, cast adrift in a suffocating sea of kudzu. A grove of transmissions stood on end in front of the trailer, and red transmission fluid leaked on the ground, sweetening the humid July Georgia air. Green mildew mold and rust splotches scabbed the trailer's aluminum exterior. A pile of beer cans grew below one of the trailer's open windows. Dirty curtains drooped, motionless. The only sound was the hovering high-pitched quivering *zizz* of the cicadas.

Poss and I stood outside our county-issued Crown Vic and waited to see if someone would realize we were there and come out of the trailer.

"Poss, hit the horn," I said.

Poss sounded the car's horn.

The shrill of the bugs floated downward as I stepped toward the trailer. About thirty feet or so from stacked cinder block steps leading up to the trailer's door, I heard a low growl. I stopped mid-step, waited, and listened. During a moment when the cicadas were taking a long breath, I put a hand to my mouth. "Hello. Anybody home?"

Two granite dogs with grease-stained backs crawled from under one of the dismantled cars. They were chained to a cinder block propping up the car's front right tireless wheel. The dogs sat, and after a few moments, they stopped growling.

I started moving again toward the trailer, but did not take my eyes off the dogs. A breeze overpowered me with the oily stench of polecat and dog shit.

The dogs stared me down. One dog sneezed and then shook his head, slinging slobber.

I placed all my faith in the chain holding the dogs.

The shrilling vibrated the air. A dog growled when I got within about a couple of bodies' length of the trailer. A step closer triggered both dogs to barking and jerking their chains, rocking their junked-car shelter.

Still, nobody came to the trailer door.

A Confederate flag decal stuck to a window right of the door. Above and below the flag said, "Heritage not Hate".

I put a foot on the first step and the dogs pulled harder against their chain. Their combined strength moved the cinder block anchor away from under the car one slow inch after another. In a fraction, the junker crashed to the ground and the dogs shot toward me. All I saw was teeth. I leapt from the trailer's steps and sprinted toward the Crown Vic. The dogs's were at my knee when there were two explosions. *POP-POP.* I stopped. The echo of the last pop lingered in the air. Then silence. I opened my eyes. The dogs lay behind me, unmoving. I squinted over at Poss. He stood behind the open driver's door holding a .40 caliber Glock.

"Son, them things were just about to eat you up."

The shrilling flowed round me in a deep wave. A woodpecker tock-tock-tock-tock-tocked.

The coil from a screen door expanded and then the door *whapped* shut, and I flinched and almost collapsed at the knees.

"Got-damnit! What the hell is goin' on out here?" A hairy man appeared outside the trailer door wearing only stained Bermuda shorts that his drooping belly pushed down. He stared at the dogs, whose heads lay in a pool of blood. "Booger! . . . Rocky!" He descended the steps unsteadily on bare feet with gnarled black toenails. He knelt beside the dogs and looked up at Poss. "You son-of-a-bitch! You killed my dogs!"

"Whoa-ho there mister." Poss aimed the pistol at the ground. "Them dogs pulled their selves loose from that junker you got over there and started after that feller. If I hadn't of shot 'em, they'd a kilt that boy." Poss holstered his gun.

I was weak kneed and my head was ringing.

The man held one nostril and blew out the open one, and then did the same for the other.

Poss walked over to him. "Mister, I'm real sorry, but I didn't have no choice. I ain't never seen nothin' like what them dogs did, pulling away from that junker."

The man wiped his nose. "Oh the girls are gonna be heart broke."

Poss flinched from the man. I could smell him from where I was standing and was overpowered by the stench of beer, cigarettes, and sweat.

The man swayed and shook his head. "Who the hell are y'all?"

Poss introduced us and told the man I was representing a man charged with some crimes. "We're looking for Portia. We were told she stayed out here."

The man fell to his hands and vomited alongside the dead dogs.

I looked away and walked around our car feeling dizzy, sweat beading onto my forehead.

Poss stood over the man as he heaved a second and third time.

Two young girls about eight and six-years-old stepped out of the trailer door, holding hands, wearing only dirty pale cotton panties, and watched the man retch. Their oily, matted hair clung over pasty shoulders. The scent of burnt marijuana blew from the trailer's door. Poss must've caught it too. He walked toward the girls.

"Girls, go back in the trailer. I told you to stay inside. Now get. Get, I said. And shut the door."

The girls shuffled back in. The trailer's screen door slapped shut behind them. Poss stood at the trailer steps for a moment. He looked at me and shook his head.

The man sucked phlegm deep from his sinuses, gathered it up into the back of his throat, and then spit – not a tooth in his head. He stood slowly, steadying himself with the side of the trailer. Then he hacked up another wad of phlegm and spit again. When he got to his feet, his penis hung out of his unzipped shorts. He smeared stringy drool from the side of his mouth onto his unshaved chin and cheek with the back of his hand.

"Where's them youngins' momma?" Poss asked.

The man hunched over and dry heaved.

"Put your pecker in your shorts," Poss said.

The man spit. He looked down over his belly and tucked his penis into his shorts.

"Y'all trespassing," the man said.

"Yeah, you should call the law out here on us," Poss said. "Well zip it up."

The man wobbled.

"Where's Portia?" Poss said.

"Huh?" His hands tremored. "Damn zipper. Motherfucking zipper." He rested his head on the trailer and dry heaved. "Shit." He spit. Then flung his hands and rubbed them.

"Motherfucking hands. Fucking hands." He plunged his hands between his thighs and squeezed his legs. "Quit shaking got-damnit. Zippers. Fucking got-damn zippers."

"Where's Portia?" Poss said.

"Huh?" The man got the zipper to move. "There." It wasn't all the way to the top, but it was close enough. "There Satan. Now it's zipped." He unleaned from the trailer. Swayed. "You satisfied now, nigger Satan?"

"Portia. Where is she?"

The man tossed his head and flung his hands in the air. "I don't cast my pearls among swine." He held up his palm toward Poss. "I rebuke thee . . . in the name of Jesus thou evil serpent. Thou split tongued demon." Then he started dancing like a chimp and making faces.

Poss lunged and grabbed the man up by the throat with one hand and squeezed.

The man twisted Poss's wrists and struggled to breathe. "You're hurtin' me."

"Not yet I ain't." Poss studied the man. After a moment, he loosened his grip. A few seconds later, he let the man go.

The man sucked in air, grabbed his throat, and coughed. "Where's Portia?" Poss asked.

"Don't know."

"Who do those youngins belong to?"

"They ain't mine."

"Then why you here?" Poss asked.

"Babysittin'."

"You lying sack of . . ."

The man cowered, stumbled back a few steps. "She left with some dude in a black Pontiac is all I know, all I'm gone tell you, nigger. A couple of days ago. She's probably in some crack house some wheres."

"When did she leave?"

"I said I told you all I know. Who cares."

Poss grabbed the man by his wrist, jerked, twisted, and bent his arm behind him, high and beyond where tendons tear and snap, I thought.

The man hollered and bent over and covered his head with his other arm. "I'm being straight with you. I'm telling you, she probably left two, maybe three days ago."

Poss lowered the man's arm a bit. "She left you with them girls?"

The man coughed. The cicadas were at their shrill peak. I was sweating through my clothes and seeing white and blue and pink spots.

"Them girls are supposed to be in school, ain't they?" Poss said.

"I don't know. They been sick."

"Who are you?"

"What's that to you? That ain't none of your business. You need to get on out of here."

Poss wrenched the man's arm up again. "I said who are you?"

"I ain't telling you nothing, you black demon from hell!"

Poss kicked the man's legs out from under him, drew his gun, and pressed the end of the muzzle to the man's ear. He was breathing hard and soaked through his clothes in his own sweat. "There are some folks that got no business walking on the face of the earth, they're so nasty. You're about the nastiest thing crawling I've ever laid eyes on."

The man still had not lost his feistiness. "You going to shoot me, nigger?"

Poss snatched him up. "Nobody would miss your sorry ass, I bet. I ought to feed you to the alligators down home."

The man laughed.

I grabbed Poss's arm. "Let's go Poss. Come on, come on. Let's get on out of here.

"I think we need to feed this sorry fool to the gators, don't you?"

"He's not worth it."

It was all I could do to get Poss to reholster his gun and calm him enough to get him inside the car.

The man pushed himself to his knees, still laughing. He raised his hands. "I rebuke thee, black devil, I rebuke thee Satan, I . . . rebuke thee . . . I rebuke thee Lucifer . . . . Thou split tongue Satan . . . Thou worthless nigger demon. . ."

We got back on the dirt road, leaving the man shouting and laughing, hunkered next to his unhowling dogs. "Thou nigger Satan . . . Thou serpent . . . I rebuke thee in the name of Jesus."

# SOFT ICE CREAM

Donnie and Arreta sat on the sidewalk smoking cigarettes outside his former room at the Silver Lining Inn. He had been staying there a month since being paroled. McDonald's bags and cups scattered their feet. Arreta's six-year-old boy, Taylor, thrilled at his Happy Meal toy. Donnie slurped round a quickly melting ice cream cone, after the boy pushed it sloppily to him. "I no want it no more, Donnie." Arreta stomped on some of the fast food napkins scattered by the wind, spit on them, "Quit it, and let me get this sticky mess you got all over you," and scraped the boy's face, scissoring his legs with hers, cinching his arms against his bowed back, bellows, head shakes.

Travis drove up in his black Dodge pickup truck. He rolled the passenger window down. "Y'all look like yesterday's trash that got thrown out. Damn pitiful." He waved. "Come on."

Donnie stood, crammed the cone in his mouth, dropped his cigarette and mashed it under his boot. Arreta flicked her cigarette into the grass, grabbed Taylor's hand and a soft duffle bag. Donnie opened the front passenger door. Arreta opened the back. They reeked of cigarettes and pot.

"Hey Buddy," Travis said. "Got yourself a toy?"

Arreta lifted Taylor into the truck. Taylor smiled. "Boom, boom. Dis my tluck. Go, go. Vroom, vroom."

"What's that?" Travis said.

"It's one of them characters from that new movie that's out," Arreta said, out of breath.

Donnie hauled himself into the seat.

"How's your momma," Travis asked.

"She's not staying with her momma no more," Donnie said.

"How come?"

"Ah, they got into it again."

"No, she's not staying with her goddamn momma," Arreta said. "She and Taylor ain't staying nowhere right now. We're homeless."

Travis glanced back at Taylor.

"Bernice is pissed because I started seeing him again."

Donnie snickered. He spun sideways and rested his left knee on the seat.

"Crazy bitch." Arreta slipped a cigarette between her lips, thumbed the lighter, but it wouldn't catch. She tossed it out the window, snatched the lighter from the middle console, lit the cigarette, and tossed the lighter back to the console.

Travis pulled into the road.

"She gives me a nervous breakdown," Arreta said, inhaling deeply and blowing. "I can't stand to be around her. We should go back there and shoot her in the face then chop her up and take her down to the lake and feed her to the catfish, or better yet take her out in the woods and burn her or dump her piece by piece in dumpsters from here to Texas."

"My God, somebody's really pissed."

Taylor played in the floorboard. Arreta hit the back of the passenger seat and brought her knees under her chin. "Goddamnit. I can't believe she kicked me out. I'm sure she's got all them social workers out looking for us right this goddamn second."

"Why's your momma all bent out of shape?" Travis said.

"Because she says I'm not supposed to be around him." She pointed at Donnie.

"Yeah, but why? I mean--"

"It'll get me in trouble – with Family and Children Services and the juvenile court. She means she'll get me in trouble with them. Call them on me because he just got out of prison."

"All for that bunch of bullshit," Travis said.

"All for a bunch of bullshit I had to plead to," Donnie said.

"How's your brother? He still in Afghanistan?" Travis said.

"He loves that shit," Donnie said.

"How long has he been over there?"

"Hell if I know. He'll probably stay over there until they bring him home in a body bag or something."

"You should have done that, Donnie – joined the Army." Arreta said.

"Why don't you just shut up," Donnie said.

Travis laughed and slammed Donnie on the back. "Donnie? Shit, he can't follow orders. And he's a total retard with a gun. I'd trust Taylor toting one over him.."

Donnie crossed his arms, leaned against his door. He gnawed on his thumb. "I can handle a gun." He spit out a bit of nail.

Travis looked in his rearview. "What the hell happened to your lip?" He looked at Donnie. "What'd you do that for?"

"I didn't do nothing. She gets them fever blisters," Donnie said.

She huffed. "You can't do that now that you're a felon. You shouldn't of pled."

"If I hadn't of pled I'd still be in prison," Donnie said out his window.

"I think you should of made the State prove its case."

"It wasn't your ass that would have been going to prison if they did," Donnie said.

Arreta sat up between the front seats. "I bet they wouldn't have."

"Well, like I've told you over and over and over, I wasn't going to roll the dice."

"Now you're a felon and not good for nothing. Can't get a job nowhere and--"

Donnie backhanded her, his knuckles splitting her already swollen top lip.

Arreta slammed against the back driver's side window. "Damn you, motherfucker." She folded over Taylor sideways, cupping her lip. "Oh, my neck. My head. I think I'm going to throw up."

"No you're not," Donnie said. "Quit all your drama, damn it."

Travis tossed some wadded fast food napkins over his shoulder. They floated to her like jelly fish and were rough as oak bark to her lip.

"Quit your blubbering," Donnie said. "I didn't hit you that hard. You just keep on running your mouth and keep on running that mouth of yours until . . . You're just like your momma."

She sobbed. "I ain't nothing like that bitch."

Travis laughed. "Like mother like daughter. I'm sorry darlin' but you just don't know when to keep that mouth of yours from pushing, pushing, pushing."

Taylor scrounged off the rear floorboard and under the seats, and offered what paper he found – an empty soft pack of cigarettes, a gum wrapper, an advertisement that apparently had been stuck under Travis' windshield wiper, a couple of receipts, a food wrapper Taylor had smoothed out with leftover dried cheese, and the cigarette she had been smoking that was burning a hole in the floorboard carpet.

"Y'all are sick," Arreta said. "Look at what this boy is doing. He ought not be seeing what y'all are doing to me."

"Well, I'll tell you what," Travis said. "Why don't you let me take Taylor back to your momma's after I drop y'all off. I'll get her calmed down."

"Your Momma loves Travis," Donnie said.

"This is Donnie's deal anyway," Travis said. "You know how these Mexicans are. We don't need any complications."

Donnie faced Arreta. "That sounds like a plan."

Arreta blew a strong stream of smoke.

Donnie said, "We piss off this Mexican . . . . I don't want to even think about it."

Taylor crawled out of the floorboard onto the seat.

Arreta pulled him in her lap and stared out the window. "I want him with me."

"This is ridiculous," Travis said.

"I won't give her the satisfaction."

Travis dropped his duffle on the dresser, unzipped it, and pulled out three semiautomatics. He snapped a loaded clip in one with the heel of his hand, pulled back the slide and let it go. He stuffed the gun in his back waistband and covered it with his shirttail. The others he put back in his duffle bag and he kicked the bag in the corner.

"I hope one of them is for me," Donnie said, bouncing on his toes.

"Don't fool with my bag. I'll be right back," Travis said. "Don't y'all leave this room."

He returned a half hour later with a carton of Newports, a twelve-pack of cheap beer, and candy for Taylor. "Where's Donnie?"

"He walked down to the store. I can't smoke them jail house Newports y'all smoke. He was going to get Taylor a hot dog or something to eat, too."

Travis slammed the door on his way out.

Travis shoved Donnie through the door headlong. He stumbled over the farthest bed, clinging to a brown paper bag.

"You stupid shits," Travis said, after closing the door. I told y'all to stay in the room until I got back. Wasn't that simple enough?"

Donnie said, "I just went--"

"I don't want to hear you no more, Donnie." Travis snagged Arreta's upper arm. "Now you're going to stay out of the way. I don't want to hear you, and I don't want to see you as much as possible. And I'm going to tell both of you right now. If either you fuck's this thing up, it'll be the last, you understand?"

Neither one replied.

Travis pointed the gun at Donnie's head. "I ain't going back to prison."

Donnie ducked, stepped back, and raised his hands. "I hear you, man, I hear you."

Travis smirked at Taylor as he flung Arreta against the wall and put the muzzle of the gun under her chin lifting her to her tip toes. In the same movement he covered her mouth with his hand, muffling her scream. Taylor scrabbled to her, cringed around her legs, bawling. "Look at me. Look at me. If something happens and you get in the way, or Taylor gets in the way you are going to get a bullet under your chinny chin, chin." He pointed the gun at Taylor. "But before you get yours, he's going to get his." Arreta stroked Taylors back.

His eyes were angry slits. His jaws were locked tight. "And Donnie, this deal better go down smooth. Is this Mexican all straight that we don't have all the money, and that the rest will be paid when I resell the meth to my guy?"

Donnie rocked from foot to foot. "Oh yeah, yeah, he's cool, he's cool, Travis. Everything's going to go down smooth. No problems."

Travis lunged and stuck the muzzle in Donnie's eye. He hulked over Donnie. Spittle leaked from the corners of his mouth. "Son, if you're lying to me . . . Goddamnit, Donnie I will have to . . ."

Donnie stammered, "Come on, Travis, man. Please . . . Please . . ."

Slowly, he got hold of his rage. He eased a step back; raised the gun above his head. "Alright. Alright." His breathing came fast and shallow. Sweat poured down his face and neck. It soaked his t-shirt. He peered over at Arreta and Taylor who were huddled in the corner. Arreta screening Taylor, who was crumpled in her lap. Travis crammed his gun in his back waist band and hunched over on the end of the bed nearest the door. Donnie lit a cigarette and sat in the floor. He took too deep a drink of beer. He coughed and sputtered.

Travis stomped to the vanity and stalked around the room gulping down cups of water. He tossed two twenties into Donnie's lap. "Take my truck and feed that boy," he said gruffly. "He's all skin and bones. What do you feed him?"

"He won't eat nothing I fix," Arreta said shyly.

He threw another twenty at Donnie. "Y'all get something to eat at Cracker Barrel and bring us something to go. Fried chicken, green beans, potato casserole. What else, Arreta? I like their baked apples. Yeah, get them, and corn bread, and sweet tea." Travis tossed Donnie the keys. Donnie dropped the catch.

Donnie squat. He reached for Taylor's hand. "Come on Taylor, let's get something to eat."

Taylor wrapped his arms around his mother's neck, burrowed his head in her breasts.

Travis stood over them. "Make him quit that howling before somebody calls the law."

"Shut up Taylor," Arreta said, through her teeth; tears streaking down her panicked face. "Shut up." She dug her fingernails into his skinny wrists and pried his arms apart. "Goddamnit, one of y'all help me before I strangle him."

"This is why I didn't want you bringing him." Travis kicked the bed.

"We ain't got no place to go," Arreta said.

"He's got no business being here."

"He can't go to Momma's."

"It's better than here," Travis said.

She wrapped the boy tightly with her arms. Her eyes were angry and desperate. "They'll take him away from me."

"Donnie, after you feed him, drop him off at Bernice's front door whether she's there or not and take off."

"No. No." She emphasized each word in a rasping pleading sob. "No, don't you do it, Donnie."

Almost inaudibly, Donnie said, "Don't be so rough with him, Arreta, please, please. He's just a little biddy thing that don't understand, and scared to death." He got down on his knees, eye level to Taylor, smiled. "Calm down Taylor. It's okay, buddy. Let's go get us some soft ice cream. You want to do that? Get us some soft ice cream? In a cone? Like we did before?" Donnie acted like he was holding a cone, licking ice cream. Taylor wouldn't budge. "Arreta, just let go of his arms." Donnie licked. "Yum, my ice cream is good. Come on, let's go get us some, okay?" He offered his hand to the boy.

"Da, da, ice tream. I go wid due Donnie." Taylor released Arreta. Donnie combed his fingers through the boy's short hair and embraced him round the shoulder. "Bye, Mommy," he said, stumbling cross footed out of the room, without a whimper about the indentations and punctures in his forearm.

"And you drop him off at Bernice's before you come back. I mean it. He ain't got no business in this mess," Travis hollered. He watched the truck leave the parking lot, secured the chain, turned the bolt. Then he turned, confronted Arreta who was sitting on the floor against the wall with her knees drawn up. "Strip." She winced. "Strip, I said." Back against the wall, she pushed herself to up, staring him down. She slipped her jeans and panties down her legs slowly and kicked them to the floor. She unclasped her hair and shook it loose. While she had her head inside her t-shirt, pulling it off and unhooking her bra, he pushed her onto the bed, and with his rough hands he spread her knees, and kissed up and down the inside of her thighs.

He reached for a cigarette, lit it. "I'm all out of breath and can't move a muscle. Goddamn girl, you take it out of me, every time."

"But you feel good, don't you. It's the best you've ever had, isn't it, baby?"

He inhaled, the ash orange in the dark, smoke exhaled with his speaking. "Every time with you." He pulled her down and kissed her too hard.

She snatched her t-shirt and put it between her legs. She padded into the bathroom and took a steamy shower, washing her hair and shaving with a disposable razor. She dried, applied lotion, put on a fresh pair of panties she carried in a zip loc plastic bag in her purse, a brown leather bag with long straps into which she threw most everything she needed. Then retrieved her jeans on the floor beside the bed and borrowed a t-shirt from Travis.

Donnie and Taylor came in the motel room hollering, "Mommy, we're home." Donnie carried the bags of food and a drink cart with iced teas. Ice cream melted down Taylor's arm. He plodded to his mother, arm extended, holding the cone, ice cream dripping onto the carpet. "Momma, lick, lick, lick."

"Donnie, what were you thinking?" She grabbed a clean wash cloth and turned on the water and wetted it.

"This is his second one," Donnie said.

She collected the cone and dropped it in the bathroom trash can. Taylor bawled. She held the back of the boy's head, opened the wash cloth, and swiped his face. He struggled, buckled to the floor, and began bawling louder. She yanked his hands and wiped. "I won't be able to get him to sleep, now, and I ain't got his medicine in my purse."

Travis woke. "I thought I told you to drop him off at Bernice's?"

"You should have seen the youngin' eat," Donnie said. "Like he was starved to death."

"Now I'll be up with him throwing up," Arreta said.

"We always take him to get soft ice cream, Arreta," Donnie said. "It's what he looks forward to." He grinned.

"Everybody's deserves to have their ice cream, ain't that right Travis?"

Arreta re-soaked the wash cloth in some fresh warm water and swiped Taylor again. "I might as well give you a bath."

Donnie laughed. "We had us a time. Didn't we Tater?"

"Shut up, Donnie," Arreta said. She lifted Taylor under his arms, carried him into the bathroom. He wet himself when she started the water. She almost slipped. "Arms up." He complied. Cussing under her breath, she yanked off his shirt. "Shoes." He wouldn't move. "Stand up. Taylor, I need you to stand so Momma can take off your pants and underwear and shoes." He wouldn't budge. "Quit or I'm going to pop your butt." He covered his ears and wouldn't look at her. She lifted him under the arms and sat him on the toilet cover. He sat with his hands still over his ears, his eyes squeezed shut, his lips compressed. She slipped off his shoes and socks, stood him, unsnapped his shorts, and pulled them down and his underwear. He moved his hands from his ears to his penis and began jerking it. "Taylor, stop." He grunted and kept jerking at his tiny penis. "Taylor, Taylor." He opened his eyes, stepped up and put his penis against her mouth. She slapped his hands and his penis. "Quit. Quit." He put his hands on the top of his mother's head and stepped toward her face. "No, Taylor. This is a no, no." She grabbed his face. "Do you understand? No. You don't do that to Mommy. You don't do that to Mommy." He slung his head out of her grip and stammered in his little voice, "You and Donnie do it." Arreta picked him up under the arms and dipped him into the tub.

Donnie came to the threshold. "I'm going to Walmart."

He startled her. "What?"

"I'm going to Walmart. To get Taylor a pair of pajamas and underwear and extra clothes."

Arreta was curled up with Taylor on the bed near the window watching cartoons when Donnie got back.

"Where's Travis?"

"I don't know. He said he was going to take a walk and smoke. Didn't you see him?"

"No."

Donnie carried a bag and rambled over to Arreta. She didn't get up. He sat on the other bed facing her. "Let me show you the stuff I got."

"Is he asleep?"

Donnie stood over her. "Yep, he's out."

She'd wrapped Taylor in a towel. "I forgot to ask you to get some night diapers. He still wets the bed." She pulled her arm slowly from under his sweaty neck, sat up, bent and unbent the tingling out of it.

"I can go back out. I don't mind."

"Naw, hon', that's okay. I'll just put a couple of towels under him." Her neck cracked like hot grease. She aired her hair to cure its flatness, fanning it with her fingers, then bent her head upside down and shook.

I got him some new clothes for school tomorrow. Won't he like this shirt? Cool, huh?"

"Yeah, he'll think he's hot stuff."

"I got underwear, pajamas, and these socks, too. I thought about getting him a pair of new shoes but I didn't know his size."

"His shoes are fine."

"Well, he got some of that ice cream on them and I wanted to get him an unsticky pair."

"He'll be fine. Thanks Donnie."

He went to kiss her, but she side stepped it. "Not tonight baby. I'm not feeling good."

"Seemed like you were feeling all right for Travis."

She got back in bed with Taylor. "That's none of your business. There's some things we all got to do . . . To survive."

"Better put some more medicine on his arm and wrap it." Donnie said.

Arreta went outside for a smoke.

After a time a key turned the lock and Travis stepped in.

"Where have you been?" she asked.

"I walked down to the store to get some more beer. Donnie, I tried to call you to come get me."

"I was probably inside Walmart," Donnie said.

"What the hell for?"

"Went to get Taylor some clothes. Hey, do you mind if I borrow your truck again for about twenty, thirty minutes?" Donnie asked.

"For what?"

"I won't be long."

Forty-five minutes later, Donnie returned with a pair of white tennis shoes with Velcro clasps and night diapers.

Travis pulled a doubled-up stack of cash from his shirt pocket. "How much I owe you for the kid's clothes and shoes?"

"Nothing. They came from clearance."

"Come on Donnie. You ain't the boy's daddy."

"You ain't neither."

"You ain't got the money to be buying shit. Here's a fifty."

Donnie backed away.

"Here's a hundred," Travis said. "Take it."

Donnie put the hundred in his pocket.

Arreta pushed up to her elbow and rubbed her eye with her palm. "You didn't steal--"

"I ain't gone pay shit from no place if I can help it."

Travis chuckled. "I'll be goddamned." He put his stack of money in his shirt pocket.

Arreta lay back on her side, closed her eyes. "I ain't gone send Taylor to school wearing shoplifted clothes and shoes."

"What do you got to be so high and mighty about?" Travis said.

Salvador, arrived a little before midnight. Donnie introduced him to Travis. Arreta listened with her eyes closed.

The Mexican carried a book-sized package wrapped in a brown paper grocery bag, sealed in brown moving tape. He set the package on the round table at the window. He peeled back some tape and punched a small hole in the bag with a small pocket knife. Travis scooped a sample with his pinkie fingernail, tested it, and nodded. Salvador taped over the hole, picked up the package, leveraged it against his underarm.

"You have the money?"

Donnie nodded.

Travis paid from his wad of cash.

Donnie stood between Salvador and Travis. "There's a little hiccup in the arrangement, Salvador."

"What do you mean?" Salvador said.

Travis looked up mid-counting.

Salvador reached behind his back and pulled out a gun.

Donnie put his open palms in front of his chest. "Now, now, Salvador, we've got most of the money for you right now, and we're going to get the rest for you tonight, I promise. All we need to do--"

"Goddamnit, Donnie," Travis said.

"We've got to sell it to our guy tonight so we can pay you the rest that we owe," Donnie said.

"Jesus Christ," Travis said. "You lied to me."

The Mexican pointed his semiautomatic at Donnie."

Travis picked up the money. "What's wrong with you? You told me--"

"You liars," Salvador said, aiming his gun at them. "This is a set up. Both of you. Police."

"Now hold on there, Salvador," Travis said. "I'm just as pissed off as you are at this lying piece of shit." Travis pulled a knife and slashed Donnie's forehead.

Donnie screamed and grabbed his head.

Arreta yanked the bed sheet off the other bed.

"If I'd wanted, I'd sliced your goddamn neck and you wouldn't be breathing."

Blood ran down like a curtain over Donnie's eyes.

Arreta cut the bed sheet with Travis's knife, wrapped it round Donnie's head.

Taylor sat up, eyes closed, rubbing his mouth. "I got to go potty, Mommy."

"Go ahead, baby. Stay in the bathroom." Arreta led him by the hand and closed the door. She tried to lock him in or jamb the door, but there was nothing from the outside.

"Put your gun down," Travis said.

"You are cops."

"They're not, we're not cops--" Arreta said.

"Does that look like I'm a cop to you?" Travis pointed at Donnie. "I'm sorry for this, this, dick head, Salvador." He looked hard at the Mexican. "I didn't know about this money shortage until just now, either. Just like you. I tell you what. Go with me to sell this stuff."

"No way," Salvador said.

"You want to make your money?" Travis said. "It's the only way."

Salvador held his gun on them. "What is your plan?"

"What would happen if you could maybe double your money?" Travis said. "Would you have to turn that in or could you pocket it?"

Taylor scuffed out of the bathroom and sat, leaning on Donnie. "You bleedin'. Wha you do?"

"I was jumping on the bed like them monkeys and fell."

"Oh. Did Mommy kiss it?"

"Not yet."

"Go ahead Mommy, kiss it and make him be'dur."

Arreta gave Donnie a peck on the temple.

"You don't want to go back to your people empty handed do you?" Travis said. "I don't want you to, 'cause they'll come looking for us, too."

The Mexican stared at Taylor and lowered his gun.

Travis wiped the blade on the bedspread, folded it, and clipped the knife to his waistband. "Don't put this all on me just because of this dumbass."

Salvador squat and wiped Taylor's hair with his hand.

"We'll take Donnie with us," Travis said. "And if you want to kill him, that's fine with me."

Salvador put his gun in his waistband and covered it with his loose shirt. "This your boy?"

"Yes," Arreta said.

He touched his head. "He is sick here, in his head? He sick?"

"Yes."

"He very, very skinny. He not eat?"

"Not much."

"You bring him to my house. My wife feed him. She make him eat. Fill him out. We take care of him." He held up five fingers. "I have five children. All born here." He looked at Donnie. "You his Poppy?"

Arreta said, "No, he's not his father."

Salvador looked at Travis.

"No, I'm not the father, either."

"This not good for him. Marta will feed him. He play with my kids. They good kids. Take him to church." He smiled big. "We treat him like he our own."

"Thank you Salvador," Arreta said.

"Okay, so give me the cash you got." Salvador held out his hand.

Donnie handed him what they had.

"I go with you to sell it," Salvador said. "Who has guns?"

"I've got a 9mm under the seat of my truck," Travis said. "We'll go in it."

"He does not have one?" Salvador asked, pointing to Donnie.

"I don't trust him with one," Travis said.

"I don't get a gun?" Donnie said.

"Hell, no," Travis said.

"Where are we going?" Salvador asked.

"Almost to Chattanooga," Travis said.

"How long will we be gone?"

"Couple of hours."

"Who is this guy?"

"Nobody to treat like we treated you."

"I'm raising the price on the meth."

"Sure, I don't blame you," Travis said. "Donnie, it's coming out of your cut."

"Shit."

"Well, what would you like? Live and take a smaller cut, or take a bullet between the eyes? Your call."

Donnie kept his mouth shut.

Arreta and Taylor went back to bed when the three men left a little before one.

The men returned at four. Salvador slept in the bed nearest the bathroom. Travis shared the other bed with Arreta and Taylor. Travis found a quilt and pillow in the dresser and tossed it to Donnie to fix a pallet on the floor.

Arreta didn't like Travis doing this to Donnie, but there was nothing she could do about it.

Travis woke her naked below the waist. Taylor was asleep against her back. She nudged Travis with her forearm. "No, Travis." He pulled her onto the floor. Her head hit the air conditioner and she blacked out.

She awoke on the floor naked, with a gouging headache; her brain, scrambled eggs. Nauseous and weak, she was splayed at the ass, her insides in shreds.

Taylor was hanging over the bed. "Mommy, Mommy, wake up, wake up. School, school. Mommy, Mommy. Wake up." Travis was snoring. Donnie was on the floor breathing heavily. Salvador was curled up on his side.

She sifted through the whirling blur, plucked her clothes and bag off the floor, blundered to the bathroom. She retched over the toilet. It was all she could do to crawl in the shower and pull herself to her feet. The hot water loosened her muscles. She palpated the gash and knot on her forehead and rinsed the dry blood from her hair.

If her hand could have found his knife, she would have sunk it into his neck, sliced off his prick, stuffed it into his mouth, screamed, "Suck it, suck it, suck it, you cock sucking bastard. Die, die, die, you ass fucking motherfucker." She would have loved to see him gag on that unnatural thing he so bragged about, seen the terror on his face, pushed it in as far down his throat as she could and watched him turn blue trying to breathe. She would have twisted the knife, pulled the blade out, slit his throat, decapitated him, delighted while his eyes went vacant. The bastard, the motherfucking cruel bastard.

She dressed Taylor in his new clothes. Travis awoke and volunteered to take Taylor to school. He pulled on his jeans, stomped into his boots. He kicked Donnie awake. Donnie had slept in his clothes. He slid his feet into his sneakers and bolted to his feet. "Go on so he won't be late," Arreta said. Donnie swept Taylor up. With tickles and giggles, they were out the door.

Donnie lay on the floor and rolled a joint. He was talkative. Salvador was sitting on the far bed. He was the only one listening to him.

Travis turned impatient and grim. He stood at the curtain peeking out in all directions.

Donnie passed the joint around.

The men settled out financially. Donnie barely got anything. He did not dare complain.

Travis shared a line of cocaine with Donnie and the Mexican from his own stash. Arreta swallowed the roach.

Travis sent Arreta with cash to pay the room bill.

As she left the office she watched narcotics officers storm the room and Travis barrel across the curbing of the parking lot in his truck, fleeing from a plain clothes being dragged, and an unmarked car.

Arreta wheeled around into another plain clothes narcotic investigator who plucked the yellow payment receipt out of her hand.

"Where are you going, Arreta?"

"Damn, Hoop. I don't know nothing about what's going on."

"That's not what Donnie's been saying."

"That pussy motherfucker."

Another narcotic officer – muscled, shaved head, earringed, and brilliantly tattooed up both arms – went inside to the desk, came back and confirmed that Arreta had paid for the room they said they had been watching.

Salvador and Donnie slugged out of the room, heavy lidded, in handcuffs. Arreta was holding her bag with all her belongings.

Hoop, handcuffed Arreta behind her back and walked her over to the room.

"What's happened to Travis?"

"Don't know yet," Hoopingarden said.

She sat on the pavement watching Donnie spill his guts to Hoopingarden. His whiny voice was like a spike going through her head.

"Yeah, I know this is a parole violation," Donnie said. "Can't we work something out? I'll be your confidential informant. Anything so I won't have to go back to prison."

"We don't have any say so about parole," Hoopingarden said. "That's up to the Department of Corrections."

"Come on, Hoop. I know everybody who's selling around here."

The Mexican kept his mouth shut. The ID they pulled from his pocket apparently did not use Salvador.

"Nothing comes up with the name on the ID and his description," a Hispanic investigator said.

A uniformed officer put Arreta in a patrol car, still handcuffed behind her back, and drove her to jail, where she was photographed, fingerprinted, booked, strip searched, forced to surrender her clothes and bag, and issued navy blue jail scrubs.

"That bastard raped me. He sodomized me. Branded me like his whore," she bawled.

"I'll tell the nurse," the jailer said, locking the holding cell door.

A social worker showed and interviewed her through telephones with the thick glass between them. "My little boy, Taylor, he's six, and at school, somebody's got to pick him up." She tried to explain why she was jailed, but the social worker cut her off and told her she would need to tell her lawyer.

No investigator came to get her side of things, how she had nothing to do with Travis's drugs.

She tried to hold it together not knowing what was going on, what was going to happen.

# WILLIE B. POLITE

The tide sits the boats low near the oily mud. The cars splash by. Momma told me to be careful riding my cruiser on the road.

"You broke my video game, you damn retard," Twan said. "Go on. Don't you start crying. You cain't just throw things around when you get mad. If you want to play with things you got to take care of it. If you cain't take care of it, I ain't gone let you play with it. Now go on to the library." He pushed me.

"What's wrong?" Uncle Cloudy said.

"He was in there tearing up the video game. If he cain't play with it right, he's not allowed to play with it at all." Twan said.

"Son, go to McDonald's and get you something to eat and come back," Uncle Cloudy said. "I'm putting this money in your pocket. Now go get you something to eat. Don't ride in the road."

"Hey Fawquita. How youuuuu?"

Fawquita walks all over town everyday in her stretchy leotards. Music comes out these covers over her ears. She got sparkling white tennie shoes. Pulls her hair out of her eyes with a stretchy band. Her arms slinging like she gone fly. *Swish, swish, swish.* Fly Fawquita, fly, fly, fly.

I ride a little ahead of her and say louder, "Hey Fawquita. How youuuuu?"

She be looking like one of them queens I seen in them pictures in the library and on the TV. Her mammies bounce all over as she walks. The faster she walk, the faster she bounce, up and down. *Boom-dee-boom-dee-boom-dee-boom.* Walk, walk, walk, walk, walk. Getting it on down the sidewalk, waving her arms, *swish, swish, swish, swish.*

"Hey Fawquita. How youuuuu?"

She pulls away one of her ear covers, where the music comes out. "Hey Tank. How youuu? It Tuesday."

"I's fine." My legs hurt peddling to keep up with her legs moving on down the sidewalk. "You's lookin' good," I says.

I shout again so she hear me over that music. "I says you is lookin' goood this mawnin' Fawquita." Fawquita be smelling like nursing milk.

She pulls both of them ear covers off her ears. She keep a walking. "What's you say, Tank?"

"I says, you lookin' good this mawnin'."

"It be Tuesday." She gets on down the sidewalk.

I keep peddling hard. Cars driving by. Black clouds breaking up. It still steamy after it rained hard.

I wave. Gots to keep one hand on the handlebar. "Hold up, Fawquita, hold up, I wants to axsk you somethin'."

"What?" she says. "What? What? It Tuesday, Tank."

"I'm holding up my money.  Stop, stop . . . can you stop?  Look at this money a white man gave me."

Fawquita stops.  "Tomorrow Wednesday, Tank. The day before today was Monday."

"Today Friday, I think."  She not even breathing hard.  Just sweating.  Her sweat smells like nursing.  I like nursing.

"Get on away from me, nigger dog," she shouts, waving her arms all over the place and stomping.

I stand straddling my bicycle next to her.  I don't see no dog.  I hear the music coming from her ear covers. It buzzes like gnats.

"Son, can you tell me where the courthouse is?" The white man had a white lady in the car with him.  She smelled like flowers.  Her lips were painted red and her eyes looked like the sky.  I had silver money in my hand. Then he axsk me again, "I say, son, can you tell me where the courthouse is?  Honey, give him a dollar."  Then she say, "He don't look right, Larry.  He looks retarded.  See him drooling."  Then the man say, "Just give me a couple of dollars, baby, quick."  The man stepped out of the car and walked up to me.  "Hey there my man.  What you got?"  I show him my silver money.  "Well this will add to that," he say.  "You can go buy you a Coke and a candy bar."  I sure do like Coca-Colas and chocolate candy bars. "What's your name?"  Momma say don't talk to strangers. I sure never seen this man before.  "Well, anyway," he say, "I'm looking for the courthouse.  Do you understand me, son?"  I nod, sure I know where the courthouse be.  That where Momma go after they take her off to jail.  "You do? Wonderful.  Look here, I'm running late, you see.  Where

is it?" I point. "Can you be a little specific?" Momma
said don't talk. He say, "Can you show me how to get
there?" The white lady with the red lips say, "He don't
know how to do that, Larry." The man say, "You know
how to get to it?" I nod. "Excellent. Well, get in." It was
a little car. He drove fast. The woman smelled better than
anybody I had ever smelled. She say, "Larry, he's got his
nose in my hair." He say, "I don't care as long as he gets
us to the courthouse." The woman was all in tight clothes
and high heels. She was tall and pointy. Like a tree
walking. The man say, "You'll have to walk back to get
your bicycle." He put money in my hand. "Here's a ten.
Thank you, boy." The sun was in my eye. The man
followed the flower smelling woman clacking up the
sidewalk.

Fawquita is waving and turning round. "Shoo, now.
Shoo. Shoo, you nigger dog. Go on. Go on. Damn dog.
Goddamn old dog."

"Where dat dog?"

"Dere he go. Big ole black mangy thing. On down
de street. Dere he go. Ole nigger dog. Get on out of here."
She waves her arms. "Get. Get, now."

"Fawquita."

"Get on out of here, nigger dog." She claps and
stomps.

"Fawquita?"

"Get on dere."

"Fawquita. Look here at this money this white man
gave me."

"Whatchyou say Tank?"

"I got a hundred dollars from a white man with this white woman with red painted lips and she walked on high heels and smelled like magnolias. And she had pointed boobies that stuck straight out like this. But you got nice big boobies that bounce real fine when you walk. I like them when you walk--"

"I ain't got no time for no corn dogs or no malt liquor."

"I was wondering . . . could I nurse from your boobies one of dese days?"

She knocks my hands away and hits me on the side of the head and knocks me into a mud hole.

There's humming in my head like bees. I'm all wet and muddy. Mud in my shoes and in my underwear and in my hair.

Fawquita is over me with her fists, breathing hard, growling like a black dog.

"You hurt me. Oh. I'm gonna tell." My legs are all twisted up in my bike.

She snatches me up. "Whatchyou doing with dat there dollar bill? Quit that cryin'. Where'd you get that?"

"That, that, white man I said."

"I ain't s-e-e-e-en no white man. I ain't g-o-o-ot no time for no white folk. White folk g-o-o-ot no time for me. Corn dogs. Hallelujah. Malt liquor. Amen."

A loud motorcĭcle goes by. One of them loud fat motorcĭcles that scares me. She pushes me in the mud again and goes on down the sidewalk, arms flying like she gone fly. *Swish, swish, swish, swish.* "Watch dem dere dogs, Tank," she says. "They knock you down sure enough."

"I don't see no dogs. Where's dem dogs, Fawquita? Where? Where?"

Cars drive by fast. A horn blows. A million black birds fly off. Squawk. Moss falls to the ground. I hear buzzing bees in my head. She took my eyes, I think.

Uncle Cloudy's got a car wash and tinted window business.

Uncle Cloudy be setting around with some dudes.

"Uncle. Tank be howling," Twan say. Twan plays video games on the TV when he not washing cars.

"Whatchyou blubbering about, Tank?" Uncle Cloudy says.

"We out of green Popsicles," Pop say. "Twan, put down that video game and run down to the sto and get Tank Popsicles and me wings. Here's some money."

"Where's your cruiser, boy?" Uncle Cloudy asks me.

"I don't know." I'm all muddy and I's cold and I's got to go poop.

"Why is he howling so loud?" Twan says.

"Boy, quit scratching yo' self," Pop says.

"I got chiggers and got to go poop."

"You need to get on home if you needs to go to the poop," Uncle Cloudy say.

"Give me a ride, Uncle Cloudy."

"Son, you live right across the street, right there." Uncle Cloudy grabs my chin and points. "Get on home, now." Uncle Cloudy gets up and grabs me by the shoulders and turns me.

"Why you all muddy and wet?" Pop asks.

"Fawquita pushed me in a mud hole."

"Quit your howling and cryin'," Twan says.

"Boy, I done told you to get on down to the store," Pop says.

Twan gets on his bike. He told me he stole his bike from some people. He told me not to tell or he would go to jail. I watch him pedal down the road.

"Here now, listen to me boy," Uncle Cloudy says. Uncle Cloudy lets me vacuum his car when I stays with him at the car wash. I like his car. It smells like cherries. Miss Francis's body looks like that vacuum cleaner. But she don't smell like cherries.

"What's that retard howling about now, Cloudy?" Skeet comes out a big truck with big wheels and black windows.

"Shut up Skeet," Uncle Cloudy says. "Y'all watch things while I walk Tank home. Come on, boy. Hold my arm. Look both ways like I told you before you cross the street."

"Okay."

"Where's your bicycle?"

"I don't know. Fawquita pushed me."

"Why'd Fawquita push you?"

"I got the chiggers."

"Boy, answer me."

"I wanted to nurse."

"Say that again."

"I wanted to nurse."

Uncle Cloudy hit me hard on the back of my head. "Boy, you better not be nursing from Fawquita." He hit me again. "Damnation, God in Heaven. That girl is nasty.

You listen to me, boy." He stopped me. "Look me in the eyes and listen to me. You listening?"

"Okay."

"You're not looking me in the eyes."

I look at his eyes. It makes it hard to listen that way.

"I hear you touching some girl's boobies I will whip you good, you hear me? Until you cain't sit no more. You hear me?"

"Uh-huh."

"Boy, quit your cryin'. Stop that cryin', now. Stop it. Hush up. Your momma is gone raise Cain about this." Uncle Cloudy starts shouting. " . . . They'll throw you in Milledgeville. Hush that crying." Uncle Cloudy takes holds my hand tight. "Come on before you mess in your britches."

"We need to make a stop at my house first, Tank, allright?"

"Okay."

Nobody was there except me and her. It was clean and cool inside and smelled nice.

"You want a Coke? Here you go, baby." She turned the TV on cartoons. After a while I got sleepy.

She was naked and big and droopy. She had lots of rolls and a big bottom. She took off my clothes. I was naked. "Have you ever had sex with a woman before, Tank? It's all right, baby. I'll show you. That's why I think you've been having so much trouble. I want to help you. So you'll keep out of trouble. I know you don't understand everything that happens around you. But let me help you. Okay?" She took my hand and showed me how to rub her. She liked it. And she rubbed me. And I liked it, too. And she moaned and I moaned. And she had me lie on top of her and she put my peter in her and we moved up and down and we started breathing hard and my peter spat and she hollered and she held me and asked me to do it again and again. She was a soft, nice, big woman. I liked it. We did it some more. Then she held me and hummed and I fell asleep.

"Boy, why you be cryin'?" Momma says. "What happened to you?

I don't say.

"Well? Answer my question, Willie B. Polite."

"It Tuesday, Momma."

"No it ain't. Today Friday."

"Fawquita say."

"Everyday Tuesday for Fawquita these days. They be needing to take her back to Milledgeville before she try to burn the church down again or stab her Momma."

"She say it Tuesday."

"Uncle Cloudy say you ain't got your cruiser."

I don't say. Momma wipes my nose.

"What happened, boy?" Momma says. "Why you come home all wet and muddy and crying?"

"I fell. Fawquita pushed me down."

"Why is that?"

"She got mad."

"Mad at you?"

"I gots the chiggers in my pants. They's about to eat me up, Momma."

"Whatchyou do, boy? You got snot all over your face."

"I axsked her a question."

"Quit jumping around. Get your hand out your pants." She pins my arms. "What did you ask Fawquita?"

"I asked if I could nurse."

Momma slaps me on the side of my head and all over my body. It stings like being hit that time in the head by them black boys.

Momma says, "Grown boy nearly thirty-years old cain't be touching no boobies. You keep your hands to your self or Gawd gone chop them off. I gone get a hickory switch to you if you be touching boobies, you hear me?"

"Uh-huh."

"What'd you say?"

"Yes, ma'am."

"You want Miss Francis to take you away forever?"

"No, ma'am."

"Quit crying. Lord, oh Lord, I couldn't live if that happened, baby. If they took you away from me, I'd die. I couldn't stand my baby being taken away from me like that."

My peter big and hard from scratching it. Momma always say not to touch it or Gawd will kill me dead. Dead. Dead. Cemetery dead. Like Grandmamma in the cemetery. She in that heaven box with her eyes closed and not moving like she asleep. She wouldn't wake up. I tried to wake her. Them men closed the door and put that box in another box and then put it in the ground and put dirt over it. Cemetery dead. I ain't seen Grandmamma since. I don't know how she gone get to heaven when she in two heaven boxes in the ground. Momma say it ain't her body that goes.

"Momma. When I was like a vegetable and the preacher put me under water to clean me for God, what did that do?"

"It washed away all your sins, baby."

"Just like a dirty potato. That what you say." Momma tap me on the nose.

"That's what I say."

"You let me wash the potatoes."

"Yes, baby."

"You smell like potatoes, Momma."

"I do." Momma laughs.

"I like to wash the potatoes."

"You a big help to Momma."

"You say sin like dirt."

"We gots to get the dirt off you now."

"God won't eat me when I die? That what you say."

"Lord, no. You ain't no potato."

"I want you to go to heaven with me, Momma."

"Jesus's Momma will take care of you for me if I'm not there."

"What's Her name?"

"Miss Mary. You remember? She be with the baby Jesus in the manger at Christmas time? She be his momma."

"She a nice lady?"

"She the nicest lady they ever was."

"Will she let me nurse, Momma?"

"She the queen of heaven. She will make sure you get whatever you need in Heaven, baby."

"Fawquita say she is a queen."

"I done told you Fawquita ain't no queen. Miss Mary really is the queen of all heaven. She will take care of you."

"I want to stay with you, Momma."

"Well, well . . . ." Momma wipes my nose with a wet towel, and hugs me and rocks me on my feet. She smells like potatoes. "We gots to get you a bath." She lets me nurse. Tingly. Momma laughs. Sings. She wipes my mouth. Then she undresses me and puts me under the water. It be warm and clear. The dirty water runs into the drain.

"Soap your body, baby," Momma says. "Use the wash cloth Momma put in there. And soap. Willie B. Polite, clean your body good."

"Yes ma'am."

Momma washes my hair. She sings and makes funny noises. Momma's funny. We laugh.

Then she rubs me down with lotion.

Dry clothes are warm. The chiggers are gone. Cartoons are on the t.v. Momma makes supper. Chicken and macaroni and cheese. Then Momma peels me an orange. I eat it, slice by slice. Juicy.

Momma says, "I don't want you walking with Fawquita no more, you hear me?"

"Uh-huh. Fawquita has big boobies, Momma."

"Willie B. Polite, you quit talkin' like that. You quit worryin' about Fawquita's boobies. She going crazy

again, boy. The po-lices will lock you up for that. You
want to go to the jail house?"

"No, Momma."

"You stop that, baby," Momma says. "Hush, now."
Momma holds me tight. "You just keep your hands to your
self."

Miss Francis put me in that room. There was no
sunshine to look at. I could not hear the traffic or the birds
outside. I could not smell the tide. No chocolate to rest in
my gum, no cup to spit. There was no talking, no music
singing on the radio. There was no TV. I had to stay there
for a long time. I rocked in the chair sometimes.
Sometimes I put my ear to the wall to try to hear the
outside. I cried. Nobody came for a long time.

"I cain't understand why y'all have to treat this boy
like this," Uncle Cloudy said. "He don't deserve this. He
don't understand what he do. Let him stay with me. He
ain't never gone get no better."

"He's being a menace down at the library, I hear,"
Miss Francis said.

"Well, I thought that's where you wanted him to
go?"

"Yes. But, he must behave," Miss Francis said.

"He ain't gone hurt nobody. He's just trying in his
way to get to know people and make friends. If you want
the boy to, to . . ."

"Assimilate into society," Miss Francis said.

"Do what?" Uncle Cloudy said.

"He needs to get out and get used to being around
people and behaving right."

"Then you're gone have to expect some growing pains," Uncle Cloudy said.

"Well, we'll continue to assess," Miss Francis said.

"That's right, baby," Momma says. "Now quit cryin', baby. Hush up, now. That's a good boy. Momma's boy. You always Momma's boy. Ain't you Momma's boy?"

"I's Momma's boy, Momma. I love you, Momma." Momma makes me blow my nose.

"You go to Uncle Cloudy's car wash and sit and read a comic book," Momma says.

"Yes, ma'am. Pop's got green Popsicles."

"And Twan lets you play his video games. Or go to the library and read. You like doing that, don't you?"

I like going to the library. The girls come in the library smelling like flowers. Their lips look like cherries and strawberries.

"Baby, I'm going out tonight. Be good for Uncle Cloudy."

I sneezed. Momma did not smell like potatoes, but like flowers. "Momma. You smell good."

"You like it? It's perfume."

"You dressed like a movie star." I sneezed and sneezed.

The library lady made me leave. "Willie B. Polite. You got to go home," she said.

"I didn't touch nobody," I said.

"No. You humming and grunting and making too much noise for the library," she said.

She didn't tell Momma. I would have got a hickory switchin'. I won't ever go back there if Miss Francis wants to send me to Milledgeville.

Julio came to the door. Momma sent me out. I sat on the porch in the chair that used to sit inside and spoon my chocolate in my lip. Momma don't like me dipping inside. She say it's nasty and cain't be cleaned. She had to go to the store and get a new rug when I spilled. Now I dip and spit outside. Now Momma fusses if I get juice on my clothes. I try to be careful. The chocolate makes me tingly. Miss Francis don't like me dipping. She tells Momma it rot my gums and make me dead. It make me tingly. How it gone make me dead?

Momma says not to tell nobody about me nursing. Uncle Cloudy knows and Auntie Bunt. Miss Francis will take me away. I want to stay with Momma.

Miss Francis have a wider bee-hind than Fawquita. She have the widest bee-hind I ever seen. She's a white lady with a round red face. Uncle Cloudy says it be because she like to drink a lot. I like to drink a lot, too. Milk makes me fart. Momma don't let me drink Co-Cola at night. It makes me pee in my bed. Momma don't let me sleep with her in her bed no more. I makes a pallet next to her bed when she asleep.

Miss Francis talks loud to me and smiles a lot. Her mouth smells like peppermint sometimes.

Julio left. Momma sometimes smokes on the porch. We sit out there 'til it gets dark. We go inside and watch a movie on the TV. Momma kisses me and puts me to bed.

I wake up. The po-po be there and take Momma with them when I eating cereal and bananas. The po-po look in the drawers, under the bed, behind the furniture, between the mattresses, in the commode, and under the sink. I pet they dog. He jumps all over the beds. I had a badge. A dark skinned boy took it from me. Auntie Bunt says she will get me another one.

Miss Francis be there at the house. Auntie Bunt be there. Auntie Bunt dresses me. We ride in Miss Francis' car. "It the hospital," Auntie Bunt says. "Tee-tee in a little cup." Auntie Bunt holds my peter and a cup. I tee-tee all over the floor. Auntie Bunt holds my peter and I tee-tee in the commode.

Then I on a hard bed and belted down and they stick me and take blood from my arm.

"I'm sorry," Miss Francis says."

"Hush. It's all right," Auntie Bunt says. "Why they doing this?"

Miss Francis says, "After that disturbance at the library and now with his momma using again."

"I just don't see," Auntie Bunt says. "It just ain't right, doing this to this boy. He don't know what he does. He a good loving boy."

They tie me down. It makes me mad.

"Quit hollerin', son," Auntie Bunt says. "Be a big boy, and Auntie Bunt will take you to McDonald's. You want a Big Mac?"

They poke me in the arm.

Auntie Bunt brushes my hair. "Hush. Hush."

I want to go home. I want to go home.

"Momma. Momma."

The lady unsticks me.

"I'm sorry." She yanks off her purple stretchy gloves, throws them in the trash can, and walks off.

"They had to take some of your blood," Auntie Bunt say. My red blood like Jesus' blood, like my red tennie shoes, like tomatoes and cherries, like Fawquita's stretchy pants, like the perfume girls' lips.

The hospital smells like sand in my nose. Like swallowing salty river water. Like the time when I fell over the rail when Uncle Cloudy took me crabbing. I tried to crawl up out of the water and holler to Uncle Cloudy, but the water kept getting in my throat. It was black. It smelled and tasted like a salty fart. I couldn't see. Uncle Cloudy snatched me out. He pushed the water out of me. The water came up out of my mouth and nose like that the time my stomach hurt, like rocks rolling around in it. Water came out and food I ate. I didn't see no rocks come out. I don't know where they went.

"Momma's away for a while," Auntie Bunt says. "She's sick. We gots to make sure you ain't sick, too. Now hush. Hush now, Willie B. Polite. Hush." Auntie Bunt rubs my head and holds my hand. She tries to kiss my head. I don't let her. I don't like her no more.

Uncle Cloudy pats my arm. "It's gone be all right, sonny boy. You calm down so we can get you out of here." I tried to crawl out of the water, but it kept getting in my throat. He snatched me out and pushed the water out of me, and the water came out of my mouth and nose.

The bed is hard. The Lady pokes me again. She takes my eyes. I open my eyes. I ain't tied down no more. Uncle Cloudy and Auntie Bunt drive me home. Uncle Cloudy buys me a Big Mac, french fries, and a Co-Cola. I sleepy. Sunshine. Shiny. Shining. I hear them motorcicles out on the street and thunder. Feel them under my feet. Under my feet. Feel them in my ears. I cover my ears. I still feet them under my feet. The air is not like perfume. Not like peppermint or soap or roses. It is like pine trees boiling and like eggs, like when I fell and the water got up my nose and Uncle Cloudy pushed it out.

"I'll take you for shrimp after I get done at the car wash," Uncle Cloudy says.

Uncle Cloudy and Auntie Bunt leave me by myself. Cartoons be on the TV. I sleepy and close my eyes.

"Momma is at the jailhouse," Auntie Bunt says. We walk over there.

Momma and me talk on the telephone with the glass between us. She cain't hug me or kiss me.

"You doing okay, baby?" Momma says.

"Yes, ma'am," I says.

"You gettin' plenty to eat?" Momma says. "Yes, ma'am. When you comin' home, Momma?"

"Quit cryin', baby. You gots to be a strong boy for Momma, okay?"

"Okay, Momma."

"Here, Willie B. Polite, blow your nose," Auntie Bunt says.

"You have Uncle Cloudy take you to the sto' and get yo' chocolate so you get yo' tingly," Momma says.

"Okay." The phone be making crackling noise.

"But don't be dipping inside the house," Momma says.

"Okay, Momma."

"Miss Francis been coming to see you?"

"She take me to the hospital. They tied me down and hurted me." I show Momma my arm where the lady poked me took out my red blood.

"I know," Momma says. "I'm sorry, baby."

Auntie Bunt walks me home.

Uncle Cloudy sits me down to see Miss Francis.

"The drug screen we did at the hospital came back positive for cocaine and marijuana," Miss Francis says.

"What?" Uncle Cloudy says.

"Tank's drug screen came back dirty," Miss Francis says.

"How?" Uncle Cloudy says.

"I don't know. I thought you might." Miss Francis says.

"I ain't the foggiest," Uncle Cloudy says.

"Well, he had to get it somewhere," Miss Francis says.

"What? Why that's somebody telling stories."

"There's got to be an explanation," Miss Francis says. "The only one I have is that he's been taking the same drugs as his mother."

"Didn't dem policemen search the place when they arrested Naples?" Uncle Cloudy says.

"Yes," Miss Francis says.

"They didn't find anything. I knows that. They tore the place up."

"No, they didn't find any drugs. That's beside the point."

"Well, why did they arrest her then?" Uncle Cloudy says.

"Because her drug screen given to her by her probation officer came back dirty."

"How?" Uncle Cloudy says.

"I guess because she is using again," Miss Francis says. "According to this test so is Tank. Now I'm putting two and two together and it leads me to believe he's somehow getting drugs from her. She's endangering him."

"Naw, naw, naw," Uncle Cloudy says. "That ain't right. That ain't right. That boy stay with me at the car wash all day Saturdays. His Momma take him to church on Sunday. We at church all day on Sunday. He don't bother nobody. He don't do nothing but read comic books and ride that cruiser of his. He go to the library sometime and read. Just read them little children story books and talk about them stories."

"Until he got kicked out," Miss Francis says.

"Huh?" Uncle Cloudy says.

"I'm going to send him to a place in Savannah for six to twelve weeks to get cleaned up."

"What?" Uncle Cloudy says. "Now that ain't no need. Ain't no need at all. He can stay with me for a while." Uncle Cloudy look at me. He make me smile. He don't smile back. "What about his chocolate?"

"We need to break him of that right now," Miss Francis says. She sit up and grab my mouth and peel my lips back with her fingernails. They scrape. "Look at his teeth." She got skinny pink lips. She pucker like she gone kiss me. Only Momma kisses me, when I go to bed.

"It all right, son, hush up," Uncle Cloudy say.

Miss Francis unpuckers, and pulls her fingers out of my mouth. "His teeth are almost rotten because of that filthy habit," Miss Francis say. "They need to be pulled. The snuff has contributed to that."

"It all right, boy," Uncle Cloudy says. He pats my knee. "It's all right. Hush now."

"Our department has a smokeless tobacco campaign," Miss Francis says. "Haven't you seen the billboards in town?"

"Naw. Only billboard I see be that lawyer one across the street from my car wash. He'll handle your divorce and drunk driving ticket for $300," Uncle Cloudy say.

Miss Francis's face turns redder. As red as her big shirt. And she spins around to her desk. She's let me spin around in her chair before. It made me loose like a noodle. Hard to walk. Round and round and round and round and round and round.

"Why don't y'all go ahead and pay to pull the boy's teeth out then?" Uncle Cloudy says. "We cain't afford no dentist."

"The Department doesn't have the money. Budget pressures," Miss Francis says.

"Well that ain't none of our fault," Uncle Cloudy says. "Seems like the State could pay to have his teeth pulled rather than send him away from home. You knows me and his Auntie Bunt take good care of him when his Momma's away."

"He needs a different surrounding for a while," Miss Francis says. "That will do him good."

"That boy is just fine the way he is, teeth or no teeth. Let them fall out on they own, in their own good time. Leave him be with his snuff. What y'all expect of him, anyway? Seem to me y'all just want to pick, pick, pick, pick, pick on this poor boy. Me and his Auntie Bunt love him. That's more than I can say for the government. Just leave him be."

"Now Mr. Polite, are you saying that I haven't always done what's in the best interest of Tank?"

"Naw, that ain't what I'm sayin'," Uncle Cloudy says. "You just gone drop him off at that home with a bunch of strangers. You ain't gone stay with him. That boy need to stay where he's loved and looked after and stay in a place that he know. Not getting upset about someplace new and new peoples. He don't know nothin' about no Savannah."

"Like I said," Miss Francis say, "drugs didn't just magically appear in his body. I'll go up there every week and monitor his progress."

"Now look me in the eyes and listen to me, Tank."

I looked in Twan's eyes.

"You take this money and you go up to that second house with that black mail box and you tell them you there to buy three twenty bags, you understand?"

I nodded.

"Just like the last time. Okay?"

"Okay."

Uncle Cloudy smell like money, he say. He gives me quarters and dollars to buy my chocolate. "When y'all gone take him then?"

"Monday morning. I need for y'all to have him here at seven."

Uncle Cloudy gets up. "Come on Tank."

I hug Miss Francis. "Bye, Miss Francis."

"Can me and Bunt go visit him up there?"

"He's not allowed visitors."

"That ain't right. This boy ain't no criminal. Why he got to be punished? Just for being slow and different. It ain't right, Miss Francis. Y'all gone see you're doing more harm than good."

Twan drove me to the corner. "Go on now. I'll drive around the block a couple of times and pick you up right here, okay?"

I nodded and opened the door and got out. I walked to the yellow house. It was dark. Only a light at the road. There was the big dog chained up to the tree. He stood and barked. The front porch light came on just like the last time. I stood real still. The skinny black girl opened the door. She waved me in. "Don't just stand out there. He ain't gone bite you. Come on." She yanked me inside.

"I'll see you Monday morning, Tank," Miss Francis says. "We'll take a drive to Savannah, okay?"

"I want Miss Lisa to take me." I says.

"You want Miss Lisa to take you?"

"Yes. Do like the last time. We had fun at her house."

"What did y'all do?"

"Mm-Mm-Mm-Mm. She's got big boobies."

"Quit rubbing you penis, boy," Uncle Cloudy says.

"What are you saying, Tank?"

"Mm-Mm-Mm-Mm-Mm."

"I think this is evidence of his unraveling, Mr. Polite. That he is using controlled substances. We've got to get him detoxed immediately."

"Come on, son." Uncle Cloudy says. "Miss Francis, he needs his chocolate. It's his one little thing."

"I likes my tingly," I says.

"You see? You see, Mr. Polite? They're not going to let him have it at the home," Miss Francis says.

"So what," Uncle Cloudy says. "A little snuff in the evening ain't gone hurt that boy none. He ain't never gone be able to do nothing. Just like a little child. Ain't got an enemy in the world. This is all he'll ever be. Just the way he is right now. I just don't see. I just don't see." Uncle Cloudy hit his leg with his hat.

"Let me see the money you got." She grabbed my hand and opened my fingers and got the dollars Twan gave me, then left down the dark hall and left me there with the kids watching cartoons and the other big dog. Then she came out of the back with a paper bag and put it down my pants and then pushed me out the door and I fell and hurt my knees and my nose bled and the dog barked and I ran fast.

"I told you I'd pick you up at the corner, dummy," Twan said.

"That big dog barked and tried to bite me. She pushed me out the door. My nose is bleeding and I hurt my knees."

"Damn." Twan took off his shirt and squeezed my nose. "Hold your head back. Well, where is it?"

"Huh?"

"The bag, Tank." Twan put his hands down my pants and pulled the bag out. He looked in the bag and laughed. "Yeah. This is it. You did good. You did good."

"Where did he get the drugs in his system, Mr. Polite?" Miss Francis says. "I'm not happy about this."

"I still don't believe he took any at all. I don't believe that test," Uncle Cloudy says. "Naples is a sick woman, I'll admit. But it don't make her a bad momma. She's always taken care of that boy. Been able to handle him better than anybody. Me, you, his Auntie Bunt. Anybody. And all the police, judges, lawyers, social workers, probation officers have done is interfere. Pick, pick, pick, pick, I say."

"You haven't been around him twenty-four hours a day, seven days a week the last few months, have you?" Miss Francis says.

"I've been around him most every day. More than any of you social workers. I ain't never seen this boy take no drugs," Uncle Cloudy says. "I ain't never seen him high or strung out. Naples wouldn't let him take no drugs. That boy ain't never used no drugs."

"Well, he had to have gotten it somewhere. It's in his system."

"I tell you I don't trust them drug screens," Uncle Cloudy says. "I've heard about 'em."

Me and Uncle Cloudy leave out of there.

"I swunny that woman smells like the marsh at low tide," Uncle Cloudy says. "Like a salty fart."

We laugh.

Uncle Cloudy's arm is around my shoulder. "Come on sonny boy."

We eat outside. Uncle Cloudy have a pork chop sandwich. I have a hotdog, tater tots, and a Co-Cola. Uncle Cloudy gets us soft ice cream cones.

A white police lady be in the house. Uncle Cloudy be there. Auntie Bunt be there. Miss Francis be there, too.

"Tank, I got to ask you some questions, okay?" the white police lady says. She talks loud and smiles.

Fawquita told on me, I know. "Fawquita's my friend," I says.

"That ain't why she's here," Uncle Cloudy says. "You listen to her questions now son."

"I want to ask you about your Momma." The police lady got a big mouth of white teeth. Big eyes like the sky, prettier than the lady I took to the courthouse. But she don't smell as pretty. She don't smell at all.

"Momma be home the day after this day?" I says.

"No," Uncle Cloudy says. "We've talked about that, remember?"

The police lady be wearing a yellow shirt.

I point. "Yellow," I say. "Yellow. Yellow." I point to my clothes. "Yellow. Yellow."

"Tank, did your Momma let you smoke?" the police lady says.

"No. I gots to dip my chocolate outside."

"What's that?"

"That's his snuff," Uncle Cloudy says. He shows the lady my can.

"Let him answer, please."

Uncle Cloudy puts the can back on the table.

The clouds make the light get dark and then bright inside through the window. The door is open. The windows, too. It's warm outside. Not hot, yet. It will be soon. Hot for a long time. Then Christmas. Santy Claus. And cold weather.

"Momma smokes her cigarettes."

Uncle Cloudy gets hold of my hands and puts them in my lap. "Quit waving your fingers in front of your face, son."

"Do you know a man name Julio?"

"He be a friend of Momma's."

"He bring you or your Momma drugs?"

"I sit on the front porch when he comes."

"What about Twan?"

"We play video games at Uncle Cloudy's."

"What's marijuana, Tank?

"Uncle Cloudy gives me Popsicles at the car wash."

"What about Twan? He give you any marijuana?"

"He gets my Popsicles. They the color of money. The same as my Saturday shoes. Uncle Cloudy lets me vacuum his car on Saturdays and I play Twan's games."

"Your Momma let you smoke little marble rocks with a pipe? You ever seen them little rocks, Tank?"

"I had rocks in my stomach when I was sick that time. All that came out of my stomach, but no rocks. Did you find my cruiser? Fawquita pushed me in the mud. You gone take me back to the hospital? Poke me again? Tie me up?"

"It's all right, baby," Auntie Bunt says. "Stop cryin', precious boy."

The white police lady asks me some more questions. Then she and Miss Francis leave.

Uncle Cloudy sits on the front porch with me. I spoon my chocolate under my lip. Ain't too many cars on the road tonight. It's raining out there over on the Island. Out there over the ocean. I feel the wind. I see the lightning. Blink. Flash. Blink blink. Flash. Blink. Flash. Blink flash.

"You got enough chocolate, sonny boy?" Uncle Cloudy says.

I work the snuff against my gum and nod. "Tingly. Momma be home in a few days."

Lightning. Blink flash.

"It's too far to hear the thunder," Uncle Cloudy says.

# AN UNACCOMPANIED
# SURVIVING ROCK STAR

It was the first week of deer season and I shot an
eight pointer – my first in eight years. I followed him in
my scope as he plodded to within ten yards of my tree
stand. He turned and stopped, looked upward. I took my
shot. He went down.

My brother-in-law and I butchered the buck and put
the meat in the deep freeze with the head and rack wrapped
in plastic for the taxidermist. We washed the blood off our
hands, arms, boots, chop blocks, knives. My brother-in-
law took the hide, a tenderloin, ribs, and hind quarter. We
wrapped bones for the dogs and tossed scraps to the barn
cats. The excess we threw on the trailer I pulled behind the
tractor into the woods and unloaded in a pit gouged with
the back hoe and covered to keep out the coyotes. My
brother-in-law drove home on his four-wheeler and I drove
the tractor and trailer into the barn.

Jerry Dean stood in the front yard when I made my
way to roll up the water hose. He was shirtless, shoeless,
sockless, nothing covering his head, stubble faced and
gaunt, all protruding ribs and shoulder bones, just baggy
dingy britches hanging down below his hips that let his
boxers show from the waist.

"Where in the world did you come from?"

"Got clunked in the head and set out at the road."

"You stoned?" He was haggard looking and dazed, breathing through his mouth. He had lost a good many teeth.

"I ain't stoned," he said with a strained croaky voice.

"My God, look at yourself."

He was swaying. His hands were trembling. He rubbed his eye with the heel of his hand. His knuckles were caked with dry blood. He stammered, "I just feel like I been beat to hell is all."

"You don't smell too good, either. Come up here, son." I threw my coat around his shoulders that I'd had on the truck bed. I went in the utility room and retrieved an insulated hunting cap and pushed it down on his head along with the ear flaps.

Jerry Dean is my sister's youngest, only six years younger than I. Most of America, if not most of the whole planet, if they've had much contact with popular American music, have had Jerry Dean's band's rock and roll anthems tattooed into their psyches at sporting events, laser shows, stock car races, Waffle House juke boxes, fraternity parties, evenings of tequila shots and pitchers of beer, boating on the lake, motorcycling, and movie soundtracks.

Once a month, a royalty check arrives and he drives to the bank and cashes it. Then he and some skanky woman that's latched onto him, with their sniffling noses, scorch the highway to his friendly drug dealer and engorge themselves.

He pushed his arms in the down coat. I zipped it up. "Dear God, where have you been, Dirty Foot?"

Through chattering teeth, he said, "In, in, in the hospital for my nerves again." His fingernails were gnawed until he had the cuticles bloody. He slipped his feet in a pair of my old boots I dropped in front of him. "I was in Atlantic City with some dudes playing poker and got to drinking--" Bent over coughing, he stumbled down the driveway behind a tree, hawked, and spit, and stumbled back. "I was playing poker, and one thing led to another--" He took a few breaths. "I remember snorting coke off the belly of these naked oriental hookers curled up in a big martini glass and . . . You ever seen that? . . . Them oriental girls are the softest--"

"Look-a-here, Jerry, you just appeared out of the mist out here?" You couldn't see the road a hundred yards from the house for the mist and fog.

"Got pushed out. They drove off," he said, wheezing, and convulsed into a deep heavy cough that folded him over and brought him crumbling cross-legged in his spot.

I pulled him up under the arms, and with his arm around my shoulder and his legs wobbly, led him to the house. He didn't have the strength to lift his legs for the stairs. I carried him into the back door, to a chair at the kitchen table, where he laid his head on his folded arms on the table. I poured a cup of coffee for us both – mine black, his with plenty of cream and sugar. After a time, he sat up and wrapped his shaking hands round the warm cup. I had to hold it to his mouth. He ate half a grilled cheese sandwich I fixed and a few bites of tomato soup I spooned him. Then I sat across from him at the table.

"Did you have a good time in Atlantic City?"

"I was talking to a couple of dudes about putting a band together. We started heading down to Florida."

I poured us another coffee from the fresh pot I'd made. He stuck his face over the steam of his cup.

"Neil Young was stalking me. He was there in that casino--"

"I thought you and Neil worked things out after . . ." ("your last hospitalization." I wanted to say.) "I guess you haven't been taking your medicine, have you?"

"Now wait, Swampy. That damn mangy hippie saddled right up next to me at the table trying to tell me how to play my cards."

"Was this before or after the Asian hooker in the champagne or whatever it was?"

Jerry Dean pointed to the chair next to him. "I told the sumbitch to leave me alone, but he went on how this was a free country and all. That's how he does. That's how he always comes at me. And dad-gum. He did it to me again, Swampy."

"What was that, son?"

"He walked off with all my money. That damn hippie walked off . . . with them long skinny fingers . . ."

"How long had you been awake on the meth?" I should have put him in the truck then. That's what my gut was telling me. I'd have to take rough measures to get him there. I was getting too old and he was still too crafty.

"The buzzard come out of nowhere and sat his ass right there next to me. Bought us Jacks straight up and smoked my cigarettes. And, and, then Merle Haggard came up, patted me on the back and said, 'How you doin' son?' I think he was singing there." His hand shook. He tried to sip his coffee. Half of it spilled down the side of his mouth.

I dabbed Jerry's mouth with a napkin. He didn't realized what I did.

"Now tell me that was one of my hallucinations." The coat was too long in the sleeves. He pushed the brim of the hat up with the coat sleeve. I encouraged him to eat the second half of his grilled cheese sandwich. He ate it and finished his coffee in a gulp. "I don't rightly remember how I got to Florida. I hooked up with a woman and gave her money to drive me back to Atlanta, then crawled in the backseat of her car and kind of blacked out. Next thing I know this big black dude was beating hell out of me, had my wallet, wanting my credit cards. I don't carry none, Him and that woman started kicking. When I woke up, hogs were rooting around in a ditch out in the middle of nowhere. I walked. Got picked up. A Florida State Patrolman woke me up wanting my name and if I was all right and wanting to know what happened and all that. I couldn't remember nothing."

"Did you get locked up?"

"Spent the night at a motel down at the Jacksonville airport. The next morning a State Patrolman drove me to the airport--"

"In cuffs?"

"Naw. What for?" He coughed into the thick sleeve of the coat. "Where's Kathy?"

"Out shopping."

His head sank into his arms on the table. "I'm worn out."

"What happened at the airport?"

"Why are you asking me all these damn questions? I got a headache like somebody's drilling into my temples . . ." He rubbed his eyes, augered his ears.

"You look and sound like you might have pneumonia."

He laid his head on the table.

I studied him for a time.

He peered up. "Do you remember . . . I mean . . . that time, you know . . . when the cops came busting in . . . tried to bust our heads wide open . . . somebody started fighting . . . cops didn't know what . . . we just hauled ass . . ."

I'd survived near obliteration by the Vietcong. Then came back to head security which meant babysitting those stoned degenerates from mayhem, injury, death, and incarceration. It seemed sometimes worse than the rice paddies and jungle survival. "I have never seen people who caused more trouble and destruction for themselves and others."

"Just turned out that way. People are crazy."

"Yeah. People are crazy."

Jerry Dean yawned. "I called Nadine to come get me--"

"When?"

"When I got to the airport in Atlanta. Hey, you got a cigarette?"

"No. That's the last thing you need."

"Give me a ride to get a carton. I'll pay you back."

"What did Nadine say?"

"She kept asking me a bunch of questions."

"She was the best thing that ever happened to you."

"All I needed her to do was come and get me. She's using meth anyway."

"Nadine? How do you know?"

"The last time I saw her she was bald and all anorexic looking. That's a sure sign people are using crank. That's not the kind of mother I want my daughter to be around or household I want her to be raised in. I've been meaning to call my lawyer about that."

"What are you talking about?"

"She was so messed up her hair had fallen out. It's meth."

I thought a bit. "Dirty Foot, that's when she was going through chemo for her cancer. That was over twelve, fifteen years ago. And your daughter is over thirty and you have grandchildren."

"You know the way she acts. I think she knows where I go, where I'd spend my money. Now that's weird shit. I think she's stolen my identification like they talk about--"

"Where have you heard anybody talk about it, Dirty Foot? Get in the truck." I stood and grabbed the truck keys. "Come on, we're going to the damn hospital."

"--Maybe she's had one of them chips put under my skin when I was in the hospital last time. I'm going to have my lawyer check on that, too."

"I saw Nadine last month at her mother's funeral. She looked the best I'd seen her in years."

"Nobody called me about that."

"She fell and broke her hip."

"Nobody told me. Nobody let me know . . ."

"It's time for you to grow up, settle down, sober up if you want to keep track of these things. Don't blame it on anybody else."

"I really could use, you know, a cigarette and, and, and, a glass of Jim Bean. I know you got some of that around."

I threw the keys on the counter. "What did you do when Nadine wouldn't come get you?"

"Well, they got a train at the airport and I got on it. I rode it all day. All over the place, I reckon. Way late into the night. I didn't have no watch on. I had fell asleep. A train cop came and kicked me off."

"Look here, by God, Jerry Dean. If you don't tell me the truth this time I'm not going to help you. If you lie to me I'm going to strap your ass to the bed of the truck, I don't care how cold it is outside, and take you to the hospital and have them admit you whether you like it or not. Then when they throw your sorry ass on the street, don't come back here. You can live your last years, weeks, or days wasting all your money whoring and strung out, and then find yourself in prison, forgotten in some insane asylum, under a bridge, or left dead in a garbage dumpster, I don't care anymore, you hear me? You're not going to tear me or Kathy up anymore, especially Kathy."

His voice was barely audible. "I hear you, Swampy."

"How in the name of God did you pay for that motel room in Jacksonville?"

"I don't know. Nobody talked about it." He put his head on the table.

"So, what did you do, roam the streets when you got kicked off the train?"

"I ran into some people under a bridge having a party."

"Then the cops showed up."

"I don't know how I got in a hospital." He collapsed into rough coughing convulsions.

"How long did you stay at the hospital?"

"Huh? Not long. Doctor said I was faking and kicked me out. Gave me some dead person's clothes and dropped me off at the Salvation Army shelter."

"Them?" I pointed. "The britches?"

"Naw."

"Then what then?"

"You're not going to believe me."

"Well then get in the truck."

"I can't."

"Then you'll be leaving in the back of the Sheriff's car."

He said, hesitantly, "Me and the Sheriff just parted ways. I just did six months."

I was ready to snatch him up and throw him in the truck bed and tie his sorry ass down. "Why were you locked up this time?"

"Driving drunk, they said."

"I thought you said you'd been sober all this time?"

"Yeah, after being locked up--"

The plane crash ten years before had re-formed him. Not reformed him religiously or spiritually, but re-formed him like a damaged instrument that has been reheated and bent back into place and whose tone has been altered in the tempering. He'd always been reckless, feeling invulnerable. After the crash, he was diagnosed with bipolar disorder and post traumatic stress disorder. He continues to vainly smoke despite having emphysema, and continues to drink beer and whiskey daily despite that he's an alcoholic (even though he denies it). He takes all kinds of psychiatric medication for his mental health, and is supposed to take pills for blood pressure and cholesterol. Largely due to the fact that he drinks heavily still, he has been hospitalized countless times for mental breakdowns and alcohol induced seizures. The alcohol negates the benefits of the psych meds.

To a rational person it's self-destructive. But to ask Jerry Dean, it's part of his image of immortality. It didn't matter if he was ninety, he was going to be true to his creed even if it killed him. He'd never accept that he balding, without muscle tone, almost toothless, and a chronic emphysemic cougher. To himself, he'd always be that hard rockin' drummer. What I tried to do was contain the self destructive behavior as best I could while he stayed with me.

What he wanted out of me was a place to flop to recover until he felt nineteen again, ageless and ready to ride in the back seat of that big red Cadillac convertible with buxom blondes under both arms on the road to Sweet Immortality Land, where there was always plenty of snort and booze, by a pool of laughing beautiful naked or scantily clad young women ready to party in his Eden with accompanying loud rock music.

"I'm not going to even ask how we got from being discharged from the psych ward to being arrested for DUI."

He rubbed his hand gruffly over his raspy jaws. "Swampy, I couldn't explain it to you anyway."

Crows cawed it seemed from every tree outside.

Jerry Dean said, "You know I didn't remember I had three past convictions for DUI. The police don't go for that John Doe explanation. They pluck you up in two seconds flat in their computer using your fingerprints. It was a terrible mug shot. They took a new one of me this time."

Mine and Kathy's home had been Jerry Dean's sanctuary ever since he was in school, an asylum from his crazy drunk momma – I hate to say that about my sister, but it's true, her and all the men that came and went in that trailer raising all matter of holy hell. During these periods of asylum, Kathy cooked and washed Jerry Dean's clothes. They watched soap operas, and he would forget about playing the drums. Then after a month or six weeks of settling his nerves (as he called it), there'd be a careless stack of cash left on the kitchen table (usually around five thousand, once ten thousand, as the boy never knew the meaning of money), and he'd leave in the night and we wouldn't hear from him until he'd show up bedraggled again, skinny and strung out, weak and shaking, needing rest and nourishment, cleanliness, a haircut, and peace.

"They treat you all right in jail?"

"Oh yeah. No trouble at all. I gave them all kinds of autographs, played the piano and sang at Christmas time. Got a nice trustee's room to myself with cable TV. And got to eat with the Sheriff and the Colonel – the good food, not the inmate mess. All the undisturbed rest and relaxation I needed. Saw a dentist, a doctor, and a psychiatrist and got back on my meds again."

"You still taking them?"

He scratched his head. "Well . . . I don't directly remember. Have you got a cigarette?"

"Sorry, don't smoke."

"I sure could use a drink, too."

"Coffee or water is all you're getting."

He started snoring on the table after a time. I couldn't awake him, so I collected him up, his head bobbing over my arm, his boney legs below the knees dangling. The boots dropped. His feet were gashed and bruised. I laid him on the queen bed in the guest bedroom with the thick coat still on him.

Kathy drove into the driveway about a half hour later. I met her at the back door and filled her in on what had happened. We tugged the coat and the rotten pants off him. She sponged the top layer off with warm soapy water and we wrapped him warmly in blankets. He never awoke. "Take them smelly filthy things out to the burn barrel and go to Walmart and buy him some warm things." Kathy was a practical woman who adored and mothered Jerry Dean. They were the same age.

I poured gas on the mud caked britches and set them afire in the barrel. After washing my hands, I got in the truck and headed out in a dazed mood. I loaded the buggy with what the boy required, hoping the sizes would fit, paid for them, and put the truck on the road, reluctant for some reason to return home.

The house smelled of homemade vegetable soup, fresh hot coffee, cinnamon rolls. Jerry Dean lay on the

couch wrapped in a blanket and comforter, asleep. Blue
flames blazed from the blackjack oak in the fireplace,
emitting little to no smoke.

"He woke a little after you left," Kathy said. "I've
never seen his hair all buzz cut like that. Did you notice
it's as white as snow and balding at the crown?"

"Did he say anything to you?" I asked.

"He just hugged me. I remember he had the most
beautiful teeth and head of hair. Remember he'd let me
wash it in the kitchen sink and I'd blow dry it? He
wouldn't let anybody else touch it."

"I hope these clothes I bought will fit him."

"He looks so . . . so caved in." She handed me
some dirty folded papers that were torn on the edges. "I
found these in the back pocket of those filthy pants."

I unfolded the papers at the kitchen table. Kathy sat
across from me. They were from a neurologist. I couldn't
read much of it because of a grease stain. The diagnosis, I
learned after some Internet research, was debilitating, life
threatening. My heart dropped. My arms slackened. I
stared at the words on the page for a time until I returned to
the kitchen and spoke to Kathy. "Does it say anything
else?" She picked the pages off the table. She called the
doctor's office and rescheduled an appointment.

"He just appeared like a poor ghost out of the mist,"
I said. "I came from the barn to the front and there he was.
The worst I've ever seen him." I shook the papers. "Looks
like I totally misjudged the whole damn thing. I feel like a
real son-of-a-bitch"

I went to my study and returned with a magnifying glass and tried to read through the grease stain on the medical papers. It was no help.

'Remember the jail bait?" I said.

"Oh my God," Kathy said.

"And I almost killed that man."

Kathy laughed. "It was just a misunderstanding."

I snickered. "So was the Cuban Missile Crisis. Her daddy came here intent on killing Jerry Dean; his girl all in rapture with a forty-year-old stringy haired drummer."

Kathy stirred the soup. "I remember you handling it quite diplomatically, Leonard."

"Jerry Dean and that little girl came romping up stereo blaring in his car, that silver Lincoln with the black vinyl roof he had back then?"

"Oh, yes--"

"You remember? Them reeking of marijuana and bourbon?"

"I thought that man was going to shoot us all," Kathy said.

"She had just turned sixteen *that* day."

Kathy pulled out the small kitchen vacuum.

"He will probably want you to go to the doctor with him."

"That's fine." She started the vacuum. I pointed to Jerry asleep on the couch. "Honey, he's asleep." She flicked it off. "I forgot he was in there," she said. I looked in and he hadn't budged. She put the vacuum away and poured fresh cups of coffee for us. "This is probably the last thing I need, I'm so jittery," she said. Then she put

plates of cinnamon rolls on the table. We forked a few
bites and sipped our coffee.

Cradling her cup, her elbows resting on the table
top, she said, "Don't you think we probably need to call
Nadine? Tell her he's here – and talk about that doctor's
report?"

Most days recently I had worked on a book that I
had promised my publisher. Now with writing demands,
lecturing at other universities and conventions on the
American Civil War, it seemed I was busier now than
before I retired as professor at the University. While I was
in my study browsing my notes I heard a wild turkey. I
wasted a good amount of time scouring the back woods out
my window through my binoculars searching for the old
tom.

Jerry Dean woke the next morning, drank some
coffee and went back to bed. On the second day he was up
again early, ready to eat. Before I came down, Kathy up to
our bedroom while I was tucking in my shirt.

"He doesn't know how he got here."

"What do you mean?" I said.

"He doesn't even remember showing up."

I shook my head and Kathy shrugged before darting
down the steps.

It looked as if two Jerry Deans could have fit into
the jeans I bought him. He was gulping down coffee and
greeted me. He wore one of the flannel shirts, thick white
socks, and a pair of my slippers, and had wrapped a blanket
over his shoulders. Kathy had fixed a large breakfast.
After he had eaten, he turned to Kathy and thanked her for

the best rabbit he had had since the last one she had fixed for him.

Kathy began clearing the table.

"Here, let me help you," he said.

Kathy put her hand on his shoulder. "No, you just sit right there, hon. I've got it. Drink your coffee."

He and I went out on the back screened porch. He shuffled, leaning on my arm. At the chair I hung onto his arms until he was settled. I fetched his sugared and creamed coffee which he took in both hands. His hands trembled. He looked round the porch and asked me where I kept my cigarettes.

"I quit."

"You did?"

"A long time ago. I smoke a pipe, but just in cold weather."

He rubbed a palm between his knees and rocked. "I could use a drink."

"Last night, you said you'd been sober since you were locked up. Let's keep it that way."

Looking confused, he said, "I did?" A few seconds later he asked, "You got any reefer then?"

"What?"

He looked over his shoulder, lean over to me, lowered his voice. "The bag of grass, you know, to settle my nerves? Like always?"

"Like always?"

He pointed. "The bong you keep in the barn. Didn't you go out and buy me some weed so I can go out there and smoke? Man, the way I feel, it'd be nice to be baked this morning."

"Do I need to slap some sense into you, boy? I never have had a dad-gum bong. I'm not your buyer or your seller."

He took a loud sip of coffee. "Take me to the store so I can buy a fifth of vodka. My head feels like a spike has been driven through it. I could put it in my coffee. Kathy would never know."

The sun was beginning to warm the porch. A smiling Kathy poked her head out. "Everything is ready in your bathroom for a shave and a shower, Jerry Dean."

I reached into the inside of my coat and handed Jerry the medical papers. "We found these in those britches you were wearing when you showed up."

The clanging of pots and pans rang through the back window. The phone pealed off, one, two, three before Kathy helloed. "Read them, if you can." He moved the papers around and squinted. "Do you recall what that's all about?"

"Let me try to get this thing in focus." He moved his lips while he read. "I've got no earthly idea what this is, Swampy."

"Do you remember going to that doctor?"

Jerry Dean rubbed his eyes.

"Nadine apparently went with you."

He shook his head stiffly.

I leaned into him. "I've got to tell you, Jerry Dean, according to this doctor . . ."

"Is it cancer?"

"No."

"Is it serious?"

"I hate to say, but yes, I think it is. I described what I knew of the disease.

He had a scared look, holding onto the arm of the chair, legs crossed at the ankle underneath the seat. He went into a wheezy loose coughing fit. After he had settled down and was able to talk, he asked, "What's going to happen to me?"

"We've got you an appointment with your doctor. Kathy can take you or I can--"

"I want her to go with me."

"You don't need to worry about a roof and food. Whatever you need we'll get it for you. Medicine, a TV, a cell phone, a computer, whatever you want."

He sat stunned for a time. "Naw, I can't put y'all out."

"Where are you going to go then? You want to go stay with Nadine?"

"I sure as hell ain't doing that. All she wants is my money. The gold digging b--"

"Wait, wait, wait, now. You can't live by yourself."

"I don't know why not."

"You can't look after yourself."

He drummed his fingers on the arm of the chair for a time.

"You got to stay sober and you got to stop smoking pot and snorting coke and meth and what other chemicals you like putting in your body."

"I can do that."

"Why you just asked me for a cigarette, marijuana, and a whiskey not a minute ago.

He crossed his arms across his chest. "I don't remember."

"You've got to take your medicine when you're supposed to--"

"I can do that."

"--And you've got to go to your doctor appointments when you're supposed to – on your own."

He chewed on the inside of his cheek and stared out at the barn.

"I guess this is just me being negative or cynical, but I think if you try to take care of yourself, your degenerate friends will show up. You'll give them a call and they'll be all too happy to bring whatever you need and you'll be high as a kite within hours of us leaving you. They won't make sure you take your meds, hell they'll take your goddamn meds and sell them. They damn sure won't take you to your doctor's appointments. I know you're going to keep on snorting and drinking. I just hope your entourage calls 911 so we can come identify your body and can give you a proper burial."

Jerry shuffled outside, and gimped up the hill to the barn. He fell once; tripped on a root. He sat, checked his ankle and hands. It was all I could do not to get up and check on him, or holler out to him. He used a tree to pull himself back to his feet. He stopped to take some breaths further up the mild sloping hill. After a while I heard him heaving up his breakfast alongside the barn.

I was in my study working on my book when I heard a knock. A showered and shaved Jerry Dean shuffled in. "So that's it," he said. "I'll become totally dependent and slowly turn into a vegetable? I'm not going to be able to walk or talk or make love to a woman. Somebody's going to have to feed me, give me a bath, change my diapers, clean my ass?"

Not even Nadine knew what we did with the money he left on the table when he set off in the night. Kathy and I never touched a dime of it. Instead, we set up an account in his name. It now had over a quarter of a million dollars. I told him of my plan for the use of his midnight kitchen table money, as Kathy and I called it: use it to add a wing onto the house for him to live. He agreed after some thought with the caveat that Kathy also use some of the money to remodel her kitchen and all the bathrooms in the house. We retained an architect and by mid-December, we had our plans.

Christmas day, it snowed four inches. It was frigid and sunny for the rest of the holidays – unusual weather for us. I called Nadine to see if they would consider letting Jerry Dean visit them for Christmas, him sober and regulated on his medication. Nadine was comfortable with the idea. I went to Richmond for three days to lecture at a Civil War re-enactment convention. Kathy talked to Jerry Dean about seeing his daughter and his grandchildren. He was absolutely opposed. Then Kathy told me he struggled up to the barn, took the tractor back into the woods, and didn't come back until past dark, soaking wet, drunk and smelling sour and of cigarettes. He said he had slipped off the tractor while trying to keep it from rolling into the pond. He messed around an hour trying to get the tractor unstuck by himself, but finally left it sitting in the pond. He wouldn't eat. She fixed him a hot shower and put him to bed. But a few hours later, he was up. He spent most of the night pacing and hacking and mumbling to himself. Kathy finally got up. They watched old black and white movies and drank coffee. She didn't know where he got the cigarettes but let him smoke on the front porch. He got so anxious, she gave him a valium hidden within two Tylenol, and poured him half a glass of bourbon. That calmed him. He went back to bed about the time the sun was coming up. She made sure he was covered and warm, and that the oxygen hose was clipped under his nose.

She was shook up. I took an earlier flight home.

The water was almost up to the engine of the tractor. My brother-in-law and I spent over two hours prying it out using a wench he had outfitted to his tractor. I spent the rest of the week over-hauling the points, spark plugs, and wires. It also gave me the excuse to change the brakes on the front wheels.

The remodeling and construction of the new wing started after the first of the year. The hole for the new wing's foundation was dug. Having experienced being almost swept away by a tornado in Nebraska and then seeing the TV news about a whole town being flattened by the same tornado, Jerry Dean wanted a reinforced concrete bunker to be constructed in the basement. The concrete foundation and basement floor were formed and poured the second week of January. The tornado shelter was formed, supported with rebar, and poured the next week. The framing went up in a week, then the metal roof. From then on, the work inside progressed steadily.

Jerry Dean puttered about the property on the tractor, smoking, his oxygen tank bungee corded to the seat. The construction workers were scared he was going to set off an explosion. He'd head into the back woods, sometimes clearing vines and small brush, pushing them into piles, throwing a flaming kerosene soaked rag on them and watching the blaze. He widened the trail to the fishing pond that our property shared with my brother-in-law's. He threw chicken liver into the middle of the pond and let it sit on the bottom for the catfish and with another rod he baited night crawlers for bass and brim. Kathy would fry the fish he caught.

He'd slip off when one of the workers would give him a ride to the store. He bought them beer and his liquor, and restock their cartons of cigarettes and cigarellos. He hid his stashes in the well house and in the barn – the same hiding places from his prior stays. At quitting time on Fridays he drank beer with the workers. They enjoyed laughing at his stories.

On the gloomy cold days that he couldn't get out, he'd ponder over a jigsaw puzzle, slept despite all the construction noise, ordered movies off the cable, watched old seventies reruns like Sanford and Son, his favorite. Even with the medicine he didn't sleep well. At night we'd awake to him listening cozily to the albums in my collection – Merle Haggard, Lefty Frizzell, Jimmie Rodgers – and plunking around on Kathy's piano or guitar and singing softly – his voice bourbon warm, nicotine edged.

February, his head's tilting to the right was more discernible and his balance more unreliable. In a consult the beginning of February, the doctor informed us of more noticeable declination and ways to accommodate him. We started looking for a nurse, a handicap van, and constructing a ramp at the house. We'd already installed a handicap toilet and handicap handles in the tub and showers in our house and the new wing. He hated the mortality they symbolized.

Valentine's Day, Kathy and I drove to Atlanta for dinner and an overnight stay at the Ritz Carlton in Buckhead. We had Jerry chewing nicotine gum by then. He did it just to appease Kathy. He was still smoking. Kathy wished to believe he wasn't. He told her he hadn't taken a drink since the last doctor's appointment. She was the same way with his drinking. I knew otherwise.

During dinner, Randall, Kathy's brother, called to say that they had fed him, Jerry had taken his pills, and when he left, Jerry was in bed breathing with his oxygen, watching TV.

The telephone call in the quiet early morning hours was startling. I'm a heavy sleeper. Kathy was hitting my shoulder. "Leonard. Leonard. The phone. Wake up. It's the phone. Wake up." My cell phone was vibrating and ringing. I sat over the side of the bed, reached out toward the fuzzy light on the night stand, and braced myself. I put the phone to my ear. It stopped ringing. "Hello? Hello?" The hotel phone was so loud it probably woke the people in the adjoining rooms. I answered it. It was Nadine. Then my cell started ringing again which confused me. Kathy took the hotel phone and handed my cell back to me. "Hello?" It was a police officer calling from the Rome hospital. Kathy spoke to Nadine. It was a short conversation. She started packing while I listened to the officer. I asked some questions, but the officer didn't know anything beyond his short script. Jerry was at the hospital

with Randall, Kathy's brother.  There'd been a fire.
Randall had apparently pulled Jerry out.  Both were getting
treatment.  Nadine didn't know anything except that Jerry
Dean was in the hospital and our house was on fire.  She
would meet us at the hospital.

The barn was nothing but black embers.  Not a wall
or vertical board was left standing – only the remains of my
tractor and trailer.  By the time the fire department got
there, the barn was so far gone they let it burn out.  All we
found was half a dozen whiskey bottles (a few that had
burst), a steel barrel of discarded beer cans, and one of
Jerry's oxygen tanks.

The glass breezeway we built between the new
wing and the house prevented the fire from spreading and
badly damaging the house, according to the fire
investigator.

The dogs awoke Randall, he told me.  He rode up
on his four-wheeler as the barn collapsed.  Quickly
becoming discouraged, he tore round as close as he could
get to the barn, and then round the house, hollering for
Jerry.  Jerry smoked in the wing after it was enclosed,
instead of going outside in the inclement weather.  Smoke
and flames were shooting out of the eaves.  Randall kicked
through the back door, which was only a plywood board
braced with a two by four.  Black smoke and the blast of
heat shoved him back.  He hollered for Jerry Dean.
Hearing nothing, he crawled inside and found Jerry Dean
sprawled out, face down.  Randall hooked Jerry Dean under
the arms.  Jerry fought against being dragged outside.
Randall collapsed just outside the doorway, overcome by
smoke.  When Randall awoke, a fireman was kneeling over

him giving him oxygen. Jerry was raving out of control claiming Neil Young started the fire and Merle Haggard was his daddy and he was going to go after that sorry bastard, Neil Young. Randall said Jerry Dean kept going on like that even as they loaded him into the ambulance.

In the closet of Jerry's charred and water damaged bedroom in the wing, we found an empty quart of Jim Bean, an oxygen tank on wheels, a melted plastic ashtray, and a partial carton of cigarettes with one clean pack stuck in it.

Jerry stayed in the hospital and then a psychological hospital for over a month. He had no memory of the fire. During an early visit he hollered and cussed, accusing me of conspiring with Nadine to steal his money and keep him locked up by telling everybody he was crazy when it was me and Nadine who were crazy and manipulating, telling the press he had a life threatening disease he had contracted from aliens from another planet. He pointed out F.B.I. men in black suits and black hats posted outside his door and everywhere in the hallway. They were to protect him because he had finally broken the code. Neil Young was the master of all these aliens that had invaded the planet. He started raising Cain about Merle Haggard being the only hope to save the planet from Neil Young and the aliens. He told me I had to call Merle Haggard on his secret telephone line. He said he had the right number scribbled on a torn piece of crumbled paper he pulled out of his pocket. He started obsessing about the number, mumbling to himself, scratching out numbers, writing down other numbers.

Then, abruptly, he lunged at me, held my shoulder and whispered in my ear,

"Make sure you don't give anybody my real name. I've been given very, very specific instructions by a very reliable person never to give my real name when held hostage, captured, or hospitalized. You see, I'm on the run. I'm a hunted fugitive. I'd like to settle down, but they won't let me. A fugitive must be a rolling stone. I'm lonely, but can't afford the luxury of having the one I love to come along. I'm on the run, the highway is my home. I'm on the run, the highway is my home." He was talking then singing the Merle Haggard song, "I'm a Lonesome Fugitive." I got up and left. As I pondered down the hall he began singing Haggard's "Momma Tried."

April was a quiet month. We finally got the insurance money. We knocked down the addition to the foundation. If the fire had any silver lining, it allowed us to adjust the plans and insert a number of improvements omitted in the first design. After Jerry was released and lucid again, he transferred three-hundred thousand from his royalty money to cover improvements to the addition, and the construction of an authentic wood barn painted red, like the old one – not some unsightly steel building I was planning which was all the insurance money was going to cover. He didn't mingle with the workers or ride on the beautifully refurbished 1950 Ford 8n tractor I found for him – the first thing I bought with the insurance money. Instead, he withdrew. He closed the blinds in the living room, hid in his bedroom, and wouldn't go out on the back porch until dark, claiming people were gawking at him through binoculars. He wandered around in sweats, mostly traversing the path down the hall to the bathroom or the kitchen. He fixed a nest in his bedroom closet and napped there or read by a small lamp with a dim bulb. Then he began to sleep in there in the night. I tried to coax him out to go to bed one evening but he wouldn't budge, saying in his growly voice that it was the safest place in the house – free of the voices and the gawkers.

By May, Jerry Dean was noticeably growing weaker since he hadn't gotten out and exercised. He needed a motorized wheelchair, but wouldn't let us get one. The only thing he'd use was a homemade cane Kathy found at a flea market on the Tennessee border. With the cane, he finally got out in the early mornings and late afternoons around the property and sometimes to pay a call to Randall. This was the longest he had stayed with us. His 60th birthday was coming up.

His behavior improved, but at its best could only be described as eccentric. His outbursts were fewer. His sense of humor returned in bursts. Sometimes we'd hear him singing in his closet where he still spent most of the time. There was one evening in early May where all the chemicals in his brain were in tune and he entertained us after supper like the young Jerry Dean used to do when the kids were home and we'd dance while he pounded on the piano or strummed on the guitar and sing late into the evening, never tiring. He sat with the guitar in his lap and sang a half dozen mischievous Lefty Frizzell tunes. The last song he played for us was a Jimmie Rodgers song he'd learned – "Mississippi River Blues." I've heard Rodgers sing that song hundreds of times. Jerry Dean took a slightly slower tempo than Rodgers. He took his time emoting the words. His bluesy tone, the way he bent and stretched the notes, was like being drawn into a dream.

At the doctor's appointment in mid May, blood was drawn and scans were taken. For the consult a few days later, a nurse escorted us into the spacious office where the doctor sat behind his desk. In another chair was Nadine. I stood against the back wall. I knew this was going to be uncomfortable.

Jerry Dean faced Kathy. "What's she doing here?" He looked back at me and held up his hands. "Swampy?"

"It's all right, son."

"Why is she here?"

Nadine was aplomb and beautiful in a tailored blue silk pant suit. She put her long fingers gently on Jerry Dean's boney forearm. "Don't you remember me coming with you to see the doctor back in the fall?"

"You're crazy," he said. He pushed himself up and fell back in the chair – started cussing under his breath.

Kathy glanced at me. "All right Jerry Dean," I said. "Calm down. Nadine is here because we need her here."

He slouched down. "Why?"

Nadine said. "I'm here because--"

"What are y'all talking about?" Jerry Dean said.

I stepped up. "Do you remember the divorce?"

"I've done everything I can to forget it."

"Well, you signed some papers."

"Everybody does, I guess." He cut his eyes at Nadine.

"Two of those are real important. You know Mr. Silverson?"

"He's my lawyer."

"And Mr. Collins?"

"He's the guy that handles my money."

"Well, you signed papers so that child support and alimony is paid automatically, and then to collect all the income sent to you from all sources, mainly your royalty income."

"Okay," he said hotly.

"Then somebody has had to handle your taxes, banking, investing, and deliver your monthly stipend which you have cashed and spent as you have liked. Autonomously."

"What?" he said gruffly.

"With a free will. Nobody has interfered in the way you have spent your money. No matter how recklessly, illegally, harmfully it was to your health and wellbeing. You have had untrammeled autonomy as to the way you have spent your money."

"Speak English Uncle Swampy. You mean to say I haven't been getting *all* my money?"

"Certainly not, Jerry Dean, because you have expenses that have to be paid every month. And despite having an irresponsible personal life, you are financially responsible. You know why?" I stared at him until he looked up at me and met my eye.

"Okay, I give. Why?" he said.

"I'm going to explain and I want you to sit up and listen. Now although Mr. Silverson and Mr. Collins have had formal management of all these transactions, including a trust for your daughter and now your grandchildren, these documents that you executed were powers of attorneys. One was a financial power of attorney. The other which is germane to today's discussion is a durable power of attorney, addressing medical decisions. In both powers of attorney you named Nadine your representative. Kathy is the co-representative with Nadine in the medical or durable power of attorney."

Jerry Dean hunched over, stared at the carpet. After a moment he twisted slowly to Nadine. "So this whole time . . . I thought I was . . . but y'all didn't tell me."

"Those were the things you agreed to, hon," Nadine said.

"I didn't know."

Nadine said calmly, "I've been able to watch over things so all your money didn't all go to legal and accounting fees. Mr. Silverson and Mr. Collins, of course assisted me. We sent Scarlett to private school and college and Europe. I hated you wasted yours on drugs and booze and women and wild parties. But your grandchildren have money in trust so they'll be able to go to college wherever they want without having to worry about the costs. They live in a nice home in a wonderful neighborhood. All because of what you've provided. I can't complain about that. There's been no waste. I've seen to that Jerry Dean. I've seen that your expenses have been paid timely, whatever they were, even though I didn't agree with them, and even when it hurt. I've gotten better dealing with it. Every thing's accounted for. If you ever want an audit, the books are open."

He turned and faced me. "So I wouldn't get gypped?"

"You don't know how lucky you are," I said. "Most of your money, without her, could have been eaten away. Thousands and thousands of dollars wasted but for her."

"You trust her Swampy?" he asked.

"Absolutely, without reservation," I said.

"And this other thing? The paper here," he said.

Kathy said, "We need . . . We'd like for you to sign it. It's for us to make medical decisions in the event you become, you know, brain dead, or hooked to machines to keep you alive."

He took up the pen. "Where do I sign?"

Nadine pointed.

He looked at her. "Who's making this decision?"

"Me and Kathy. Is that all right? We all discussed it. Neither Kathy nor I could do it alone."

"You didn't want to be apart of this decision, Swampy?"

"You never wanted me to take you to the doctor. Anyway, I couldn't make the decision, son. I could never unhook you."

He signed the document. "Unhook me. That's what I want. But I hope I won't give y'all the need."

He withdrew to his bedroom the rest of May and June, spending his time on the computer, sometimes buying a book, mostly biographies of rock musicians he knew or had run into over the years, Keith Richards was one in particular. He only came out of his closet or room to go to the bathroom or eat or get a cup of coffee. I tried to get him to walk through the new wing and inspect the progress, or view the construction of the barn. He claimed he wasn't going to move into the addition, so he wasn't interested. He said, the wing was for me and Kathy. He liked where he was. He didn't want to talk about it.

A few weeks later in June, early the day before his birthday, a stack of one hundred dollar bills were rubber banded on the kitchen table with a note that he had "The Mississippi River Blues." He was going to New Orleans. He had gotten a gig down there. It was first time he had ever left a note when he had left in the night. I awoke Kathy and then called Nadine.

Nadine checked her computer. "Then you couldn't have bought gas this morning."

She traced his whereabouts by accessing his cell phone by computer and dialing the last number he called. At first she got some guy who wouldn't tell her his name. She told him it was an emergency and that she was Jerry Dean's wife and needed to talk to him. The guy laughed and acted like he never heard of Jerry Dean and hung up on her. I called and acted like a detective and tried threatening the guy into cooperating – that he could be charged as an accessory of manslaughter if Mr. Johnson died if he was concealing his location. He told me to do whatever I had to do, he didn't know where Jerry Dean was, that he picked him up and dropped him off at the airport. That was all he did."

Nadine called the bank and explained the situation. Tracking him was like racing traffic lights. Each time Jerry Dean made an ATM withdrawal she got an email that showed the location. He bought his airline ticket by credit card – destination unknown. He made an ATM withdrawal for the maximum.

Six hours later he withdrew cash and checked into a hotel casino in Las Vegas – his usual, according to Nadine. Since I'd never been there and cared not a wit to go, the name of it meant nothing to me. Nadine called the hotel and spoke to the owner. She said that they had spoken together on several occasions about reconciling bills after room damages and other unseemly matters she didn't go into. They were on a first named basis and began regaling each other about past events and how enjoyable their dealings had been with the other. Then she broached the subject of whether he was aware of Jerry Dean having checked into his hotel. He was not aware, but after a check of his computer, he confirmed that Jerry Dean had – under his usual alias. He told her the very room they had him established. She then informed him about Jerry Dean's health and how he had no business being there unaccompanied.

"Dominic, he needs to be in a wheel chair. He's very unstable on his feet and could trip or collapse at any moment. I need you to get one of your staff to provide him some kind of assistance, one of those scooter chairs immediately, and see that he gets to wherever he wants to go, except no prostitutes. If he wants to see a show or if he wants to gamble, please escort him and see that he is provided with whatever *nonalcoholic* drink he wishes and that he is fed a healthy meal. He has left his medication here in Georgia. He is a risk to himself and to your establishment. I want to make it clear to you, Dominic, that we have spent a tremendous amount of money at your hotel and casino, and that if any injury comes to him in any way before I get there, I will hold you and your hotel and casino fully responsible. Forgive me for being harsh, but he is in very fragile health and doesn't know the extent, and I think you understand that he's going through a hard time with a last moment of . . . yes, that would be the best way to describe it. So can you not tell him that I have called? Let him think that it's your idea and keep one of your security men on him so he's not taken advantage of. I will make sure you and your staff is compensated for this act of goodwill. Thank you, Dominic. That's very kind. I will see you tomorrow morning."

The three of us took a private jet to Las Vegas. We were picked-up in a limousine and checked-in to the hotel. Nadine met with the shift security supervisor when we arrived. A guard had been stationed outside Jerry Dean's room door. His movements that day had been tracked. She met the owner when he arrived that morning. The owner contacted the hotel's physician and instructed him to check on Jerry Dean and administer his medication. He would visit Jerry and inform him that we were in the hotel and ready to take him home once his visit in Las Vegas came to an end.

When Jerry Dean failed to answer his door, security used their key and let the physician inside. Jerry was in the tub near full of champagne. The glass coffee table in the living room was dusted with cocaine. Another unopened bag of cocaine lay on the table with a half dozen empty little bottles of vodka and another half dozen little bottles of Jack Daniels standing neatly side by side. There was a pool of bloody vomit outside the bathroom door. Another in front of the commode. The bathroom floor was full of empty Dom Pérignon bottles. A rolled up twenty dollar bill and the remains of snorted cocaine flaked the edge of the bath tub.

A paramedic inserted a long needle into Jerry Dean's chest. Air was compressed into his lungs. His body jumped violently when electrical jolts were shot to get his heart going.

I was not encouraged when they revived him. This was not what he was going for. I felt embarrassed interfering in this last pure act of his creed. He was supposed to go out on his own terms, stubbornly in his own image of a rock and roll star, alone, drunk on good whiskey and engorged on good blow.

They strapped him to the gurney and helicoptered him to the hospital. We made our way in a limousine provided by the hotel.

That week, I stayed in touch with Messrs. Silverson and Collins about matters for Nadine. Scarlett flew out with the grandchildren, her husband, and his mother. With her legal duty out of the way, Kathy and I decided it was best we return home, the ultimate decision we rightly felt should be made by Nadine uninfluenced by us.

# KYLLE

*Never give anyone the satisfaction of denying you something you need, and for that, what you have to do is to learn to need nothing. Starve the wanting part of you.*

Dorothy Allison,
"Mama"
*Trash*

I

In the Ramada Inn along I-95, six miles north of the Georgia-Florida border, Kylle's parole party rocked into its sixth hour.

Kylle and Chandler fixed a few lines of meth on the toilet tank with a razor blade behind the locked bathroom door. Chandler pecked Kylle on the corner of the mouth and handed him a rolled bill. "Compliments of Raul." Kylle bent and snorted half the line in one nostril, the other half in the other. Then he sprung and held his nostrils and snorted and shook his head. He wiped his nose and licked his mouth and fingers. "Things been going all right down in Yulee?"

Chandler plucked the bill from Kylle's hand, knelt on the toilet seat, snorted the other line. "Raul's treated me all right, I guess. I had to suck his dick a couple of times, literally and figuratively." Chandler held a nostril and

inhaled deeply, coughed, inhaled the other. "I'm glad
you're back to help me deal with him."

Kylle sniffled and licked the inside of his lips. "I'm
getting tired of hanging around here. What about
you?"Chandler dusted the tank with his index finger and
licked the residue. "Whatch you want to do?"

"I don't know."

Chandler cupped and rubbed Kylle's crotch. "Want
me to get us a room?"

"Better not."

Somebody pounded on the thin door. "Kylle, you
in there?"

Natalie.

Chandler chuckled. "Speak of the devil."

"Kylle? Kylle? You in there? Whatch you doing?"
She twisted the door handle and pulled at the door.
"Unlock this door, damn it."

Chandler unlocked the door.

Natalie twisted the knob and Chandler fell out. He
weaved and laughed. "Hey Nat. Want a snort?"

"When did you get here, bitch?"

Chandler asked Kylle under his hand, "You want
me to frisk her?"

"What?" Natalie stepped by Chandler. "What the
fuck did that bitch say?"

Kylle leaned on the doorjamb, rubbed his nose,
sniffled, and yawned. "Nothin'."

Natalie slapped Kylle. "I can't believe you. You
just got out for that shit. What you gone do when you got
to pee in the cup or pull a hair follicle?"

He pawed her a step back. "Go on. Quit pestering me."

She jabbed, hooked, missing, panting as Kylle leaned left, right, then bounced on his toes circling, slapping her on the side of the head. "You can dish it out but you can't take it." Slap. "You can dish it out but you can't take it." Slap. Natalie swung with a roundhouse, missed, swung with a roundhouse, missed. She stumbled, catching herself before her head hit the floor. She turned and lunged. Kylle caught her in a headlock, spun her, and then with his shoulders and hips, smudged her against the wall. "Why you got to be this way?"

"Quit it, Kylle, goddamnit."

He slung her.

She charged again.

He dodged, snagged her hand and bent it in to the wrist. All he had to do was apply a little more pressure for it to snap.

She winced, bent over. "Quit." She tried kneeing his groin. Missed.

He kneed her in the stomach.

She screamed. "Bastard. Bastard motherfucker."

The other kids in the room coiled round them.

Panting, her hands shook. "I ain't putting up with your bullshit anymore--"

He stood her by her toe tips, hanging by the throat, his hand the rope.

She gulped air. "I know Chandler's your fuckin' bitch--"Raising her a half inch, the gulping stopped.

She grappled his wrists.

He knocked her hands away and drew his Ruger from his back and stuck its black muzzle between her eyes. "I could pop a bullet in your head right now so easy, you fuckin' cunt."

Chandler yawned. None of the kids moved. Somebody screamed for him to stop. Most just blinked half asleep and swayed like Spanish moss in a breeze.

He let her get a breath but still held tight. He flung up his sloppy tank top. A large bandage covered his abdomen. "Forty stitches. You'd like to poke me again, wouldn't you?"

She puckered to spit.

He covered her mouth and nose, "Uh-uh. Uh-uh," whipped her head this way and that, bounced it off the wall and stared at her, counting to himself, *one thousand, two thousand, three thousand, four thousand, five thousand . . . . How long would it take for her to start squirming for breath? Eleven thousand. Pretty good.*

"You want to breathe do you?"

"Mm-mm."

"You want to breathe?"

Scared eyes. She nodded.

Six*teen thousand.* He moved his hand, leaned on her with his forearm, kept the Ruger pointed against her head.

A tall medium-skinned black boy with long dreads, wearing a teal football jersey, lurched from the circle of kids and offered Kylle a toke of his joint. "Come on man, be cool. Put your tool away. Let little sister go."

Kylle squinted. "Who you?"

The kid raised his open palms above his faux diamond ear studs. "I ain't nobody, man. Just want to have some fun like everybody else. Come on, let little sister alone."

"You the cocksucker been fuckin' her while I been locked up?"

"Naw, man--"

"Last nigga I heard braggin' about getting white pussy ended up eatin' out of a straw for six months."

"I ain't disrespectin'--"

"Why you in my business, then?"

"Man, I don't want to be in no-o-body's business, you know what I'm sayin'? I just want to drink and smoke some reefer and party with all these fine ladies here."

The kids mumbled agreement.

The black kid said, "We don't need no po-po."

"Let her go, Kylle," Chandler said. "Vitamin don't mean nothin'. He's a friend."

Kylle scanned the kids and smirked. He leaned and his mouth rested against Natalie's ear. "If I can't have you, nobody else can. Just remember that." Then he bit Natalie's ear, she screamed, and he stepped back.

Natalie buckled. The black kid, Vitamin, caught her.

Kylle watched Vitamin and Natalie's chunky best friend, Lisa, in her Goth attire, crook their arms under Natalie's and walk her toward the door to the adjoining room.

He raked his skinned head. "Don't be mad, baby. I'll call you later. I'll get us a room and we'll have our own private party like old times."

Natalie hurled his senior ring. He deflected it just
before it hit him above the eye. It lay against the bare foot
of an Asian girl wearing faded jeans low on her hips and a
red silk camisole. She smiled. He almost bent down but
his pride told him to fuck it and he walked away to find
Chandler.

The room vibrated again. Booming hip-hop. Girls
in bikini panties. Smoke thick and bitter. Shirtless boys
swilling from kegs and chanting, *drink, drink, drink, drink*
. . .

Kylle watched Natalie and Lisa run out into the
pouring rain.

The Asian girl tapped him on the shoulder. Her hair
flowed down to her waist. She held up his ring. He swept
her up against his bicep and kissed her. She opened her
lips. Rode his thigh. He reached into his pant pocket and
popped an ecstasy into his mouth.

"What's that?" she said.

"A happy pill."

She whined. "Oh, I want one."

He opened his mouth and slid it from his tongue
onto her tongue. She smiled and moaned, swallowing the
pill with a swig of beer she snagged from a kid walking by,
and wiped her lips with her hand. Kylle's knees shuddered.
The room spun. Fettered still to his temper, he moved in
rhythm against the girl and caressed her hard nipples. Her
fingers slithered into his pants. Later, he thought. Let her
cool off. The both of them. He might get a tattoo. Some
place on his body that would be painful. His shin, maybe.
The back of his neck.

Chandler shoaled up behind him. "What the fuck are you doing?" Chandler elbowed the girl. She toppled onto the tawny carpet and gave them a confused look, while pulling down her camisole.

All of it crashed in on him like a wave. "It's getting hinky." He shoved past Chandler and stepped over the girl, slashing out of the reeking room and into the gnat-biting darkness. A thick cockroach wriggled upside down on the walkway outside the door. He stomped it and skiddered to his car.

The rain still beat down and would get caught in gusts that blew sideways like curtains. He sat soaked in the silver Mustang he'd bought off some Yankee on St. Simons that panicked alimony money. The Newport filled his lungs. Then he snapped the car in drive. It muscled away and the dual pipes thundered as the storm, blown in from the Atlantic, choked the sewers.

II

Three days after the party, Kylle and Chandler were in Kylle's car, going down a chalky road, listening to the squawk from a portable police-band radio. They had hit a half a dozen houses. No dogs, no alarms systems, no neighbors, no risk the people would be coming home because the kids at the party had told them their parents or their grandparents were out of town, at doctors' appointments, work, or A.A.

Logging trucks and tractors used the road mainly to harvest the pulpwood and stumps in the swampy tree groves. After a time, the dirt road crossed railroad tracks that had been the scene of a double murder. Kylle and

Chandler stashed some of their drugs and cash in plastic containers in a hole at the edge of the woods where one of the bodies fell. Every time they got to the tracks, Chandler told the story of the murders as if it were the first time Kylle had heard it. As Kylle dug up the Rubbermaids, Chandler chewed his fingernails and spit out the story.

"The old man dropped right where he stood. One shot in the back of the head. Boom. Turned his brain into fuckin' mush. Dropped face down right here in the weeds beside the cab, you know, right here where we're standing. Didn't even know what hit him. That'd be a bitch to be alive one second and dead the next without even expecting it."

"Probably the best way to go," said Kylle.

"The spot is haunted now," said Chandler.

Kylle stood. Sweat poured down his face and arms and back. "So it's a good thing we're stashing this shit here then. The ghosts will stand guard, I reckon."

"Fuck you, asshole."

A man and a teenage boy came up the road on two four-wheelers with a couple of black dogs trailing behind them. Kylle and Chandler ducked behind some palmettos, unable to bat away deer flies and sand gnats biting their scalps and mosquitoes swarming their faces and arms.

The silence returned after a few minutes.

"I wished you'd shut your trap and help me with this." Kylle covered the containers with the musty black loam, palmetto fronds, soggy tree limbs, moss, oak leaves, and pine straw.

Chandler threw Kylle a dirty motel towel. "Any place where blood's been spilled violently is haunted, most of the time--"

Kylle mopped his face, neck, and arms. "That's pure horse shit. Your fucking brain is fried. If that's what they're teaching you at college you need to get your money back."

"Kiss my ass. Tammy said--"

"That bitch don't know what planet she's on most of the time. She's like a possum. She wakes up in a new world every day."

"--she saw the wrecker parked right there next to the tracks like the day of the murder one night she drove out here."

Kylle grinned. "You lying sack of shit."

Chandler chuckled. "Yeah. Just wondered how far I could string you along about the haunted part."

"Well I guess you know."

They got in the Mustang.

Kylle geared the car and gunned it. The back wheels spun, throwing gravel and dirt. They barreled down the tunnel of trees, white dust boiling, powdering the car and the palmettos and ferns along the road. The car did not slow for a covey of doves that burst from gnarled vines or through the shadow of a hawk circling in an updraft, or hogs rooting for worms in the moist road ditch, as Kylle and Chandler's urgent purpose lie deeper in the swamp.

After a time, Chandler bumped Kylle's right hand and leaned in. "You ever worry them kids will turn us in?"

"Naw. As long as we keep those stupid fuckers supplied with pot and pills, nobody's gone say a thing."

"I feel kind of bad about that old lady," Chandler said.

"Shit. Don't. That hair-lipped faggot grandson of hers fucked-up my community service. I had it sweet there at the mission. Inside. Air conditioned. Then the bitch lied and I ended up picking up trash on the side of the highway sweating like a damn pig, eaten up by bugs. I almost got snake bit. Fuck that shit. Goddamn bitch. The bitch. Pissed off my probation officer when I wouldn't go back and he locked me up. The judge, she hates my guts anyway."

"She's gonna die."

"The judge?"

"Naw. That old lady. That's what her grandson told me. She's got a brain tumor or something. Cancer. They were at her chemo in Jacksonville."

Kylle's cigarette rested between his thin lips. Smoke drowsed from his nose. He shrugged. "We all got to die sometime. Old people. They never throw nothing away. We got enough pills to keep your Brantley County bitches stoned for a month."

"What about that kid where we got all those guns and swords? I saw the pictures in the house. His dad a Marine or cop or something?"

"Both."

"Huh?"

"He's both. He's some big wig at the Law Enforcement Training Center at Glynnco."

"Fuck."

Kylle lowered his window and snapped his cigarette out. "His kid just moved down here from Maryland or somewhere. He got into some deep shit up there and Momma sent him south to live with Daddy to keep him from getting locked up."

"It's good to have a daddy with connections."

"You should know."

"Shit, it was my dad's turn to cook for his supper club last night. I had to bartend for those old bastards."

"What'd y'all fix?"

"Crab stew, shrimp, corn, crab cakes from Barbara Jean's, baked potatoes, New York strips on the grill."

"Goddamn."

"They all left knee crawling, elbow walking drunk," Chandler said. "If there'd been a roadblock on Frederica, the twelve could have locked up nearly the whole courthouse crowd." Chandler grabbed his gym bag and rummaged through it. "Oh shit. I forgot. I brought you a cigar. Old man Dixon gave it to me."

"Thanks, bud." Kylle sniffed the cigar. "Expensive." Kylle bit off the tip of the cigar and hunted for his lighter. "Any women there?"

A blur of passing evergreens, hanging vines, waist-high palmettos. The mystery of creatures beyond, elusive as quicksilver. A hackled hog unspooling a cottonmouth from the knuckles of a cypress root. A wild cat half unseen behind the veil of Spanish moss. The corrugated back of a gator spying out of black water with its golden eyes. The pungent odor of a meandering polecat.

"I'm not supposed to say," Chandler said.

"Oh, the double raccoon secret bullshit. How many?"

"Hypothetically speaking, there may have been two or three."

"And hypothetically, you made the arrangements."

"Crank for the girls goes a long way to keep the boys happy with poontang. Funny as hell seeing those old bastards getting all steamed up while they got lap-danced and seeing them wheelbarrowing the girls across the floor. Dixon about threw out his back. They thought they were gonna get free snatch and blowjobs, but I got that straighten out right quick. Old cheap motherfucking bastards."

"Of course. And they had to negotiate that shit through you. You're a fucking prince."

"Damn straight," Chandler said. "I'm no fucking philanthropist. No altruist."

"Hold up, hold up. A what?"

"I don't give my shit away. You taught me that."

"Sure, sure. Hell, fuck no," Kylle said. "You never give nothing for free."

"I'm just as much a fucking capitalist as Dixon's bank and your fucking bondsman." Chandler pulled out a roll of twenties from his pocket. "Look at this. I made a couple of percent from the girls' action. It greased some of the old boys to pay off the bets they owed me and I took some more."

"Yassir." Kylle said.

"Yassir. Land of the Haves and Have Nots. Only The Apartheid Causeway between 'em."

"You fucking read too much," Kylle said.

"Hey, let me tell you what happened last Sunday morning," Chandler said.

"Shoot, cocksucka."

"Some Sea Island bitch dad's representing in her divorce came waltzing into the kitchen."

"Fuckin' for the retainer," Kylle said.

"Hold up, goddamnit. Listen, this bitch's face had been pulled back so many times, goddamn gnarly. No tan lines, fake tits, bald as one of those Playboy bitches."

"She had a Brazilian box?"

"That's what I said."

"Smooth as butter."

"Fuck you."

"You don't know what you're missing, Chandler."

Chandler huffed. "I'm not even listening to you. She had a cup of coffee with me and bummed one of my cigarettes. It was just as if it was our Sunday routine. She lifted the front section of the paper--"

"Your future stepmomma."

"Fuck you, asshole. In a little bit she said, 'Sweetie, I just come down wondering if you had a little ol' mood booster.' 'Well goddamn peaches, why sure,' I said. I offered her half of my bagel and a glass of orange juice. Oh, that pissed her off. I guess she thought she'd get a free snort."

Kylle said, "A bitch don't get nothin' for free."

"Fuckin' right. She finally pulled two twenties out of her big shiny purse. I handed her a baggie--"

"We need to--" Kylle said.

"Shut up for a minute. Then Mrs. Botox snorted it right there between us, gave me a kiss with some tongue, I almost knocked the shit out of her, then she shook her bare ass back up the stairs. I had to get the hell out of there, her whittlin' dad's pecker, screaming, just the way he likes 'em-- "

"This is what we need to do--" Kylle said.

"--Another fucking crazy morning in the neighborhood."

Kylle found the lighter. "Preaching to the choir, brother."

"It's just a façade. The island's really one fucked up, fucked up place."

"Let's go down to Daytona for spring break," Kylle said." "I know a dude we can stay with."

"Yeah. Okay. But, what about that kid?" Chandler said.

"What kid?"

"The one whose daddy is the fuckin' Fed."

"Shit. It didn't take the kid long to start doing the same shit down here, though." Kylle steered with his knee as he flicked the lighter, once, twice, three times.

"Here," Chandler said. "Let me do it for you." He lit it and held the lighter in his right hand and draped his left arm over the back of Kylle's seat while Kylle spun the cigar under the flame and drove.

"He uses his allowance from momma to buy enough shit from me to float through the days until he graduates." Kylle inhaled and blew a narrow stream of smoke. "He's gone try to be a macho Marine like daddy. Says he wants to go to Iraq or Afghanistan and kill Hajis. I hope he gets his stoned head blown off. Retarded motherfucker."

Chandler dropped the lighter in the console and leaned back against the door. "Yeah, but if I'd known his dad was a Fed beforehand, man, I wouldn't . . . We could be fucked bad--"

"Naw," Kylle said.

"--A fucking arsenal."

"The kid told me his stepmom got the Tec-9 during some Customs seizure. She was supposed to have turned it in--"

"Thinks he's a bad motherfucker," Chandler said.

"He's a fucked up dumb motherfucker that would be in deep shit if the cops found out. Serious federal time. All we got to do is keep Mr. All Fuckin' American supplied with all the free dope he wants until he goes Jarhead."

Chandler sat up and flipped the lighter between his fingers. "Still . . . Shit, that could cost us more . . ."

"Naw, naw. I got it all figured. He won't want to get his ass in a sling anymore, either."

"I guess."

Kylle grabbed Chandler under his chin, pinched his cheeks, and wagged his face. He puckered and leaned within a few inches of Chandler's lips. They laughed.

Chandler sat back again and watched Kylle smoke.

After a time they drove out of a thick row of pines into a swath bare and dry after its trees had been harvested. Kylle realized for the first time there was a pond about a half-mile off the road. He wondered about the fishing there.

Kylle said, "Me and my dad never did anything together except talk about doing things together. Not that he wouldn't, he couldn't. I don't remember a moment in my life that my daddy wasn't locked-up for gutting from rectum to Adam's apple the bastard who molested my sisters."

"Goddamn, Kylle," Chandler said. "You never said . . ."

Kylle blew a stream of smoke and held the cigar between his fingers atop the steering wheel. "He was on death row for a long time until some judge commuted his sentence. I saw him more those six years he was on death row than at any time in my life."

Chandler pulled his knees under his chin and leaned against the door.

Kylle told Chandler about visiting his dad in prison, about how his mom would load him and his two sisters every third Sunday of every month in her brother's station wagon and drive them the 90 miles to the prison in Reidsville. The two hours it took to get there were hours of excited anticipation, like Christmas Eve. They knew the destination was the big prison, but it was as if they had no sense of what a prison was. Reality would not hit them until they were in the parking lot. Then the curtain would pull back and the lights would shine and they would finally hear the gate snap locked, and see the razor-wired fence coiled round the building. The drive back would be quiet. Kylle would crawl in the back seat and fall asleep. He would wake sweating through his collar and stuck to the vinyl seat after dreaming that his dad and he had gone fishing on the river and caught a whole line of catfish. With the seams of the seat indented in his cheek, he would sit up, try to rub the crick out of his neck, see his mom still driving and trying to keep her eyes open. His sisters were usually asleep like kittens in the front seat, the youngest slumped against their mom, the oldest against the youngest. The inside of the car was a wind tunnel. As it was Sunday, the only thing on the AM radio was an evangelical preaching about the wages of sin, eternal damnation and salvation. It never gave Kylle hope. Nothing gave him hope after enduring those goodbyes and drives home month after month.

"The last time I saw him was the weekend before my twelfth birthday. The guard who escorted him to visitation ate cake with us and sang.

"The next day when me and my sisters got off the school bus, my Aunt Shirley met us at the bus stop. When I saw all the cars parked in the driveway and on road in front of our house, I knew something bad was wrong. I don't know why I remember this, but I remember my uncles standing under the aluminum carport smoking. And then I remember going in the back door, and my mom was sitting at the kitchen table crying real loud into a washcloth. Me and my sisters went to mom and we all three hugged at the same time. My little sister asked, 'Why are you crying, Mommy?' My sisters started crying because my momma was crying. My mom calmed down after a while and then she told us, 'Babies, your daddy's dead. Some prisoner stabbed him.'"

A glade lay a few hundred yards off the dirt road between the swamp and the heavy power line that ran west through Brantley County over to Waycross. Kylle and Chandler came here to be left alone.

"I still have the fishing dream where me and my dad catch all those catfish on the river."

Kylle and Chandler stored the rest of their stolen loot and some of their drugs in two six-foot long plastic coolers dug into the gray sandy ground behind some briar bushes and a thicket of palmettos. The coolers were full of pistols, rifles, bullets, loaded clips, pocketknives, pills in ziplock plastic bags, rare coins, real silver forks, spoons, and knives, and now two long samurai swords. Shirtless, wringing sweat, shorts drooping, they covered the coolers with the damp loam, two thick pine logs, and their piss.

The treefrogs' *quank-quank-quank-quank*ed in time with the pulse in Kylle's temple. The swamp like the inside of a pneumonic lung.

They packed cash in two other smaller plastic containers and stuffed them inside an armadillo mound that they'd exhume later with a hook Kylle had welded and shaped.

The sun fell behind the western pines and water oaks. Their shadows cut across the dank glade. A sliver of orange globe expanded above, but it was twilight already in the thick woods. The moss-laden limbs and vines provided a shield from the outside world. Nocturnal beasts stirred.

Kylle and Chandler howled as the Tec-9 and the AK-47 chewed-up scrawny pines. The guns slung dozens of shells with each loud burst. Wispy strands of Spanish moss floated to the ground. Pine chips flew and ricocheted, leaving gnarled stumps. Kylle saw Natalie and her nigger rescuer (same as the image of the one that shanked his daddy) convulsing in a pile of skin and guts and bone splinters. They passed the Crown Royal bottle to each other with rebel yells and drank without wiping the lip, firing their guns until their ammo was spent and the barrels glowed blue heat and pale vapors replaced the concussions.

Then staggering and laughing, spitting and groping, rolling among the shells, wrestling like rutting bucks, Kylle heaved Chandler to his back and pinned his bare shoulders. "Say calf rope. Say it. *Say it, goddamnit.* Calf rope. Say it. I got you pinned. Calf rope, motherfucker."

Chandler wriggled and scudded away on his hands and knees, kicking up oak leaves and pine needles. He squalled, "Let me catch my breath."

Kylle grabbed Chandler's baggy jean shorts and pulled them down to his ankles.

"You cocksucker," Chandler hollered.

"Yeah, what you gone do about it?"

Chandler lunged.

Kylle lifted his hips off the ground and crab-walked backwards.

Chandler lunged again and tackled Kylle by his shoestrings, rolled to his knees and straddled Kylle. With his forearms, he pushed all his weight onto Kylle's shoulders. "I got you in calf rope now, motherfucker."

Kylle rose from his abdomen, not to be pinned, never to be pinned. After a few seconds, he reached behind Chandler's head and pulled him down. He felt them lock in a hinging at the waist, and with it, a heat, a pressure from Chandler, hollow from Natalie. Chandler before him, glistening in sweat, the oak leaves *shishing*, an unburdening breeze, they, in this moment, breathing, there. That pressure, that heat. The hinging. He slid his hands up Chandler's arms, up over his shoulders, round, taut.

III

Kylle had been staying at a motel on Highway 17, across the street from the abandoned paint factory, after being let out of Alto. Chandler knocked on the orange door a little before seven. Kylle pulled the curtain back and peeked out. Chandler, in starched khakis and untucked blue oxford button down, rocked from one sockless loafer to the other.

"Hold on," Kylle said. A low cloud morning. The weather pressure squeezed a migraine. He lit a cigarette, unlocked the warped door and cracked it open. Wearing just his boxers.

Chandler pulled his brown hair back tight with his hands. "Ain't you going with me?"

Kylle rubbed his eyes. "Where you going?"

"Yulee." Chandler looked around. "A pick-up. Remember?"

"What? I thought you had a class at the college."

"Tomorrow. Come on."

"Naw, man. Think I'm gone puke."

"Aw man, get dressed. You'll be all right once you get up and going."

"Go on. I don't feel good."

"We'll get you some coffee and Goody's or something," Chandler said.

"Naw."

Chandler pushed the door.

Kylle held tight. "Quit being a pain in the ass, Chandler. Go on."

"I don't want to go by myself."

"Then don't go." Kylle coughed.

"You know I can't do that. Raul will feed me to the gators if you don't show."

"Ah, you been dealin' with him ever since I been locked up. He ain't gone mess with you."

"I told him you were coming," Chandler said. "He's expecting you."

Gulls stood and flapped and squawked on the old swimming pool that had been filled in with black dredged sand. A chain link fence still surrounded it, some sections gouged and drooping.

Chandler stretched to look over Kylle's head. "Who you got in there with you? That Asian bitch?"

"Nobody."

"Nobody? Really?" Chandler slapped the wall beside the door, inciting dirt daubers from their fluted nests under the rotting eaves. "It smells like piss out here. Let me in, goddamnit."

"I'm going back to bed."

"That why you didn't come stay with me last night?"

"Man, quit being a drama queen. Go the fuck on."

Chandler tramped back to his Jeep, mumbling. He shouted back to Kylle. "I should have never given that little slanty-eyed bitch your number." Then he flipped Kylle off as he tried to peel away.

Other than a few oleanders and unpruned crepe myrtles and palms here and there, no tree grew on the motel's grounds. Where there were not scuffed out sand splotches, St. Augustine grass lay scorched and overgrown with dollar weeds and clover, and throughout, veined mole tunnels.

A black man in shorts and a dirty white sweatshirt walked beside the road against traffic carrying a five-gallon bucket and a window squeegee, whistling the National Anthem. Kylle had seen the Whistler riding an old cruiser bicycle or walking, whistling church hymns and marches. His volume could overcome the noise of jackhammers, train engines, and pulpwood trucks, and, like a shaft of light, pierce closed car windows.

Kylle remembered giving the Whistler a ride across the causeway once. It was a steamy afternoon, the sky full of boiling clouds. The Whistler reeked of fish and onions. They smoked Newports and rode with the windows down. They drove into a black wall of hard rain. Rain whipping the smoky onion interior. Kylle and the Whistler, brothers of rain and cigarettes.

Just as quickly, they were out of the rain, reaching the mainland, Highway 17, the Fendig billboard warning convicted felons in English and Spanish that possessing firearms could subject them to federal prison too. The Whistler said, "Somebody stole my cruiser right off the front porch of my Auntie's house and it only two blocks from the po-lice's station. You got a couple of Newports you can spare?"

This morning, with the sun rising and the Whistler in silhouette before the orange slit of sky, Kylle swayed like a skinny pine and blinked hard. Stoned, stunned, or by reflex or unknowing, whether in dream or no, his right hand crept to his heart and remained there until the Whistler walked in front of Mack's Barbeque, sustaining the last notes of the Anthem. *For the land of the free-e-e-e. And the ho-o-o-me, of the, bra-a-a-a-ve.*

Kylle shivered. "Ho-o-o-ly shit." Then the last long savoring drags before he flicked his cigarette to the parking lot, turned, and slammed the door.

Fleas jumped as he slogged over the sandy carpet to the bathroom. He stood over the toilet and brooded over his stream of water. Under the weak bulb over the sink, he pulled back the bandage and studied the sutures. The wound was tender and inflamed, oozing puss. "The crazy bitch." He bit his lower lip and tore off the rest of the bandage. Winced as he dabbed bourbon on the stitch line with toilet paper. Concentrated to hold down the bile that burned upward. Taped on a fresh gauze square. Guzzled a mouth full of Jim Bean once, swallow, twice, swallow, three times. Swallowed, bleary-eyed, crawled in the sour bed, embalmed and leaden, wondering whether he could unmoor himself from the old siege, like talons of some giant vulture gripping his heart, the overbearing weight that bore him down, the shadow that shut out all light all joy. If he gripped the Ruger on the bed stand right now, would a bullet through the roof of his mouth be painless, instantaneous? Or would he just fuck himself up, brain damaged, lying in a fetal position, prisoned to machines and tubes, bed-sored, until his muscles evaporated and his organs gave out? Would death be a soulless unconsciousness, Jesus' warm golden paradise where he might be embraced by his dad, or the unquenchable fires? Or would he be born again into some river insect hatching, skittering, and dying all in one day, or a red-assed monkey, or some water-headed catfish-skinned sentient from another galaxy with long fingers and an albino body like a starving toddler?

The accruing gray dawn seeped around the frayed edge of the brown curtains paisleyed in orange and gold. Sweat beaded his forehead. The muscles down his spine were like taut chain. He brushed away a fly that landed on his face, augured gnats in his ear canals, kicked a cockroach crawling over his foot. A wiry eight-inch lizard assumed the wall above his head like a cell's baleful sentinel. Sometime, in all this, he repined into a head sore dreamless half-sleep.

The owner pounded on the room door at eleven. "Check-out time, Kylle."

Bourbon filmed his mouth. His temple throbbed as if he'd been bludgeoned with a tire iron. The sutures bowed him in. Fresh mosquito and cockroach bites stippled his arms, legs, and neck. His ears rang a high-pitched *e-e-e-n*.

He snatched a tee shirt off the floor and armed into it. Legged into wrinkled jeans. Pulled on a pair of raveling white socks stained black at the ankles. Stomped into his prison issued brogans, scuffed and dull.

Without looking back, he cracked open the door and his boot provoked a crab to sidle from under the air conditioner to the corner. "This shit hole is all yours." Then he staggered out of the room, leaving the bed sheets peeled loose, and shielded his eyes from the blanching glare.

Chandler unlounged himself from the hood of the Mustang. "Y'all all fucked out?"

Kylle bent over and grabbed his side and sneezed. "Goddamnit, shit."

The stench of low tide. Down wind from the paper mill, turpentine plant, and power plant. Another day's dose of poison. The heavy air fuming sulfur, chlorine, coal ash, and some other putrid chemical that Brunswick seethed in the processing of stump hearts, which he could not name, a miasma stinging his nostrils. He held his abdomen and flung his duffle into his car.

"Damn, you look like shit," Chandler said.

Kylle cleared his throat. "That's about how I feel."

Chandler scoured beside him. "Where's your company? The slantyeyed bitch."

"What?" He slapped Chandler on the back of the head. "Man, don't be a shit ass."

Kylle followed Chandler in his Jeep to a Waffle House hemmed in by a tidal creek and strip of marsh, and an abandoned Texaco self service station. Somebody had chained a three-legged wiener dog to the Brunswick News dispenser. The chain was long enough for the skinny dog to sit shaded under a rusty folding chair. Next to the chair, courtesy of the County's inside smoking ban, was a metal table with a plastic Waffle House ashtray full of butts.

They slid into a booth next to the window. Chandler read a newspaper left in the booth. He told Kylle of the front page story about a string of burglaries on St. Simons. "Cops got no prints. Of course not."

Kylle propped his head on his hands and inhaled the steam rising from his black coffee while some country singer growled and gargled on the jukebox. The siege was full blown, like being eaten alive inside by millions of microscopic piranhas. The Ruger lay under the driver's seat out in the Mustang. Otherwise, he could have blown his head off right where he sat.

"You look like death," Chandler said. Kylle thought at first he said, "You would like death."

He looked up and all was cataracted. He closed his eyes and massaged his temple and tried to come to terms with another day.

After a time, the waitress brought Chandler's food and refilled Kylle's coffee. "Here you go, hon," she said. Chandler slid the paper aside and wolfed down scrambled eggs, waffle, bacon, grits, hash browns, and milk.

Kylle leaned against the glass and closed his eyes, and every ding of spoon and click of fork and knife, every cough and murmured word, every shuffled foot and flip of newspaper, pierced his ears and reverberated inside his head. From time to time a waitress hollered an order downrange to the cook and this prompted the slamming of refrigerator doors and the blending of eggs for omelet and the cascade of plates being unstacked and tossed like cards along the metal counter. That he could be deaf. He would have liked death more, at this moment. The soulless, unconscious kind.

They stopped at a Jiffy store. Kylle bought a packet of Goody's. While he stood at the Mustang pumping gas, he flipped his head back and poured the headache powder onto the back of his tongue and chased it with a shot of flat Mountain Dew.

A cream colored Ford Fairmont whipped in behind his heels. Five Mexican men were inside the hubcapless car. Two in front, three in the back. The windows were down. Gray putrid smoke poured out of the tailpipe, which was kept from dragging by clothes hanger wire. Chandler went to the car's red front passenger door and leaned into the window. Kylle couldn't hear anything said over the Fairmont's clacking valves and Ranchero music.

Chandler leaned out of the car window. "The son of a bitch says I shorted him this morning."

Kylle turned around to the Fairmont. The Mexican at the back passenger door pulled back the front of his shirt to display a revolver.

"Tell the bastard that he should of counted the money during the transfer."

Chandler spoke to the driver in Spanish.

Kylle said. "Maybe one of these little greasy bastards stole it from him. Tell him I said he ain't getting any more from us."

Chandler translated.

The driver turned and rested his arm on the back of his seat and stared at Kylle. He spoke slowly and in a thick accent. "You call me a liar? I don't do business with liars or cheaters."

Kylle pulled the nozzle out of the car and twisted the gas cap shut and then stepped toward the back passenger door.

The driver nodded his head to the one in the back seat who pointed his revolver at Kylle's chest.

Kylle studied the Mexican. "You know, I don't like doing business with people who aim a gun at my chest."

Chandler stepped back and shook his head. "Fuck, Kylle, you're pushing the limit, here. I'll just give him the damn money."

"You didn't short him, did you?"

"No. Hell no."

"I ain't gonna let him rob us."

"Paying him is better than being dead."

Kylle asked the driver, "Raul, how much did you say we owed you?"

The Mexican held up five fingers. "Quinientos."

"Quite a shortfall," Kylle said to Chandler.

The Mexican said, "Five hundred dollars."

"Five hundred." Kylle said. "Quinientos. Quinientos."

"Simón."

Kylle followed the black diesel fumes of a dump truck with a loud muffler gunning through a yellow light. The siege compressed into rage. The great black cat that prowled under his skin. He exhaled when he realized he'd been holding his breath for however long. "We been transacting business quite a while haven't we?"

"Pos, si," Raul said.

"And we ain't had no trouble with one another."

"No."

"But now you're saying we shorted you five hundred today?"

"Simón. Five hundred dollars."

Kylle rotated his head and the muscles in his neck crackled like oak splitting. "And you want it right now."

"Si. Pinche buey. Five hundred."

Kylle looked around the car. Chandler was nowhere to be found. "Now? Right here?"

Raul, the driver, nodded to the other two back seat passengers. They pulled pistols from under their shirts and held them in their laps. One of them said, "Vámonos chingando a este pinche cabrón." *Let's kill the sonofabith.*

"Well, if that's how you're gonna be." Kylle triggered the nozzle handle, spraying gasoline in the face of the Mexican pointing the revolver and into the lap and faces of the other Mexicans in the back and over the front seat and the shoulders of the driver and the front passenger. The Mexican in the back dropped his revolver in the floorboard and screamed and clawed his eyes and kicked his fellows in the back. Kylle kept spraying as he reached into his left jean pocket and drew his disposable lighter. He let go of the handle, dropped the nozzle, and then thumbed the lighter wheel and held the flame a few inches from the front passenger's right shoulder.

"Vámonos, vámonos," the Mexican shouted.

The driver snapped the Fairmont in gear and the car squealed away into the road, pulling out in front of a tractor trailer with a load of new cars. Glass shattered, steel bent, plastic busted, Mexicans screamed. The truck braked hard and its momentum pushed the car, barely missing a minivan, a motor home, a dude on a chopper, but clipping a Florida couple in a Cadillac with a handicap placard dangling from the rearview mirror.

Kylle tucked the lighter into his pocket and watched the Mexicans heaved up the road, metal grinding, brakes moaning, Norteno accordions blaring, *ay ay ayyyyyy.* "Yessir. How far are you willing to go? That's what separates chicken shits from the real criminals."

The truck stopped when the Fairmont's front corner panel busted the new road level Pizza Hut sign.

Kylle picked up the nozzle and hung it back on the pump.

Seconds later, the Mexicans kicked open the passenger side doors and all scrambled out just before the Fairmont burst into flames. Two of the Mexicans guided the blind screaming ones stumbling, and the five dodged the six lanes of slowing traffic, holding their ribs and bleeding heads, limping behind the motor inns and restaurants, huffing toward the woods and the interstate.

Chandler jogged from the cover of the coin air pump wide-eyed and jittery. "Goddamn that was fuckin' nuts."

They went inside the store.

"What the hell happened?" asked the convenience store attendant.

"Looks like a bunch of Mexicans pulled out in front of a truck," Kylle said, handing over his twenties without looking up.

Something within the Fairmont exploded and rattled the store's pane glass. The attendant covered his head and dove under the lottery game cards. Chandler almost spilled his Slurpee when he ducked behind the pork rinds and cheese crackers.

After a few seconds, the attendant hoisted himself from the white and gray marbled linoleum squares, grunting, and went into a spasm of deep wet coughs. "Goddamn. I about messed in my britches." He gawked out the glass. "Looks like Baghdad out there."

"They tried to rob us," Chandler said. "Pulled a gun on my friend here."

Kylle slumped and cut him an eye.

The crew cut man rung up Kylle's gas and Chandler's Slurpee. He wore a blue vest festooned with a yellow support the troops ribbon pin, a red and white ribbon with a blue star, and NRA and Marine Corps pins. A television monitor above the plastic booths by the soda fountains and coffee machines blared Fox News. "Must have been a bunch of illegals the way they fell out of that car and run off." He patted the back of his belt. "They'd a come in here trying to rob me I'd a sent 'em to the cemetery."

"I bet you would of," Kylle said.

"You damn right I would," the man said. His forearm was inked with a faded green-gray tattoo of an out of focused tiger or cobra or scorpion. "I just called 911. Maybe you could give 'em identifying information or something."

"Naw. It all happened so fast," Kylle said.

The man's gut hung over the cash register. "News every day says we're being invaded by 'em. Politicians won't do a damn thing." He handed Kylle his change. "Damn Mexicans bringing drugs in by the truckloads. Ever week almost, the paper's got some drug bust down on I-95."

Chandler gave the man a ten-dollar bill for scratch off lottery tickets.

The man slipped the bill in the cash register drawer and then unspooled the cards pointed out by Chandler. "And they're having their babies in our hospitals and crowdin' our schools with a bunch of kids that we got to teach how to speak English. And you and me are paying for it. They don't pay a damn thing. I ask ya, how do you come to a country to live and don't speak the language?"

"I don't know," Kylle said.

The man handed Chandler his cards. He leaned with his palms on the counter. "I say build a wall along the border and shoot ever one that tries to climb it or tunnel under."

"Well, I don't think they're gonna catch that bunch," Kylle said. He turned toward the door. "We'll talk to ya."

"Yeah. Well, nice talking to y'all." The man put on his reading glasses and turned around to the wall counter below the snuff and chewing tobacco rack to read the newspaper. "Y'all come back."

Chandler set his Slurpee on the hood of his Jeep. "Goddamn, Kylle. Crazy motherfucker."

The Fairmont was charred and covered in flames. Thick smoke billowed from the melting tires. Sirens and fire truck horns blared, descending from east and west. Cars and trucks and vans had stopped in every direction, and winter tourists in shorts and sandals, ball capped plumbers and electricians, pulpwooders in cutsleeved shirts and overalls, sunburned roofers, bighipped housewives, leathered Harley riders, and high school kids leaving the to-go windows at Burger King and McDonald's stood along the road ditch like a gaggle of pelicans shitting on a shrimp boat dock. They crossed their arms over their chests or videoed or photographed or cell phone squawked while they watched the car burn.

The driver had backed his truck from the Fairmont. He sat on the doorstep of his cab smoking a cigarette, cradling a small fire extinguisher.

"Damn Chandler, can't you keep your goddamn mouth shut?"

Chandler scratched a lottery ticket with a dime. "What'd I say?"

"Don't say nothing. And how the hell did those heathens know where we were?"

"Mmm." Chandler scratched another lottery ticket.

"I said how did they know where we were?"

Chandler held up his cell phone. "Listen. Raul called me and said he'd shorted me this morning. Insisted that he bring me my money."

"And you believed him and then you told him where we'd be."

"Well . . . I told him I'd meet him at the Cracker Barrel across the street."

Kylle shook his head. "Didn't that sound a little suspicious to you? You're going to get us killed or busted. You don't set up some meeting off the cuff like that. You checked the stuff he gave you this morning, didn't you?"

"Yeah."

"And you knew you hadn't shorted him, that's what you told me, right?"

"Yeah." Chandler sucked on the straw of his cherry Slurpee.

"You got to be more careful. It should have signaled a set up to you. Either he'd be wired or you were going to get ambushed. And you see which one he tried. Brought muscle with him. The cemetery and the jail are full of stupid criminals." Kylle opened his car door. "Remember who had the fucking gun aimed at his chest."

"Yeah. I'm sorry."

"Sorry? Fuck sorry. Think, goddamnit."

"Well, if you'd gone with me this morning instead of laying with that little Asian bitch none of this would have happened."

Kylle clamped his arm around Chandler's neck like a vise. "Chandler, it's moments such as this that I ask myself why I don't take you out to the Gulf Stream buoy and leave you."

Chandler held up a lottery ticket. "Look. I won a hundred dollars."

Kylle unhanked him and Chandler rubbed the back of his neck and ran into the store and came out moments later strutting, snapping a hundred dollar bill in both hands.

"You're the luckiest son of a bitch I've ever seen," Kylle said.

Chandler buried the bill in the middle of his paper money and jammed the roll in his front khaki pocket. "I'm way ahead of the odds."

They got in their cars and Chandler followed Kylle to a tattoo shop on Highway 341. It was on the same side of the street between the Pentecostal church and school and the dirt road to the gun range, and across from the liquor store and the railroad switching yard.

Chandler had three fears: clowns, being locked up, and needles. He watched, shivering and stuttering, wondering how Kylle could sit there calm and quiet while a needle drew the Chinese symbol for love on his left pectoral.

IV

Natalie would not answer her cell and would not return Kylle's messages. He'd been trying to talk to her since the day after the party. One time a black boy answered the phone.

"Who's this?" Kylle asked.

"This Kylle?" the boy asked.

"I want to talk to Natalie."

"You a stubborn motherfucker, I'll give you that."

"Don't cuss me, nigger."

The boy hung up, howling.

Kylle called Lisa on her cell. She told him Natalie wanted nothing else to do with him. He was lucky she did not swear out a warrant and get him thrown back in jail where he belonged. Lisa refused to relay any message of his to Natalie. She hung up on him when he began cussing her.

V

Kylle and Chandler had half a dozen deliveries to make that evening along I-95 from St. Mary's north to the Darien outlet mall. It would only take them a couple of hours. Chandler wanted to go see some of the strippers across the interstate from the outlet mall when they finished. Kylle grumbled that they didn't have time and he didn't want to leave all that cash in the car while Chandler visited his skanky customers with their floppy tits and cellulite asses. Kylle had other plans that he kept to himself for the time being.

After their last delivery, when their hidden car compartments were full of cash and empty of pills and weed, they headed back south on I-95.

Chandler lit a joint and inhaled, holding his breath before exhaling. After a time, Chandler realized they were in the vicinity of Natalie's house. "You're not thinking about going to Nat's, are ya?"

Kylle blew cigarette smoke through his nose and grinned. "Hey, there's an idea."

"No, we ain't." Chandler leaned on the passenger door and picked at the acne on his forehead. Unruly black whiskers blotched his face.

Kylle knew that Natalie's mother would be at work at the hospital. He hoped her little brother was at a friend's, too. He flipped open his cell phone, and before hitting the speed dial, he turned to Chandler. "Here's what we're gone do. Get your cell phone out."

"Why?" Chandler asked.

"Just do what I said."

Chandler unclipped his cell phone from his belt.

"You're going to call Nat—"

"I don't wanna call—"

"Hell yes you're callin'. I call, she'll see my number and won't answer."

"You're aiming to fucker the shit, aren't you?"

Kylle hit Chandler in the face with the back of his hand and knocked the joint out of his mouth.

"Goddamn, Kylle. What'd you do that for?" Chandler unbuckled his seat belt and bent forward, his head between his knees, foraging the floorboard.

"Do what I said, Chandler, or I'm gone beat your ass right here in this fuckin' car."

Chandler groped for the joint.

"Forget about that damn joint for a second."

Chandler sat up. "What?"

"Tell her you're on your way."

Chandler bit his lower lip.

"Give me your goddammn phone," Kylle said. "You're too fucking stoned to dial."


VI

Kylle parked his Mustang at the Baptist Church down the street from Natalie's house. He pulled his Ruger from under the driver's seat and slid it in the back waistband of his jeans.

"Why you bringing that?" Chandler asked.

"Don't want to leave it in the car."

Chandler surveyed the church grounds and down the street. "Nobody's going to bother it around here."

Kylle hawked up phlegm, nodded, and spit on the wet asphalt. He unlocked the trunk and stashed his gun under the spare tire.

Chandler zipped up his hooded sweatshirt to the damp cold. "Hold up. I got to take a piss." He ran up to a line of shrubbery behind the church, over by the children's swings, slide, teeter-totter, and monkey bars.

Kylle locked the car with the key remote, then walked up to the shrubbery next to Chandler, unzipped his jeans, and pissed in the black sand, too.

Kylle zipped his pants. "Come on."

Chandler pulled his shorts down and squatted, hanging onto the swing-set pole. He and Kylle laughed as he shat into the sand under a toddler swing. Kylle said, "You are one stoned nasty bastard." Chandler wiped himself on the cold wet metal poles.

"Come on, let's go on back to the car and go get drunk at my house," Chandler said.

"We're already here. We'll go after."

The pavement flushed in dull pink by streetlights every fifty yards. Kylle and Chandler kept in the shadows as they skulked along the grassy road ditch toward Natalie's house. All the dogs were barking on both sides of the street.

They climbed the chain-link fence and Chandler knocked on the back sliding-glass door.

Natalie moved a wooden curtain rod from the bottom door track and unlocked the door. Chandler stood in a small patch of light thrown onto the patio from the inside lamp and watched her slide the door back. Natalie brushed her bangs out of her eyes and stared at Chandler for a second, then peeped outside left and right. "You sure you're by yourself?"

"Yeah, I swear," Chandler said, shaking his head. "I just come to bring you this peace offering like I promised--."

"I got a test tomorrow. I'm trying to study . . ."

He handed her a baggy. "I ain't gone stay long."

Natalie stepped back. "Oh, thanks for the weed. Apology acc--" As she slid the door shut, Kylle jumped out from behind an oleander and pressed against the door.

Natalie pushed against it, but Kylle had the leverage and was too strong.

Natalie ran for the house phone.

Kylle jumped around her and pried it out of her hand.

"Damn you Chandler," Natalie said. "Fucking pussy." She backed against the wall. "Son of a bitch."

Chandler picked up the baggy on the floor.

Natalie tossed her head and raised her hand. "I want to know, of the three of us, who likes it up the ass better? Chandler, you the pitcher or the catcher? I'm always the catcher. Just the nature of my anatomy. But you boys. Don't think I didn't know. Kylle, how's it up the ass with you?"

Kylle backhanded her. Her head snapped back. Blood trickled out of the corner of her mouth.

Chandler opened the sliding door and caught Kylle's car keys.

Natalie smudged the blood from her mouth. "Shit, don't leave, Chandler. I don't care what they say. Three's a party not a crowd--"

Kylle backhanded her again.

She kept talking "--especially between the three of us. We got so much in common. You boys come here for a threesome? I ain't into that."

Kylle slapped her the hardest the third time. She spun and stumbled into the wall and came up again rubbing her cheek. "But that don't make no difference to you, does it? You'd just force me, huh Kylle? That what you come for? Beau'll be home any minute."

Chandler shook his head. He slid back the door and walked into the darkness.

Natalie sidled around the corner of the wall and tried to get down the hallway, but Kylle snagged her arm, brought her back to the plaid living room couch, and held her, their heads reclined on the maroon crocheted afghan draped over the back.

She covered her mouth. "Quit, Kylle."

"I just came by to see if you got the roses I sent, baby. I just wanted to see you."

"I threw the fucking things away."

Kylle laughed. "Boo-whoo."

"Fuck you, Kylle." She wrung his arm from over her shoulder and scooted away.

"Where's your nigger boyfriend?"

"You're nuts, Kylle."

"Nuts?" He lifted the front of his shirt. "You're the one that cut me, remember?"

"You deserved it."

"Come on, let's put all that shit behind us, okay?"

She stood. "I'm tired of it, you fuckin' psychopath."

He pounced, knocking a cup of ice tea off the end table. She flinched. He caught himself and then stepped back again. "I'm sorry. Baby, I'm sorry. I love you, baby."

"Get the fuck out," she said.

"Come on, baby."

Her upper lip ballooned. Her face splotched. She rubbed tears with the back of her hand.

He smoothed his hands over her arms. "Sh-sh-sh-sh-sh. Natalie. Come on, baby. I'm sorry. I didn't mean to hurt you. I love you. What we've got is special. Come on." He massaged her shoulders. "Relax, relax. I promise I won't be mean anymore."

She hugged herself.

He wrapped his arms around her, patted her back. "You're gone hyperventilate like that."

"No, Kylle. Stop," she whispered. "Quit. Let me go."

"Natalie. Relax. Come on. Please. I promise."

"No." She pushed him away.

"I just want to talk to you. We've gone through these rough times before."

She shook, wiped her nose, coughed. "I'm tired of it."

"I love you, baby."

"You don't know what love is."

He grabbed her breast and squeezed.

She spit in his face and ran down the hallway.

He grabbed her at the threshold of the bathroom.

She rolled to her back and kangaroo kicked, missing, cracking the drywall, but then tagging him with four quick kicks in the gut and ribs.

He back kicked her in the ass, jumped, straddled her neck, and yanked her by the hair and wrenched her to her feet. "Gotdamn cunt. Motherfuckit." He punched her in the face.

Her head rolled and jerked like a puppet.

His hand gripped her mouth like a vice. "Calm down, bitch. Calm down, I said."

She scowled and panted. Blood poured from her nose.

"You feel better, now?"

He blew. "You got me good."

Spittle ran down his chin. He smeared it on her shoulder.

"Calm down," he said. "Calm down, damnit."

He pulled his hand away. Chuckled. Kissed her. "You are one mean little bitch. I've always liked that about you."

She squirmed, brought her knee up, tagging him on the side of his knee.

He collapsed and rolled, holding his leg, laughing. "Goddamn shit."

She scrambled up the hall.

He pushed himself up and hobbled after her. Then heard three gunshots. Something hit the wall and knocked metal and glass and the telephone crashing to the floor.

His ears rang. His insides felt as if the explosion had gone off in his belly.

He limped around the corner and peeked into the living room.

Chandler stood over Natalie holding the Ruger with thumb and finger. Blood splattered the wall, Chandler's shirt, face, legs, and hands.

Natalie lay on the floor. Blood poured out of her head, soaking the beige carpet. Her leg twitched. A gurgled moan. Air exhaled. Then stillness.

Gravity's hand slammed the air out of Kylle, dislodged him. "Oh, my God. No. Christ no, no."

Chandler paced, still clutching the Ruger, snatching clumps of his hair and mumbling and stuttering.

Kylle yanked Chandler by the shirt, ripping his sleeves. "Christ, what the fuck did you do?"

Chandler covered his ears. "Fuck. Fuck. I lost it. Jesus, oh Jesus. Christ. Fuck, fuck, I lost it. I didn't mean to shoot. I just wanted to scare her. Oh, Jesus, no, no, no, no, no." He swallowed the barrel, squeezed his eyes, and held his breath. Kylle slapped Chandler's hand and the gun flung across the room.

Chandler collapsed into Kylle's arms. Kylle unpried him and Chandler fell to the floor.

Kylle roared at the ceiling. "No, no, no, no. Christ, no."

Chandler grabbed him by the ankles, drooling. "I love you, Kylle. I love you. I'm sorry. I-I-I--"

Kylle kicked loose and sank alongside Natalie, wrenching tears.

Chandler walked on his knees sobbing and rubbed Kylle's shoulder and arm.

Kylle clasped Chandler's throat and his nails pierced into flesh, drawing blood that inked his fingers.

Chandler twisted his head and tugged at Kylle's wrists. Piss streamed out his shorts, down his leg. His eyes rolled back in his head and he ceased struggling.

Blood leaked down Kylle's fingers a moment more. Then he threw Chandler down and booted him in the head to agitate him into breathing.

Chandler gagged and wheezed, crawled into the kitchen and retched on the marble tile.

Kylle laid his face in the blood and stared into Natalie's fixed eyes. He slipped his arm under her neck and pulled her to his chest, screaming and rocking.

# A FREE DOG AIN'T FREE

There ain't a damn azalea bush in our trailer park:
Azalea Gardens. And Tonya, my old lady, beat hell out of
my truck driving it, scalded at me for losing my license
after getting caught driving drunk again.

I had to work to pay the bills. Tonya couldn't cover
them with her ten-hour-a-week cashier's job at Wal-Mart.
Then all the fines and court fees on top of the bills. If I
didn't pay all them fines and fees my probation officer
would have my ass locked up. Then, where would Tonya
be? Back at that truck stop waitressing where I found her, I
guess. That's what I kept telling her when she'd bitch
about the shift I worked at the carpet mill. It's a damn
good job for a man that didn't finish eleventh grade. At
least I have a job. At least I didn't lose it those seven days
I sat in jail. I mean, I had the vacation time. Scott at the
plant found somebody to cover for me. If anybody asked,
he didn't mention me being locked up. Scott's been good
to me the past few years, especially since my little girl,
Natalie, got murdered by her drug dealing boyfriend.

I should have killed that bastard when I had the
chance. I heard all about him beating Natalie up and giving
her pot and pills and her winding up at the emergency
room. Him selling dope and packing a 9mm, and breaking
into houses, and in and out of jail. A thug.

My oldest boy, Keith, called me from Iraq all upset, wanting me to do something. His sister, Dorie, called me from her job at Hilton Head, crying and carrying on, too. It was impossible for me to do anything here in Calhoun, four hundred miles away. My hands were tied being on probation back then for my first DUI and having no driver's license.

I called their momma, but she told me to stay the hell out of it. She'd take care of it and hung up.

But Dorie and Keith kept calling me, saying, "You got to do something, Daddy, before she ends up dead or in prison."

I had a plan at one time. My nephew, Gary, drives a truck taking carpet down to Miami. He goes right by Kingsland every Sunday and Wednesday evenings on Interstate 95. He comes back every Tuesday and Friday. He and I talked about me riding in the truck down there with him. We would call the thug and pretend we wanted to buy some drugs from him. Then we'd gag and duct tape him, shoot him in his head, and then chunk his sorry dead ass in the river for gator food. Sounded like an airtight plan. Who'd miss a creep like that? The meth addicts he sold to? Then he killed Natalie before I could get down there. So smart, he took the cops on a high speed chase down the interstate through Jacksonville. Now he's locked up where I can't get to him.

I've never been much of a daddy. I'm a sorry one for putting things off. Like the thing with Tonya bringing home that wild killing machine.

I was at work, of course. Working overtime so another boy could go deer hunting. I didn't mind. I needed the money. It was a Saturday. Tonya toted the garbage off to the dumpsters. She picked me up at around ten, bitching at having to be out alone, driving after dark, complaining that my truck wasn't dependable, wanting a cell phone in case the truck broke down so she could call for help. I just let it go through one ear and out the other like usual. I was beat. Just one day off coming to me. I looked forward to a couple of beers, taking my boots off, and watching TV in my recliner with my dog Happy in my lap.

The kids named Happy when they were little. He was the only thing I got in the divorce with their momma besides my underwear, jeans, shirts, boots, and truck – the one I still got. It was me and him for five years before Tonya came to live with me. When he wasn't in my lap, he slept in his bed behind my recliner in the corner. If Tonya came near me while he was in my lap, he'd growl and snap. It gave me a chuckle. She carried an eight-inch fixed blade bowie I knew she'd probably like to jamb down his throat when he did that.

Happy was a little part everything. Big sad eyes that got me every time. Short tan coat. Solid. Weighed about as much as a couple of 30-30 rifles. A little bigger than a football with a curly tail.

When Tonya picked me up that night, after bitching about not having dependable transportation and no goddamn cell phone, she said, "I got a surprise for you, baby."

I've always hated that phrase. It's like getting an envelope from my probation officer or the court. Natalie's momma, before she would tell me she was pregnant would always begin by using that phrase.

Tonya drove my truck with her usual lead foot or I might have jumped out.

"I got a surprise for you, baby. I was at the dumpster dropping off the trash and there was this pretty dog there. It looked like somebody just left him. I fed him my Wendy's hamburger I had left over."

Oh shit, here we went.

"What kind of dog?"

"I don't know. A white dog. It was awful. You could see his ribs."

"I'm glad you fed him, baby. What's for supper?"

"Cheeseburger Hamburger Helper."

"I can't eat that. Is that all you can cook?"

"If you want something else, you cook, then."

"What have you been doing all day? Stop at the store and pick me up a twelve-pack. Then we'll get some tacos."

"What if your probation officer wanted you to pee in the cup?"

"Tomorrow's Sunday, darlin'. She ain't coming around on church day."

"It'll show on Monday."

"Every muscle in my body aches, baby," I said. "I'm too old to be working all these hours. You got your Xanex and Oxycodone. I got my beer. Now please stop at the store and get me a twelve-pack."

She huffed. "I ought to call your P.O."

"Then where would you be? I'd be locked up and you'd be homeless."

Tonya banged her hand on the steering wheel. "Goddamn you Woodrow." She pulled into the first

convenience store on the right side of the road. I gave her a
folded fifty I secreted in my billfold. She snatched it out of
my fingers, slid down the seat, slammed the truck door, and
stomped into the store.

I laid my head back and closed my eyes.

The next thing I knew the truck door opened and a
sack of twelve beers racked me awake and packs of
Marlboros pelted my left cheek. Then Tonya hopped in the
truck and slammed the door, rattling the windows. She tore
open her pack of Marlboro Light 100s, lit her cigarette, and
scratched ten lottery tickets using her acrylic thumb nail.

"Where's my change?" I said.

She leered at me, her cigarette dangling in the
corner of her mouth. "Shove it, Woodrow."

I pulled out a beer and opened it.

Tonya threw the lottery cards out the window.

"See, you wasted ten dollars of my hard-earn
money."

"Get over it," Tonya said, cranking the truck. "I
won fifty last week, two-fifty two weeks ago."

"That's the first I heard."

"I don't tell you everything, darlin'. I pay my rent.
Your cock ain't been complaining, has it, baby?"

She backed up without looking over her shoulder,
skidded, snatched the gear in drive, and peeled out. Beer
spilled down my shirt and pants. I wanted to slap the shit
out of her.

I crammed the rest of a taco in my mouth and
opened my third beer as she braked hard off the road and
the truck swooped sideways into the trailer park drive. The
porch light was on, but I didn't see a dog. As Tonya pulled

to the side of the trailer, the truck's headlights lit up a white pit bull tied up to the trailer hitch with a thick nylon rope.

"You lied to me."

"I did not," Tonya said.

"The hell you did. You know what a pit bull looks like."

A bowl of water and an empty bowl of what probably had been food sat next to the mongrel. He was no frail malnourished animal as Tonya described. He was all pit bull with a hard intimidating muscular frame. I didn't trust pit bulls. I'd been to too many dogfights and seen them in action.

"I can't believe you brought home a killer," I said.

"He's gentle as a bunny," she said. "I used to have one when I was a girl. Daddy raised him up with us."

"Yes, your daddy raised fighters. That one was probably just a runt he couldn't train."

"You don't know what you're talking about, Woodrow."

"I'll tell you what I do know. If you see one of those in front of a house, it means that the people are cooking up crank. It's the universal calling card for meth houses." I side-armed my half empty beer can inches over the dog's head. "Jesus Almighty God, that's all I need. I don't need no more trouble than what I already got."

"Woodrow, he ate right out of my hand. He ain't no killer," Tonya said.

The dog's eyes were ice blue in blood red circles.

"Right now he ain't. He's got you fooled. They're crazy. Bipolar like Jack Porter on the other side of the trailer park. One second they're calm. The next they've got your neck in their jaws, slinging your head against the ground."

"We'll just get the do some medicine so he won't be bipolar."

"Tonya, that's their nature. That's not their mental illness. That's who or what the do is. You don't give him happy pills. I've seen these killers climb trees to get after people and maul 'em."

The dog kept opening his mouth but nothing would come out.

"What's wrong with him?"

Tonya walked over to the dog and bent down. "He sounds like he's got something stuck in his throat. Like he's trying to bark. Oh, God, Woodrow, do you think he's got something lodged in his airway?" She laid the dog down and looked down his throat. "What's going to happen? He looks like he's having trouble breathing. Woodrow what are we going to do?"

"He's okay, Tonya."

"What? Do we need to worry?"

"No. He's fine. He can breathe fine. He just don't bark."

She knelt beside the dog for a moment and petted him. Then let him up. "Well, I guess he won't be barking all hours and disturbing our sleep then."

"His vocal chords have been cut."

"They do that?" Tonya said.

"Yes. His vocal chords have been slit." A chill went down my back.

"Who'd do such thing?"

I got my beer and tacos from the truck. "Get rid of that assassin. Right now, Tonya." I opened the trailer door.

"Screw you, Woodrow."

"Tomorrow morning then. Take him to the pound, take him back to the dump, take him anywhere. I don't give two hoots to the wind. Just get rid of that mongrel. I don't want him anywhere around here."

"I ain't," Tonya said.

"Tonya, I got a terrible feeling that dog belongs to some people we don't want to be messing with."

"Woodrow, you're full of crap."

"No I ain't. Look, that dog is made to sneak up on people like an assassin. He ain't no watchdog. He's bred and trained to maim and kill."

Tonya sat. The dog jumped and wagged his ass and licked her in the face.

"Have you ever been to a dog fight?"

"No," Tonya said.

"You can buy pups with their vocal chords slit and dudes will bring their dogs to a guy who's usually there who'll slit them while you wait."

"That's crazy, Woodrow. This is a birth defect."

"No, I'm telling you God's truth. I've seen it. That dog belongs to some nasty ass drug dealer. He got loose from some meth house. Mean mothers with guns who'll use 'em. Probably huntin' for him right now. They see him tied in our yard they'll think we stole him. Then we're both dead, you hear me?"

Tonya mumbled and stuck her ass my way as she and the dog licked each other.

"Tonya? Tonya?" I went into the trailer. Happy came out of his corner and greeted me. He followed me back to the bedroom where I got my Glock out of the nightstand. He followed me out on the front porch. "You get rid of that goddamn mongrel killer or I'll get rid of him."

Tonya covered the dog with her body. "You'll have to shoot me first."

I was in no mood for this. All I needed was the cops out here. We all knew who'd wind up in jail. I just wanted to eat my supper and drink my beer in peace in my recliner with Happy in my lap and see if I could find something good on the cable TV and fall asleep.

I've told Scott at work about Tonya's antics. Forty, he'd never been married. He never had a sister. He said, "No damn woman is worth going to jail for, Woodrow."

I walked back inside the trailer and put my pistol back in the nightstand. Then I took off my boots and plopped down in my recliner with a taco, beer and a cigarette ready and the TV clicker, and tried to find something on the Discovery Channel or Animal Planet.

After a time, Tonya sashayed in, flicked off her sandals, palmed a beer out of the refrigerator, shuffled next to the TV, and took a throaty gulp. Then she set the can on top of the TV, flipped on the stereo, turning the volume up, and started peeling slowly out of her jeans and t-shirt, belly dancing in time to the music.

I became uninterested in the TV and turned it off.

She turned her back to me, unfastened her bra, twisted, and sling-shotted it at me. I wrapped it around my neck. She faced me, began massaging her breasts, licking her nipples, teasing me with her tongue like the interstate exotic dancer she'd been before aging into the waitress job. She still had the moves and, I thought, still had the body. As the music boomed, she turned and pulled her purple satin bikini panties down, giving me a slow wavering back view, hypnotizing me with the long stem rose tattooed out of the crack of her ass. Aroused and defenseless, Tonya's panties landed skillfully on my face.

I fed that pit bull for nearly five months, him tied up to the trailer, sleeping under it, lounging under it to get out of the sun and rain.

Tonya named him Dakota. She got thirty-foot of chain from the hardware store. The kind of chain they use on kids' swings. Where he paced became hard bare orange clay. Like I expected, that dog went through fifty pounds of dog chow a week.

I worked sixty hours most weeks. As my days scuffed and bruised and sweated forward, I got my community service done, paid my fine off, got my court fees paid, was knocking things out of the way. Making a dent in my back child support. Feeding me and Tonya and the dogs. Paying the lot rent. Thinking about getting Tonya that cell phone. After a while, I realized Tonya hadn't been fussing at me about my shift hours, about picking me up and dropping me off, and had even calmed down about getting her a cell phone. The truck was even running better. With things going smooth, I started wondering if Tonya had her a sugar daddy on the side. But, to tell you the truth, I was really too tired to care.

Then, while I was at work one day, Happy got too close to that goddamn killer. I imagined he tortured and mauled Happy to pieces – the murdering devil. It happened right there in front of the trailer, Tonya said. She called me at the plant and told me.

"Take the thing to the pound, now, Tonya. I'll bury Happy when I get home."

"I done buried him."

"Where?"

"I done took care of him, Woodrow," Tonya said.

"Where'd you bury him?" I said.

"You don't need to worry about that, baby. It would have just upset you more."

I didn't say another word. I wanted to bury my own dog *myself*.

I told Scott.

"I'm going to kill that murdering mongrel when I get home," I said.

"Don't lose your temper now, Woodrow." Scott had known Tonya longer than me. He hated her with a white passion, and took to calling her Conya. "Conya'll have your ass locked up."

"I should have killed the murderer that first night. Next thing that murdering devil will do is get hold of one of them kids in the trailer park and then where will I be? No sir. I'm killing that dog tonight, if Tonya hasn't taken him to the pound like I told her."

"I'm telling you, Woodrow, Conya's lied to the law on more than a half a dozen old boys I know. Conya knows exactly how to work it."

"I know," I said.

"You need to calm down and get loose from that bitch, Woodrow."

"Then how am I gone get to work? She's my driver."

"Get your co-dependent ass a bicycle. Walk."

"Hell son, its fifteen miles one way, and all the hills. I'd get run over."

"You need to get rid of your bitch before you get rid of that dog."

The killer was chained to the trailer when I got there. I went directly to the bedroom nightstand, and got my gun.

Tonya stood in the door of our bedroom. "Don't you do it Woodrow. You better put that gun back in that drawer right now. I'll have your ass locked up." She slapped and clawed my cheek. I caught her wrist, twisted and bent it back. "You better not, Woodrow." She rammed her knee twice just above my groin. It took my wind. I let go of her wrist. The she hauled off and landed a couple of solid elbows to my nose.

I forearmed her under her chin and at the bridge of her nose. She toppled on her ass. Her head hit with a crack against the bathroom door frame.

"I've got to do something before that thing kills somebody's kid," I said. "Now calm down and get out of my way."

Holding the back of her head, she scrambled around me again. "You sonofabitch. I'll get a warrant on you."

"Tonya, damn you." I grabbed her arm.

She hollered. "You're hurtin' me."

She jumped up and went to grab the gun.

I slapped her.

She grabbed her face. "Your bastard sonofabitch. You dirty bastard. If you kill him, I'll leave you."

"Oh hush your ugly mouth." I pushed her out of the way of the door.

She punched me and jumped on my back.

I scraped her off and flung her to the sofa.

She sprang up and spit into my face. "I threw your goddamn mutt in the dumpster, you stupid bastard." Then she ran back into our bedroom and slammed and locked the door and kicked and cursed and threw things.

I turned on the porch light and jostled out the front door and down the steps.

The dog's chain jangled. I came around to the end of the trailer, saw him standing taut, and snarling at me with those ice blue eyes. When I got about six feet from him, I raised the pistol and capped him one time in the head. He fell like a stone. Blood flowed onto the clay and pooled under his head.

I went out to my utility shed, got a shovel, went out in the woods behind the trailer, and dug a hole. Then I unchained the murderer, drug him into the hole, packed the orange clay over him, and spread pine straw over the orange dirt.

Tonya, her clothes and pills, and my truck were gone when I got back to the trailer.

I collapsed in my recliner with a couple of beers and fell asleep watching Alaskan crab fishermen risk life and limb in frozen seas on the TV.

The next day I didn't have to work. I smoked and drank coffee and watched TV and got out of the recliner only to go to the bathroom and refill my coffee cup or get a beer.

In the weeks to follow, I caught rides to work with buddies and nephews and nieces, anybody who had a vehicle and some time, that wouldn't mind getting me to and from work. I gave them money for gas. Some weeks it turned out cheaper than putting gas in my old pickup.

Things were quiet. I had a nice routine: work, eat, and sleep.

About eight weeks after Tonya left, I went to work like normal. It was a Saturday. Another overtime shift. Scott was there. We were working six hours into a twelve hour shift when he collapsed right there beside me. It was a massive heart attack, I learned later. The EMTs arrived, firemen, and the cops. He just dropped right there beside me, I told them. He fell and never woke back up. None of us on the plant floor knew what to do but call 911, and that's what I did. The cop took my statement and then he took my name, address, social security number, etc. I guess he radioed that in, because he came back to me and said,

"Did you know you have outstanding warrants?"

"What?"

"You got two outstanding warrants."

"For what?"

"You got an arrest warrant for simple battery and another one for cruelty to animals. Misdemeanors. They were taken out a few weeks ago by a Tonya Evans. You know her?"

"I'll be damned. Yeah. My ex old lady. She brought home a pit bull from the dump. It murdered my dog. I shot that killer before it killed somebody's kid. She took my truck. I didn't take a warrant out for that."

"Well, that's your business. All I know is she's taken them warrants out on you."

"The truck ain't worth nothin'. I stopped payin' the insurance on it last month."

"It might be in impound."

"Shit. It'll cost more to get it out than the damn thing's worth."

I studied the cop. There wasn't no way in hell he could run me down with that big old gut of his.

"Did the impound yard call you?" the cop said.

"I don't know. I'm at work all day every day."

"You got an answering machine?"

"Naw, naw I ain't got no answering machine."

"Cell phone?"

I shook my head. "Naw."

"Well . . ."

"Well . . . So you got to arrest me then, I guess."

"Yep. Don't like to, but got to do it, partner."

"What if I want to take out a warrant on her for taking my truck?"

"You need to see the magistrate judge for that."

"Cain't do that in jail."

"They'll set you a bond once you're booked in."

"I think I'm on probation."

"For what?" the cop said.

"Driving drunk. I don't even have to report no more."

"Radio didn't say anyhing about probation, so I don't know."

"That's all I need is to get revoked."

It was cool in the plant, but the big boy poured sweat. I guess it was his Kevlar vest.

"Well, bond out and then go see the magistrate judge about swearing out that warrant for your truck, if that's what you want to do."

He pulled out his handcuffs slow and eased me around, guiding me by the shoulder. "Check and see if your truck's in impound first."

"Yeah, I reckon so," I said.

I put my hands behind my back.

"Scott, that boy in the floor yonder, told me, 'A free dog ain't free.' They ain't, are they?"

The cop shook his head. "Never are."

# GOOD INTENTIONS

*The road to hell is paved with good intentions.*
—John Ray (1670)

I

       Emerald. Ike loved her name. He stood in line with the other members of the church and greeted her after she'd opened her heart to the preacher's invitation and accepted Jesus as her Lord and Savior. She wore a green velvet dress that Sunday morning a week before Christmas. Against her light brown skin and green eyes, Ike felt the dress made her look rich and educated.

       Ike believed as his Momma and Daddy taught him, that you ought to give people the benefit of the doubt because there's more to things and people than the eyes can take in at first. He took that to heart like everything else his Momma and Daddy and his preacher and Jesus and the Bible said.

       Forty-one and a deacon like his Daddy, he had been to most every Sunday and Wednesday night service at the same Baptist church since he could remember.

       Emerald started attending Ike's Sunday school class, began singing in the choir, was baptized, and joined the church.

February. A misty gray Sunday morning. Emerald was wearing her dress. The preacher was dancing down the aisle, he said the church was tingling with the Holy Spirit. An angel had visited him in a dream the night before and told him that something magnificent was going to happen in the church today, that there was going to be singing, dancing, clapping, tambourines, organ, glorifying the Lord. In the middle of a solo, Emerald, silenced the church.

"During my days of perdition—"

"Bless her Lawd," came support from the deacons and members of the congregation.

"—I sang in clubs and juke joints," Emerald said. "And I'm here to testify that the Devil do exist."

"Tell the truth, sister. Yes, Jesus, speak to her. Tell the truth."

"Dark places."

"Yes, Lawd."

"Places of drinking—"

"Tell it."

"—and women and men dancing and fornicating—"

"Yes, come out with it, sister."

"Men and women disrespecting theyselves and Gawd's Commandments—"

"Amen. Hallelujah, sister. Testify. Tell us, tell us."

"And I have seen debauchery and lewdness and black folk taking Gawd's name in vain."

"Yes, sister."

"And I too was that sinner. I sinned before Gawd. I disrespected the bodily temple He bestowed on me by drinking liquor and smoking crack cocaine and marijuana."

The whole church stood with their arms up, shouting hallelujahs and amens.

"Folks, I have seen the Devil with my own eyes—"

"Amen."

"Smelled him with my own nose—"

"Yes, Lawd. Hallelujah."

"Like our Lord in the desert, heard him with my own ears."

"Tell it, sister."

"Lucifer be a seducer."

"Yes, Lawd."

"And he be a deceiver."

"Praise Gawd."

"And he promises many riches, many castles, fame, golden palaces—"

"Lucifer be a seducer," someone repeated from the congregation.

"And a deceiver," another shouted.

"Praise Jesus. Speak to her Lord."

Emerald said, "But all Lucifer gave me was sorrow and addiction until I hit rock bottom, in the streets where I sold my body to support my habit, until I woke up one mawnin' in prison."

"Speak to her Lord. Make her Your instrument of thy deliverance oh Lawd."

"Oh, I thank the Redeemer for reaching down to this poor sinner," Emerald said, "with His grace to cleanse my heart so when He calls me home on that day I will be with Him in Heaven for all time."

The piano softly played the prelude to the song that Emerald was to sing. The congregation sat. Sweat poured down Emerald's face. She mopped her forehead with a handkerchief. "I'm gonna sing a song that means a lot to me. I've had a little sinus trouble the last couple of weeks. So y'all pray for me. This is an oldtimey hymn. I hope it speaks to y'all's hearts like it speaks to me. It's 'Hide Thou Me'." Then in a mournful tempo Emerald sang in a round deep voice that filled up the whole church and spilled out the door and windows.

To Ike, Emerald's voice was like a prophet. There were many *Amens* and *Hallelujahs* and *Speak to her Lawd* and *Yes, Lawds* from the congregation as she sang. Hands supplicated to heaven and people mumbled prayers with tears of mercy. Ike knew that Emerald knew what it felt to be discouraged, and to be down and lost, but to be found and claimed by the Redeemer. The Holy Spirit bonded him to Emerald that night.

It wasn't until a year later that he worked up the courage to ask her to marry him. He'd never been alone with her, never been to her apartment even. It surprised him when she said yes. They married at the church two weeks later.

Happiness being married brought his desire for children of his own. He didn't bring it up until their first wedding anniversary. Emerald said she'd had her tubes tied after her fourth child, a time she'd have done anything to get a rock of crack cocaine, an addiction that killed her third and fourth children at birth and sent her eventually to prison for five years.

Ike did not swear oaths, believing in the literal word of the Bible. He also believed it was only for God to judge people. It made him sad to think about all Emerald had been through, but took it that God had a purpose in bringing her into his life. He had been in jail once, too.

In the mid-eighties, he'd gone to Atlanta—the only time he'd ever gone outside of southeast Georgia—to visit his sister Viola who lived there with her new husband after she graduated from Spellman College. Ike was riding the bus, reading his Bible. A black woman got on the bus with her little boy. A skinny black man with greasy hair under a black leather cap followed them. He sat next to the woman and leaned his mouth inches from her ear, talking to her just loud enough that Ike could make out a few words. The woman had her boy in her lap. She cupped her hands over her boy's ears and tried to ignore the man herself. It only made the man talk louder. When the woman turned and slid away from the man, he started jabbing her in the arm with his long fingernails. The woman stood and the man grabbed her pocket book, which she had hooked on the arm she had wrapped around her little boy. The man jerked again, knocking the boy to the floor. Ike shot up and grabbed the man's wrist and squeezed. The man tried to jerk loose and went for something in his coat pocket. Ike bent the man's arm back until he heard a crack and then another, louder crack. The man screamed. The bus braked hard. The woman yelled for Ike to stop hurting her husband. The boy sat on the floor, crying. The bus driver came running back, asking what was going on. The woman kept hollering. The man cussed, hollering his shoulder was broke. People ran out of the bus. Soon police officers stormed in. They slid the man in an ambulance and handcuffed Ike. He got carsick cramped in the back of the police car with his arms behind his back and bent over and twisted. He prayed.

At the jail, he was strip searched, fingerprinted, and photographed. He told the officers what had happened, that he was just trying to protect the woman and the boy. They shoved him in a cell with a young white man who said he was in college and told Ike, "Man, chivalry is dead, like God, didn't you know?"

"God ain't dead," Ike had said. "I just couldn't let that man do that."

"It don't matter. You see where it landed you."

Things got straightened out. Ike was released the next morning. He heard his name called out.

"Easterwood, Isaiah. You're being let go." He stood. The jailer approached with a ring of large heavy keys and unlocked the door. "You're a free man. Charges have been dropped."

He called his sister. He had no choice. She picked him up at the city jail. She asked some questions, but he didn't talk. He rode in a cab to the bus station and got on a Greyhound that afternoon and never went back to Atlanta.

II

When Ike married Emerald she was ten years out of prison, off parole, clean and sober, and working steady. Her four grandkids stayed with her more than with their mothers. She said her girls didn't have sense enough to raise them. She made sure the grandkids had clean new clothes and shoes and food to eat. Ike admired that. But what he couldn't understand was Emerald's two daughters. They were always having some kind of trouble getting or keeping a job, trouble with their boyfriends or their babies' daddies, or with the law or social services. Always in the center of some kind of mess or trouble, everybody hollering and cussing, laying out of work, disrespecting themselves and others, and not going to church and reading their Bibles every day. He kept his mouth shut.

Ike had worked twenty-one years fixing the diesel trucks and tractors for the Camden County Public Works Department in Kingsland. He'd had but one boss during that whole time. Mr. Carl managed the garage and just pointed to the trucks and the tractors that needed worked on, and then left Ike alone. He never gave Mr. Carl any trouble. He did his work, was never late, never stole, and had only taken sick leave a few weeks after he got hit by that semi-truck one foggy December morning, the first cold morning of 1996.

With the settlement money from the wreck with the tractor-trailer truck, he bought a two bedroom vinyl siding house behind the Brunswick hospital so Emerald would be right there close to her work, kids, and grandkids. But with the grandkids there most of the time and all the turmoil with Emerald's daughters and their boyfriends and other folks, Ike stayed at his sister's house in Kingsland or at his parents in St. Mary's during the week. He stayed at the Brunswick house on Friday and Saturday nights, sometimes Sunday, too. He came to accept that the arrangement worked out better, saving him on gas and wear and tear on his little truck.

After work, when there was enough sun during the week, and on Saturdays, Ike mowed people's yards while his partner handled the customers, the money, and the blowing and edging.

Ike liked his jobs. Neither one required much talking. It gave him time to recite Psalms, meditate on his Sunday school lessons while he hummed or sang church hymns under the machine noise.

Time went by as time went by as the Lord gave it. Everything started getting tense when Emerald hurt her back.

She worked at the nursing home cleaning up after elderly people, people with Alzheimer's, and other people unable to get around and care for themselves. She got hurt lifting folks out of wheel chairs, on and off toilets, off the floor, into and out of beds. She started having constant pain in her back and hips, and numbness in her legs. It got to where when she came home she didn't have the energy and hurt too bad to keep up the house. Ike couldn't understand why her girls didn't help. He didn't say anything. He did what he could around the house when he was there. It worried and hurt him when she stopped going to church and the weekly Sunday afternoon dinners at his parents' house. She said she couldn't stand all that sitting and riding in the car. She went out at sunrise on Saturdays and bought groceries at Wal-Mart. Other than that, though, she stayed in bed most of the weekend. Much of the time she was as ill-tempered.

One Sunday he brought her a covered plate his mother had fixed, coaxing her out of the stale smelling bedroom to the living room to eat and watch TV. While she ate he went back to the bedroom and changed the bed sheets, then started a load of clothes in the washing machine, and then carried the garbage bag from the kitchen to the can outside.

"The kids been here?" he asked from the kitchen that Sunday.

"I run Tya off last night. Caught her taking money out of my purse yesterday. I ought to call the po-po and have her ass locked up."

That would just cause more problems, he thought.

"That boy she be running with be calling from the jail. I keep telling him I ain't taking no collect calls. I just finally unplugged the phone."

He stepped into the living room. "I got some money. How much do you need?"

She adjusted the blinds. "Car be needing some gas."

"I'll fill it before I leave," he said. "You going to work, tomorrow?"

"When y'all gone cut the grass?"

"Sometime this week when we be over this way."

"Where's the zapper?" she asked.

He pulled a twenty-dollar bill out of his wallet with wet hands. He found the remote control jammed between the armrest and the cushion on the gold velour couch. He handed it to her along with the twenty.

She didn't look up. She turned on the TV and flipped through the channels, settling on a black and white movie.

"You see the chiropractor this week?" he asked.

"I'm supposed to see her two times this week." She held up the bill he'd given her and waved it back and forth. "Twenty dollars every time."

He walked back to the kitchen.

She hollered out to him over a TV commercial, "Why don't you reach in your mad money and pull me out one of them folded hundred dollar bills. I be needing more than this. I knows you got it."

He placed the clean forks and spoons in their plastic compartments in the top drawer. "You can get by on that twenty till I get back and cut the grass."

"That ain't enough to put gas in the car and buy food."

He looked in the freezer. "There's enough food in this freezer to get you by until then. I ain't got no money for you to blow on them lottery games."

"I don't blow my money on that. I just buys a couple of tickets every Saturday."

"This drawer in here is almost full of old lottery tickets."

"The girls buys 'em, too. With their own money."

Uh-huh, he thought. He asked, "What medicine you taking?"

"Pills, pills, pills . . . "

"Where you get 'em?"

"Work, mostly."

He peeked around the doorway. "How much you take today?"

She turned and studied him for a bit. "Well, damn, maybe it ain't none of your business, Detective Ike."

He stared at her and shook a medicine bottle.

"What you got? Where you get that?"

"Right here on the kitchen counter."

"Give it here."

"You ain't got to be so hateful. Why you gotten so hateful to me, Emerald?"

" Bring me that bottle of pills." She almost fell out of the chair. "They mine. Bring them to me or I'll cut you."

"This bottle say X-an-ex, X . . . an . . . "

"It's Zan-ex you ignorant . . . "

"What's its supposed to do?" he said.

She twisted in her chair, annoyed. "It's for pain."

"How much do you take?"

"Couple this morning. It depends on the pain."

"That all you taking?"

"No." She studied a chicken wing.

"What else?"

"Why you need to know all a sudden what I be taking?"

"In case I got to call 911 or something."

"Shit, you ain't around enough for that."

He sat on the arm of the couch and watched her eat. After a moment, during a commercial, he asked, "What else you taking besides that Zan-ex?"

"I be taking other medicine, too, so I can sleep."

"What's that?"

"I don't remember."

"Where you keep it?"

She didn't say anything. She just sunk her spoon in a bowl of fruit cobbler.

He noticed her head kept dropping and then she would catch it. "Sleepy?" he said.

"Hm?" She stared at the TV She had it turned so low he could barely hear it.

"Food good?" he asked.

"Huh?"

"Food good?"

"Mm-hmm."

He loaded the dirty dishes and cups and pans into the dishwasher and started it. The small bathroom smelled like urine and fish and mildew. He scrubbed the toilet, sink, tub, and linoleum floor with Pine-Sol. Emerald was in the bedroom asleep when he finished. While he scoured the kitchen counters, he heard the shower start. He turned off the dishwasher.

It was dark by the time he filled her car with gas. It was filthy. He threw some cups, fast food wrappers, and a couple of empty Newport cigarette wrappers in the garbage can at the pump, shook off the sandy floor mats, and wasted five dollars to sit in the car while water jets and brushes knocked the first layer of pollen and black sand off the exterior.

On the way home he drove through a thunderstorm. Rain whipped like curtains and pelted the car.

Weeks passed in the same routine.

Emerald got no better. She hadn't been to church. He drove up to Brunswick early Sunday. The house was dark and quiet. Emerald snored on the couch in the gown and housecoat she'd been in on Friday afternoon when he'd left to clean yards.

He bent down and shook her shoulder. "Emerald? Em? Em? Wake up. It's Ike."

"Hmmm?" She rubbed her mouth with the back of her hand, rolled left then right, but didn't open her eyes.

"Emerald. It's Sunday. I come to take you to church. Wake up."

"What? Whatchyou doing?"

"Sunday. Church. Get ready. I'll take you."

"Naw, naw. I ain't going to no church. I cain't sit on them pews. Go on."

"Wake up. I'll make you some coffee. Everybody's been askin' about you. They want to see you. Want to hear you sing again."

Emerald rolled to the back of the couch and covered her head with the pillow. "I ain't singing for no more motherfuckers for free."

"Aw, now. You don't mean that."

She sprung around and pushed Ike. "What did I say, nigger?"

He was stunned.

"I said I ain't going to no church. Not today, not never. Now get out of my face, motherfucker." She stood and stumbled, held the wall, then weaved down the hall to the bedroom. Shut the door. Fumbled with the lock, but eventually locked it.

Ike stared at the floor. She'd left the TV on. His throat tightened, his eyes welled with tears.

After a time, Ike shuffled out the back door. Ignoring the TV, the fast food wrappers and bags and cups falling into the kitchen floor out of the black plastic garbage bag, the dishes heaped in the sink, the skillet and boilers of crusty food on the stove, the grass that needed cutting and the leaves blown.

He drove the thirty minutes south to his church. He missed Sunday school and came in late for the service while everybody was standing and singing.

Miss Emma, his mother's neighbor, hugged his neck. "Here's my man."

He rocked and clapped in time with the others in the back pew. Tears mixed with the sweat pouring off his face.

III

A Sunday afternoon at his parent's house a couple of weeks later, Ike's sister Viola had him cornered on the back screened-in porch. "Isaiah, I'm worried about Emerald."

His mother was putting the dinner dishes in the dishwasher with his niece while his father napped in his recliner under the portraits of Dr. King, President John Kennedy, and Robert Kennedy, with the Braves game blaring on the television.

Ike said, "I am too. When I got there Friday, the house was a mess, clothes everywhere, dishes piled in the sink, and her girls won't lift a finger to help her."

"Me and Momma have offered—"

"I know."

Viola lit a long cigarette. Exhaling, she said, "I've been hearing things."

"I don't want to hear no gossiping."

"I don't care what you don't want to hear. This is something you need to know. I've been hearing bad things for a while. I haven't told you 'cause I knew you'd say that. I wanted to check things on my own."

He unstacked two green plastic chairs and sat in one. Viola stood, looking out on the back yard. "I'm really worried about her."

The phone rang inside. Ike's mother answered it and cackled.

Viola said, "I've tried calling. She won't answer the phone and won't call me back when I leave a message on the answering machine or with one of her girls."

"She treats me the same, always has."

Viola was the first and only person in their family on both sides to go to college. She went on scholarship and now worked as a social worker in Jacksonville. She was always on the go.

"I've gone to the nursing home several times," Viola said. "Of course nobody will tell you anything. I never have seen her car there. One of the ladies at the church saw her at Wal-Mart a few weeks ago. Did you know they cut her hours because of her back? My friend said she was afraid they were going to fire her. Did you know that?"

He adjusted in the chair. It was tight on his hips. "No."

"Has she gone to the doctor?" she asked.

"To the chiropractor."

"Other than the chiropractor."

He coughed into his fist. "I don't know."

"My God, Ike, don't you know anything?"

"I ain't up there with her that much. I'm working most of the time, when I'm not at church."

"And she ain't at church either."

"Says she can't sit or ride in the car or sit in the pew."

"Don't sound like a *can't*, but something else."

"I don't know. I just try to stay out of her business. Keep my mouth shut."

"You're her husband." Viola swatted at a mosquito hovering close to her ear. "I know a back surgeon in Jacksonville, another one in Atlanta."

Ike looked across the back yard. "Atlanta's too far."

Viola crossed her arms. He didn't like her long red fingernails. They weren't real. That made him dislike the nails even more, like the tattoos Emerald's daughters got to defile their bodies. Jezebel vanity and foolishness. "Well, I gave her his name and number when I left a message on the machine."

"I appreciate it," he said. "One of her girls probably erased it and she didn't get it."

"I can call the doctor's office and make an appointment for her. You think I should?"

"Naw. Hold off. I'll tell her."

"If her back is that bad she's probably going to need surgery."

His heart and stomach jumped. "Surgery?"

"Yeah, but what I'm concerned most about right now is her meds. She shouldn't be taking any narcotics."

"Why not?"

"Because she's a drug addict."

"She *was* a drug addict," he said.

"Isaiah, you're *always* an addict. Has she been going to her meetings?"

"To what?"

"NA. It's like AA for drug addicts."

"I don't know, Viola."

She gave him a mean look and shook her head.

He noticed she had stopped wearing her wedding ring. You could still see the ring indention on her finger.

She wasn't divorced, but nobody knew where her husband had gone. It had been three years. Her little girl was nearly nine now and barely remembered her daddy. That was the only thing Ike liked about staying with his sister and niece during the week—there was a man in the house. But then there was no man in his house. And apparently that was causing some problems.

"I'm worried if she's in that much pain that she'll start self medicating," Viola said. "I've seen that dozens, hundreds of times. Then you're going to lose her, Ike."

"What you mean, self medicating?"

Viola's daughter poked her head out the door. "When you coming inside, Momma?" She stepped out on the porch. Viola pushed her back inside. "I'll be there in a minute, baby. Let me talk to Uncle Ike for a minute or two." She closed the door and looked at him.

"Well, she has access to a lot of medicine where she works . . . "

"She knows better than that," he said.

"She may know better, but the sickness in her head, the addiction. Pain all the time . . . Back pain is rough."

He didn't know what to think.

Viola inhaled deeply, exhaled, and took another draw before opening the screen door and flicking the cigarette out into the black sandy yard shaded by live oaks. He hoped this was the end of this talk and they could go back inside the house where it was cooler and he could lie down on the couch and watch the Braves. Then his sister faced him. She was a tall big-boned woman. Ike was over six-foot-three and weighed almost two-seventy-five. When Viola wore heels to church as she did now, she was taller.

"I'm really concerned about Emerald self medicating. Do you know what I mean?"

He nodded. He didn't know if he did or not.

She said, "Do you know a guy named Antonio Sapp? From Brunswick. A drug dealer, mostly. He's called Itchy on the streets."

Ike shook his head and scratched a hard to get place on his back. The house he'd bought for Emerald was his only connection to Brunswick.

"The word I've gotten is that . . . " She reached in her purse and retrieved another cigarette and a lighter.

He watched the smoke rise from the first cigarette lying in the yard.

She lit her cigarette and stowed her lighter in her cigarette case. "I had somebody run his criminal history. He's got a record. Burglary, assault, drug offenses. He went to prison back in the eighties and then a stint from ninety-five to two-thousand. Now he's a maintenance man for one of the motels in Brunswick on I-95. I can't remember which one right this instant."

"Is he one of the girl's boyfriends that be calling the house all the time?" he asked.

She tucked her cigarette case in her purse and set the purse on the other plastic chair. "No."

"Well?"

"I talked to an officer in Brunswick. He knew about Itchy, knew where he lived, and gave me his address."

"So?"

"He's an old friend of Emerald's. He's one of the girls' daddy."

Ike raised his eyes and looked at her. "How do you know all this?"

She opened the screen door to let a wasp out. "I called Itchy's old parole officer. He told me." She looked at Ike, exhaled smoke through her nose. Her daughter stuck her head out again.

"Momma, when we going?"

"In just a minute, baby. Go inside." The girl stepped back and closed the door.

Viola said, "I rode over by his house at different times. I got to tell you a few times I've gone by there the last couple of weeks, Emerald's car has been parked out front on the street."

"Maybe one of the girls drove it over there."

"I guess, but don't think so," she said.

He stood.

She flicked her half-smoked cigarette out the screen door. It hit the trellised wall of wisteria their dad had built when they were kids. "We like you staying with us. It's a big help and eases my mind you're there. I don't mean to interfere. It's your marriage. That's what's important. But you're at our house more than you're with her . . . " Viola had her hand on the doorknob. "I didn't want to hear any of this, either." Then she went in the house.

After a time, Ike went inside the house. The television was off. The house was quiet, except for the dishwasher running. Ike looked out the front window. The cars were gone. Everybody had left to go back to church. A covered plate was on the kitchen counter. Ike turned on the television. The Braves game was over. He flipped through the channels. Nothing was on he liked. He turned the television off. Then he lay on the couch, closed his eyes, and fell asleep.

IV

Tuesday, after work, Ike called Emerald at the house. He talked to one of her daughters. She didn't know the whereabouts of her momma, but the washer had gone out. He told her to have her momma call the Sears man.

Ike called again on Thursday, after work. He talked to the same daughter. He heard kids in the background. Emerald had gone to the Laundromat and Wal-Mart. She didn't know whether or not her momma had called the Sears man about the washing machine. He told her he'd check the washing machine when he got there the next night. He'd cut the grass and change the oil in Emerald's car, too. Just before hanging up, he asked to have her mother call him, but the phone went dead while he was talking.

He drove to Brunswick on Friday after work. Emerald was there. His partner and he cut and edged the yard, then they checked the washing machine, but couldn't get it to work. He asked Emerald to call Sears. She was on her way out the door to take her daughters and her grandkids to Darien to her sister's, and said she would call the next morning. He bought his partner supper at McDonald's. Then he bought oil and an oil filter at Wal-Mart for Emerald's car. He stayed up as late as he could for her, falling asleep on the couch.

He woke before the sun, meeting his partner at the Waffle House for breakfast before beginning a hot day of cutting people's yards on St. Simons Island. He got home at about seven. Emerald's car was in the carport. She was asleep in the bedroom. He changed her car's oil. The inside of the car smelled of spit-up, McDonald's, and soiled diapers. He got a plastic garbage bag and loaded it. There were broken and discarded happy meal toys, fast food wrappers, soiled diaper wipes, a folded-up wet and soiled diaper in a plastic grocery bag which wasn't tied shut, a half empty potato chip bag, numerous empty corners of clear plastic baggies, a chocolate pop-tart that had melted on the cloth backseat, and empty plastic Mountain Dew and Dr. Pepper bottles. The ashtray was full of lottery receipts and scratch-off cards. He found an empty Coca-Cola can under the driver's seat, wrapped in aluminum foil with a tube stuck in it. Next to it was a disposable cigarette lighter and an empty prescription pill bottle with the label peeled off. He vacuumed the car's inside. There were a number of stains in the tan carpet he didn't have the cleaner to get out, and new cigarette burns in the front seats he'd have to fix later. He had to go over the outside with Comet twice to get it cleaned to his satisfaction, which uncovered new gashes and scratches and dents to touch-up. Then he went inside the house, stuffed his wet and dirty clothes in a plastic bag to take to Viola's, and showered. Emerald didn't wake up. His clothes were in the closet of the other bedroom so he didn't have to open the door and worry about waking her.

He dined out for shrimp and fish and iced tea for supper at Jinright's on Highway 17, down from the house. A slice of cheesecake would have satisfied his sugar urges, but he'd been managing his diabetes with diet to avoid the insulin his parents and sister injected every day.

The Braves were playing on the west coast. Somebody called the house a couple of times after eleven o'clock. When he answered, they hung up. He figured it was one of the daughters' friends. He fell asleep on the couch with the television on.

An infomercial blared when he awoke early Sunday. He guessed it had played all night. He shaved, showered, and dressed in his brown suit, the only suit he had left at the house. He locked the back door and closed it softly. He stopped by McDonald's for a sausage biscuit and a coffee to go, and then drove his little white truck the thirty miles to St. Mary's for Sunday school and church.

He yawned all through church, napped on the couch at his mother's, and after dinner decided to stay with Viola instead of driving to Brunswick. He called Emerald. The phone rang, but nobody answered. He felt the urge to drive back to Brunswick then, but waited and called again an hour later. Emerald answered this time. He told her he was going to stay with Viola. She sounded drowsy. She said she had been at the Laundromat washing and drying clothes. She wasn't sure she was going to work the next day. He asked whether she had called the doctor. She said she couldn't get through. She had forgotten to call the Sears man. He said he would call. She didn't say anything about her clean car.

Before leaving for Sunday evening church services, Ike asked Viola for that man's address. He wrote it down on the back of a torn envelope his parent's electricity bill came in.

He went to Brunswick after work on Monday. Emerald pulled in right after him. She had two of her grandkids with her. She fed the kids fish sticks, french fries and apple juice. They watched an hour of cartoons. Then Emerald gave the kids a bath and lay them in the single beds in the other bedroom. They showered and watched TV After the news, she went to her bed. He slept on the couch.

She gave him a suspicious look when he drove up in the driveway on Tuesday evening. "Two nights in a row?"

He smiled. "That okay?"

"Your house, too, I guess."

She fixed crab cakes and hush puppies for supper. Her daughters came over. They sneered, but never spoke a word to him. They argued with their momma about working and money and getting the grandkids to and from daycare.

He went outside and watered the yard. A patch of dollar weeds had erupted. The azalea blossoms had dropped off. The crepe myrtles he'd pruned in January were going to bloom in June and fill in good.

When the kids left, he turned off the water and went back inside and cleaned the kitchen while Emerald showered. She came out to the kitchen as he was putting away pans and dishes.

"You going to be here the rest of the week?" she asked.

"You need me to?" he said.

"I'm all right."

"The girls didn't even speak to me."

"Did you speak to them?"

"No."

"You the adult."

"They adults, too," he mumbled, bearing down on the counter, trying to wipe away grease from the stove. He didn't look at her. "They stole any more of your money? They need to quit all that running around and get to church."

"My kids. That ain't none of your business." She walked out of the kitchen.

"I'm tired of them causing a ruckus all the time, cussing and wearing hardly any clothes like street whores."

She turned on the TV and hollered back from the living room. "Who you calling whores? Nigga, you better watch your goddamn mouth." She came back into the kitchen and got her purse off the top of the counter.

"Watch your mouth," he said.

"Don't tell me to watch my mouth, motherfucker."

"I didn't call nobody whores," he said.

"That's what you said, Mr. Deacon, all high and mighty."

He faced her. "That's not what I said, woman. You ain't listening." His voice sounded loud in his ears.

"Oh, I'm listening," she shouted. "Bunch of shit coming out of your goddamn mouth."

He turned toward her, raised his right hand, and back-handed her in the mouth. She screamed and held her face.

"I told you to watch your mouth. You ain't gone take the Lord's name in vain in *my* house."

She fumbled in her purse. He grabbed her arm. Her purse dropped.

"Stop it, Ike. Let me go. You're hurting me. Goddamnit. Quit it, damn you."

He let go.

"Ain't no nigga man gone hit me." She squatted and pick up her purse and coming up, she flicked open a box cutter and waved it at his chin.

He raised his arm again.

"You try hittin' me again nigga, I'll motherfuckin' kill yo nigga ass."

"Put that away, woman."

He lunged at her. She came down with the blade and sliced his forearm. He slapped her again. She flew across the kitchen and hit the refrigerator.

"Devil ain't gone have his way here," he said.

She turned and waved the blade at him.

"Put that box cutter down, I said."

"I'll cut you again, nigga," she hissed. "And have your motherfuckin' ass locked up. Don't you try coming at me again."

He did not move.

She backed out of the kitchen and down the hall, breathing hard, her black eyes hard and mean, holding the box cutter tightly, pointed at him.

He wrapped a dishtowel around his arm and followed her, a body length between them.

She backed into her bedroom, closing the door and locking it.

He stood there for a time. Then he walked up the hall, and went out the back door to his car.

As he waited for traffic to go by to get onto the main highway, Emerald's daughters drove up, stopped, blocked him, and got out cussing and screaming, banging on his hood. "I'm gone kill your ass, motherfucker." One girl carried a small chrome pistol. She lifted her arm and, with the semiautomatic turned sideways, started firing. He lay across the seat and shifted his truck in reverse. Bullets dinked the truck's windshield and passenger door, and ricocheted off the side mirror and hood. He lifted his head just enough to see out the back window and drove backwards as fast as he could control the truck, while shots fired. He stopped two blocks down the street, looked over the steering wheel, and saw the girls jump in their car. He didn't look to see if they were heading his way, but sat up, put the truck in gear, and raced down dark roads for fifteen minutes before he felt comfortable that he was not being followed. Then he drove south on Hwy. 17 and then on Interstate 95 to his sister's in St. Mary's. He didn't tell Viola.

V

Ike waited three days, until Friday evening, to call Emerald to apologize. He left a message on the machine.

He called her on Saturday around six after cutting grass. He didn't leave a message. He cleaned up at Viola's house and drove to Brunswick, getting there a little after eight. Emerald's car was not at the house. He stepped in the back door from the carport. The house was dark. Her bed was unmade. The sink was full of crusted dishes and plastic cups. Drops of blood still stippled the floor. Dirty clothes piled outside the washer and dryer closet. Somebody from Sears had called him at work to re-schedule the service call because nobody was home when they'd come on Thursday.

He didn't spot Emerald's car when he drove around the housing project where her daughters lived down the street from the Hercules plant. He drove by the Laundromats on Norwich Street and Altama without sighting the car. On the way back to the house, he stopped by a McDonald's and got a Big Mac meal and a strawberry shake to go. The Braves were on the television. He fell asleep on the couch before the game ended.

He awoke around midnight, went to the bathroom, and then walked up the hall and picked up his keys and wallet off the floor next to the couch. He pulled out the paper in his wallet that had the man's address. Antonio Sapp. Itchy. Union Street. He did not want to drive out there. He called Viola. She told him just to get what things he had left there and come back to her house. It wasn't going to do him any good to look for her. He agreed.

He locked the house door, got in his car, and headed to Highway 17, back to his sister's in St. Mary's.

On Fourth Street, Ike spotted Emerald's Marquis parked under a streetlight in front of the Club Lock Down.

Ike turned round at a corner used tire dealership and parked along the road in the club's sandy lot.

The Marquis's back passenger window had been busted out and replaced with plastic and duct tape. The hubcaps were gone and the driver's side mirror dangled. Somebody had pried out the trunk lock and the trunk was being kept down with a bungee cord. The front corner panel on the driver's side was dented in and there was a long gash down the driver's side.

An acrid odor spewed out of the window crack as a man and a woman inside hunched over the console and passed a glass pipe to each other.

Ike tapped on the window. The couple passed the pipe. Ike tapped again. The couple passed the pipe. Ike tried opening the door. It was locked. He took his key and unlocked it. He opened the door and snatched the man out of the car and threw him to the ground.

"It's a cop," the man said. "Run."

The woman fell out of the car and ran across the street and into the darkness.

Ike knelt on the man's chest.

"I cain't breathe, man."

"Where's Emerald?"

"Who?"

"Where'd you get this car?"

"I rented it."

"Who'd you rent it from?"

"A crack dealer."

"What's his name? Where's he at?"

"It's his old lady's car. They stay out on Union Street."

"What's his name?"

"I don't know."

"What do they call him on the street?"

"Itchy. Itchy. That's all I know him by."

"What's his old lady's name?"

"I never know her name, man. She got light skin, green eyes. Crack whore."

VI

Then Ike entered a month of work, fasting, and prayer while living with Viola, trying to take her advice and staying clear of Brunswick and letting Emerald lead her own life even if that meant she was drinking and drugging herself to death. "There's nothing you can do about it," Viola said. "She'll just bring you down with her."

And he prayed, and worked until his body and mind could not function. Then he ate and slept and woke the next day and did it all again and tried to not think about Emerald.

Late in the third week Ike began to pray, "Oh Lord, look down upon your poor sinner, and protect me as the Devil rains downs his wickedness, forgive me thou poor sinner my trespasses . . ." then raspy voices, *Emerald, Emerald, ha, ha, ha, ha, ha . . . Oh thou poor sinner. Seek thou God's forgiveness. Where is thou's wife? Ah-Ah-Oh-Oh is she lost, ah-ah-oh-oh, ah-ah-oh-oh. Is thou wife seek debauchery and drunkenness? Where was thou, husband? Thy wife's protector. Thou coward, sinner, debaucher, and drunkard, by abandoning thy wife. Why so far from thy calls of help, from thy cries of anguish. Rescue thy wife. But I am despised by thy wife. When she sees me she mocks and scorns me. She curses and shakes her head at me.*

The next day the same voices invaded his morning and evening prayers. Five days and each time Ike began his prayers they were drowned out by *God calls by day, but thou does not answer; by night, but thou does not give relief. Oh poor husband, rely on the Lord. Let Him deliver thee. If He loves thee, let Him rescue thee. Then do not stay far from me, for trouble is near there is no one to help.*

Each day while he tried to meditate the voices grew louder. By the sixth and seventh day all he heard underneath his daily work was the voices. They became his dreams and awoke him in his sleep. He told his sister and consulted his preacher. His preacher prayed over him. The sisters sang hymns and prayed and they ate the covered dishes they brought. After the Thursday evening deacons meeting, the brother deacons got down on one knee and laid hands on Ike's shoulders and prayed with deep voices. But despite these good people's earnest supplications the devilish voices taunting Ike would not quit. The voices taunted him through hard unceasing sweaty work under greasy trucks and tractors and in the evenings cutting yards until sunset.

*Thou canst defeat Satan. For Emerald's flesh is devoured in drugs and debauchery. Man shall leave his mother and lie with his wife; it is sin to lay with another man's wife. Thou art not a man if thou does nothing and let another man lay with Emerald. Wouldst thou be a coward? It is sin to allow a wayward wife . . . it is sinful . . . It is said, A worthy wife is the crown of her husband, but a disgraceful one is like rot in his bones. Wouldst thou be a sinful husband? Emerald is among Satan's numbers. Oh thee believer I have seen, I have seen . . . Where is thy God? Thou art forsaken, oh poor sinner. Rescue thy wife and cast thy soul into the pit. As long as thou keep silent thy bones shall waste away, thy strength shall wither as in dry summer heat, thy heart will become like wax and melt away within thou, and like water, thy life will drain away. I declared my sins, my guilt I did not hide, and the Lord took away the guilt of my sin. So much for you, thou deluded*

*husband for thy wife seeks intoxication and the pleasure of
the flesh. She shuns thy pain and grieves not, repaying evil
for thy good. Pursue thy wife into the darkness, even with
good intentions, and be afflicted with a deadly disease from
the sick bed thou shall never rise, and never shall mercy
rest upon thy heart.*

He left from God's house in the late afternoon to
find his wife.

VII

Ike opened the screen door and knocked on the
front door of the house. Nobody came to it, so he knocked
again. After a moment, the front porch light came on and
the door cracked open. A short, shirtless, dark-
complexioned man wearing shorts peeked through the six-
inch crack.

"I come for Emerald."

"Yeah?" asked the man, sniffling.

"She ain't here," said the man. He kept sniffling.

"I'm her husband." Ike pointed. "Her car be right
there on the street."

"Whatever, man. She ain't here. Don't know her."
The man closed the door.

Ike stood at the door. He knocked. The man didn't
answer. Ike knocked again. He jiggled the doorknob. It was
locked. He shouted, "Emerald. Emerald. It's me, Ike. I came
to take you home. Why you in there? Emerald. It's Ike." He
pounded on the door.

The man hollered back, "Nigger, I said she ain't
here. I gone call the po-lices."

Ike stepped back from the door and ran into it with his left shoulder. The door flung opened with ease. He stood in the middle of the dark front room. The man was on the couch. Assorted junk, lawn mower engines, a bicycle, and tools, were strewn on the floor and against the wall.

"I come for Emerald. Where she at?"

A shotgun style house with a front room and a hall ran the length of the house down the left side to the kitchen in the back. Between the front room and the kitchen were a front bedroom, then a small narrow bathroom, and then a back bedroom.

Ike walked past the man on the couch to the dark hallway. The man ran out the front door.

The hallway was black, except for a dim light coming from the back of the house. He let his eyes adjust.

He called down the hall. "Emerald?"

He groped and let his hand follow the wall. The door to the front bedroom was cracked open. He pushed it. "Emerald? I come to take you home." Shadows moved in the room.

A man's voice. "You need to go home, preacher man, before somebody gets hurt. Breakin' into other people's house."

"I didn't come to hurt nobody," Ike said. "I just come for my wife. Emerald? Is Emerald here?"

"Ike, go home," Emerald said. "This ain't your house."

He stepped into the room. Some of the pink light from the front streetlight seeped into the room's window. A man reeking of liquor and cigarettes pushed Ike out of the bedroom and up against the wall. "Nigger, you better get your ass home." The man's words came out fast and sharp like the sound from an air wrench.

Ike froze. He could not speak.

The men were less than two feet apart, but Ike could not make out the features of the man's face. He was a head taller than the man who moved quickly from side to side before him, jabbing him in the chest and stomach with his fingers.

Emerald yelled, "Stop, Itchy. Go home, Ike. Don't cause no trouble. I ain't going home."

"Go on. Go on. Go on." The man kept jabbing.

"Go on home, Ike," she said.

"She ain't going no where with you," the man said.

Ike tried to deflect the man's jabs, but he couldn't see well enough in the darkness.

The man snarled, "I'm gone fuck you up, nigger."

Ike sidled down the wall toward the back of the house. The man kept shouting at him and jabbing his chest. The more Ike backed, the louder the man hollered, and the meaner his words. "Get your nigger ass out my house motherfucker before I cut you. Get on, now. Now. Now." Ike kept moving. "You going the wrong direction, preacher man. You deaf?" The man kept jabbing, jabbing, jabbing, searing Ike with the Devil's finger. *Protect me Lord.*

"Not the back, Ike," Emerald hollered. She sounded like she'd come into the hall now. "You can't get out the back."

Ike kept moving toward the light in the back of the house. Then he realized the man was not following him.

Emerald said, "Where you going, Itchy? What you doing? What you looking for? Just let Ike out. Just let him go out the front door. Come back in the bedroom and shut the door, Itchy. Let him go out the front. He'll go out the front." Then she hollered to Ike. "Ike, go home. Go home, Ike, before somebody gets hurt."

Ike turned. A nightlight was plugged in the wall socket next to the sink in a small filthy kitchen with a sink full of pots, cups, and dishes. The back door, next to the sink, was blocked with a stack of motel air conditioners. He heaved the top air conditioner onto the cluttered kitchen table, knocking junk onto the floor.

"You dumb motherfucker," Ike heard the voice behind him, steel snap, Emerald screamed, and then a boom and another boom, and the wall and cabinet at his right ear exploded, sending Ike over the table in the middle of the kitchen, stunned, bleeding from the head, arms, and back, gouged with wood shrapnel, and unable to hear out of his right ear.

"Where are you, preacher man? Did I kill your sorry ass?"

Ike winced as he pushed himself up to his hands and knees. He turned his head and wiped the blood pouring into his eyes. The man looked as if he had a long thick pole raised. "I told you to get your sorry ass out of my house and you didn't you dumb motherfucker."

A blow to the back took Ike's breath and dropped him to his knees. Quick jabs with the end of the stick cracked his ribs.

"You gone get up? Huh? You gone get up? That'll teach you to come into some man's house and think you can be Superman." He jabbed Ike in the back. Jabbed him again. "Get up, preacher man. Get your ass up."

"I-I-I-I"

"What? What? What you say?"

"I can't see. I can't get my breath."

"I don't care if you crawl out of here. Get going."
He prodded Ike with the stick. "What's wrong with you?"

Sticking out of the sink was the handle of a large
kitchen knife. Ike grabbed the handle and pointed the blade
at the man. The man swung, hitting Ike in the head twice.
Ike buckled and swung the knife blindly. The man
screamed and fell to one knee. He hit Ike with the pole
once more. Ike lunged and stabbed the man in the leg. The
man backed out of the kitchen.

Ike's hands and knees quaked and he wheezed
trying to catch a breath. Blood poured out of his nose and
streamed from the top of his head into his eyes.

He had wanted no trouble, no trouble, he had
wanted no trouble.

Hazy pink light hinted the way out toward the front.

*The way of the wicked leads to ruin. They will not
survive judgment.*

The man backed slowly toward the front with the
stick held above his head. Ike, stooped over, shuffling
sideways, protecting his injured ribs and arm, held the knife
out at arm's length, and kept a couple of body lengths
behind the man. Emerald was howling. "Stop this. Stop
this, now, Itchy. Let him out. Oh, stop before somebody
gets killed. Oh, God, stop this." And she moaned. Ike could
not distinguish her words. The man pushed her in the front
bedroom as he and Ike made their way toward the front
door.

When Ike passed the bedroom door, Emerald jumped on his back and began hitting him in the head and clawing him. Ike stumbled in the dark. She jerked his neck and used some kind of twisted cloth to strangle him. Emerald grunted, "You bastard, you motherfucking stupid fucking bastard." He grappled the cloth loose enough to breathe. "Let go, woman. Let go." Emerald yanked and pulled. The cloth untwisted and unraveled. It was her dress. The green velvet dress, but ripped and crusty, stinking of cigarettes and beer, fish and sour body. Emerald coiled the dress around her fist and whipped him over the head with it. "Die, you motherfucker. Die. Die. Die." He bent forward and smashed her against the wall, but she held on to the dress. "Die, die." He tried to get hold of one of her hands, but she bit him through the fleshy part between his thumb and index finger. She raked his eyes with her fingernails and then bit his ear. "You bastard, you stupid bastard. I hate you, I hate you, I hate you." The man swung the stick, hitting Ike in the stomach. When he reared back to swing again, Ike thrust the knife forward. The man hollered and covered his chest with one of his hands. Ike kicked and slashed. Emerald still whipped and screamed. Ike slashed and stabbed and hacked. After a time, he could not tell how long, Emerald let go. The linoleum floor was wet and slick. He stepped over Emerald and kicked the green velvet dress loose from his foot. The man leaned in the doorway, coughing. Ike watched the man scramble across the street and collapse in the school playground.

Wheezing hard, Ike followed and kneeled by the man who thrashed and gurgled and waved the stick, a thick walking cane, in his outstretched fist.

Ike tried to stop the blood gushing from the hole over the man's heart. The blood gushed out of the man's chest onto the black sand. The walking cane fell. The man coughed up blood. A few seconds later, the man lay motionless, staring vacantly.

Ike pushed himself up and nearly blacked out. Blood saturated him. He got to his feet, and still carrying the butcher knife, he held onto his ribs and limped across the street. He could not bear to go in the house. Bloody hand prints on the door. Emerald was dead. He knew. Oh, God, he knew. He hadn't come here to kill. What had happened to him?

He collapsed against his truck tire, paralyzed in the legs, shivering all over, gasping to catch a breath, unable to focus.

He brought the knife blade up to his eyes and stared at the coagulated blood. *Oh, God, what have I done?*

*Thy God stands behind the door knocking no longer. Thy God calls not thy name. Thou art unworthy to dine in His house or to rest like a child on His throne.*

Sirens blared it seemed from every direction. Dogs howled and barked. People gathered outside their doors in their night clothes curious and confused.

*Thou are not blameless. Thy rebelled against thy God, thou did strut away from Him. Thou did not give thy God the praise and the victory.*

Ike sucked in air and gripped the knife handle in both hands and situated the blade tip so it could slip between the two ribs protecting his heart.

After much concentration, the thrust into the chest seem like an involuntary jerk, as if someone outside himself did the stabbing. His whole body seized, blood gushed down his chest, stomach, pooled onto the sand. His ears rang, his vision dimmed, his lungs like heavy weights.

*I am numb and utterly crushed.*

He palm hammered the knife butt, driving the blade's steel edge which punctured and tore vessels, arteries. He breathed heavily, coughed blood.

*My iniquities overwhelm me, a burden beyond my strength.*

He mumbled supplications, expecting no response.

# RIPTIDE

President Bush landed on the deck of the aircraft carrier I lived on in 2003, and declared "Mission Accomplished" in Iraq. We thought we'd done something that day. We'd succeeded in destroying tyrant Saddam before he unleashed the mushroom cloud. We were going to be greeted as liberators, as Cheney assured us. This was a slam dunk, like CIA Director Tenet boasted. The bad guys were on playing cards and would be hunted down.

Now, when I get off work, I sit at a cushioned stool, marooned in a certain bar in this town and talk to some of the guys, endure the empty headed Fox jerk offs with what they call the news. The bar owner (we'll call him Cash) runs Fox or the Braves game, or a football game in season, above the bar as long as the bar is open. It's a small bar tucked close to the water. No pool tables or cheerleader waitresses serving passels of hot wings. No, this is strictly a bar for the Marines and Navy guys. The walls are plastered with signed photos of Blue Angels dating back to the seventies, some of Cash's old Marine buddies from Vietnam, photographs from Desert Storm, and now some of us from this second Iraq war and Afghanistan. Cash's regular crowd used to be the survivors of D-Day and Pearl Harbor, Guadalcanal, Okinawa, the Batan Death March, the ones left from Korean and Khe Sanh. Now it's us younger survivors.

I'm kind of notorious in the bar because I'm in that photo with the president in his flight suit, carrying a flight helmet, strutting between the two lines on the flight deck. At the end of our line he shakes hands with the Admiral and Captain and Exec. I'm the black officer standing in the vicinity of the Admiral, saluting –my gaunt left profile in the photo, in the best shape of my life. After that snapshot was taken, the President turned to me and we shook hands, and I said, "Thank you, Mr. President," to whatever he shouted. I can't remember now, and "Nice to meet you, sir. Welcome to the Lincoln, sir." I was gung ho then. I hate that picture, now. I'm ashamed at myself.

This is my day, now. Up at four. Work (if you want to call it that) at five, manacled to a desk for eight. I stew at Cash's until about nine or ten, and then go to my empty house, dwelling rather, no tomb. I'm desked for the rest of my Naval career. No more flying since my Sea Dragon crashed and broke my back and legs. My vision is now non 20-20. I'm tinker-toyed together with titanium rods, plates, screws. My energy is plundered by chronic pain. I'm deemed a hazard in a cockpit. No more scudding over the sea, no more chance for promotion – twenty-five months to full retirement. But the Navy is willing to offer early retirement. They're dangling it in front of me like it's a baited hook and I'm a hungry Grouper. Fear or habit pushes me to the next day, the next week, month.

My father (the Admiral) and mother spend their retirement days in San Diego keeping their golf and tennis dates straight. They travel abroad a lot, too. I'm ill-suited to leisure that involves whacking a small ball and chasing it around.  I'm happiest when I'm in the sky, flying – have always been.  Down on the ground is when things get bogged down.

My grandfather would not understand my parents.  He sharecropped in south Alabama, lived in a home never furnished with central air or heat.  He broke ground, planted seed strapped to mule and plow, picked cotton with gnarled calloused hands.  Opportunity for success was in the harvest.  He kept his head down while plowing, planting, or picking, one row at a time.  Taciturn, joints wearing down, back breaking.

But, what happens when you run into roots and boulders underground in your path that you can't move?  I'm not a man of the land.

Cash had a Mynah bird named BoBo he garrisoned at the bar.  About every two or three hours the bird was inspired to converse.

"Laugh, Dad," said BoBo.

"No, you laugh," said Cash.

"No, *you* laugh."

"*You* laugh, damn you."

"Ha, ha, ha, ha, ha, ha," BoBo squawked.

It was this conversation I heard as I brooded over the next day's appearance at the courthouse for jury duty.  I'd never had been called for jury duty.  I'd always been out to sea, never living in one place long enough to be hood winked into having to sit in judgment of some poor bastard who was being prosecuted.  I was trying to decide, over a couple of Scotches whether to lose the summons or comply. I was tired of complying, always complying, my whole life complying.

Cash handed a beer down the bar and turned to wash and dry glasses. He saw me scrutinizing my summons and stepped up to me wiping his hands with a towel. "What you got there, Tommy?"

"Jury summons." I handed it to him.

He pushed his glasses from the top of his forehead onto the bridge of his nose. "You are hereby summoned, da, da, da, for jury service. Signed, Clerk of the Superior Court. Yep. Sure nuff looks that way." He gave it back to me, thumbed his glasses back on top of his head, picked up a shot glass, a hand towel, and started polishing it.

"What would you do?"

"Call in and say you can't come in because of pressing military business. Or plead hardship. Or say you can't sit for long periods of time because of your back that was injured during military service. That you're a disabled veteran."

"Think that'll get me off, huh?"

"Probably. Might. Good chance. Hell, you got a better chance than most."

"Goddamnit," I blew. It felt as if my back fusion screws were drilling clear through my flesh and the rods running along my discs were picking up the vibrations of some seismic event.

"They'll send out the police or deputies or something if I don't show, I suppose. Put me in jail for contempt or something."

"You worry too much, Tommy. They got too many more important things to do than come hunting for your ass. Shit, I'd lose that cock sucker. You could say you never received it. Claim you could never sit because of your injury suffered while serving your country. Blame it on the Post Office. Take the damn day off, the week. Go fishing. It's supposed to be a cloudy day tomorrow. Better yet, find a woman, get yourself laid or something. I got Viagra and Cialis, whatever you need. Take your pick. It'll keep you satisfying her for hours. Drive her crazy. Got some ecstasy, too. Slip a bit in her drink and she'll be like a thousand dollar whore."

It'd been how long since I'd had sex? Four years, plus the three months I was out at sea? I'd become a monk, an ascetic, cloistering myself in my minimalistic cell where I paid my bills and where I laid my head. Celibacy is not something I thought about, until now. It does make life simpler, conforming to an ascetic lifestyle, and God knew that's what I strived for – no confusion, no suffering, no attachments, no clutter, no demands, no obstacles. Women had become asexual human forms who inhabited the earth. I awoke, went to work, ate what little I needed without joy, spent time at Cash's, went home, read until I fell asleep (I didn't even own a television), and awoke the next morning and did the same thing.

I mailed the child support without fail and obsessed over the medical insurance premium being automatically withdrawn from my paycheck. I'd visited my kids, but it didn't matter to my daughter. She was five, born mentally retarded (I don't know a more sensitive way of describing it) blind, with a serious heart defect which hospitalized her multiple times a year. My wife, a quiet woman who dreamed of a house full of children, through her screams and sobs told me the day before I left for sea, "Tommy, you should have let me abort the pregnancy when the amniocentesis came back showing that she was going to be born with these terrible defects."

"That was both our decision, as I recall," I said coldly pulling my uniforms out of the closet and packing my bag.

"No it wasn't," she shouted.

"Settle down."

"You have a way of re-remembering things," she said. "You said you would not allow me to abort your child, no matter what because it was a life."

"She is a life. A precious life, no matter what."

A beautiful petite French woman six inches shorter than me, she stepped in front of my chest. "You and your Catholic morality. Now its our little baby that has to suffer for your morality. Our innocent baby who didn't ask to be born into this world." I stepped away. She slapped me over and over and shouted. "Just for your sense of morality, Tommy. To make you feel better, not anyone else." She grabbed my arm. Her fingernails dug into my flesh. She wanted me to say something, but I didn't. With her little fist, she pounded my chest and yelled at me in French, "I hate you, you bastard. You're nothing but a cold blooded bastard." I didn't resist. "I hate you, Tommy. It's not fair. I hate you. Do you hear me? You're away at sea all the time. You're not at home caring for this special needs baby. It's me. Me, Tommy. You don't know what love is. Love is caring for people. You and your morality and rules. Your family is supposed to be first, Tommy. We're your family. Stay with us. Help us."

"I have to go. We go through this every time. You know I have to go. That's my job. That's how I help. You have a nurse that helps you. I got you a nurse to help with the baby. You know I love you and the baby."

Her face was flush, worn, tired. She wiped her cheeks with the back of her hands; looked at me for a long time. Not the woman I married, pulling back her hair. "You're a coward. I've had enough, Tommy. Enough. I can't do this anymore. With you. We won't be here when you come back."

I picked up my bags. "We'll talk about this later," I said. Then I walked out.

"We won't be here when you come back."

I didn't hear from her for weeks. The divorce papers were delivered in the middle of the Indian Ocean. I agreed for her to have what she wanted, which was the divorce and everything else. What did I need? I had everything I needed on ship. Six months later we were legally no longer Mr. and Mrs. Riptided from my family and unwilling or uninterested or unmotivated to swim perpendicular to the current. It wasn't because I didn't care. I was paralyzed by anxiety and gloom, an overbearing shrouding darkness that I'd never encountered before that sucked me under and out to sea. I forgot how to move, to swim out of it. Six months later, my chopper crashed, I mean I crashed my chopper, two good people died, three good people were hurt so severely they required surgery and spent weeks in the hospital. I deserved everything I got, everything I'm getting. I'm resigned to being boiled down to my essential purpose here, at least for my son and my daughter's sake: a paycheck. I'm that cog in the wheel that churns them out. All I have to do is get up in the morning and show up at my desk and do my work until the end of the day and show up the next day and do the same thing all over. That's as it should be; as it always has been by fathers through the centuries.

"Another, please, Cash," I said, holding my glass out. "A double, please, so I can sleep."

"I got some pills."

"No thanks."

A tall white guy, muscular, black short hair combed straight back, leaned up to the bar wearing jeans, deck shoes, sockless, and a white polo shirt. "How's it going, Cash?" He tapped on BoBo's cage. "Laugh BoBo." The bird ducked down and darted up, ducked and bobbed, unblinking. "Laugh BoBo."

Bobo said, "Here kittie, kittie. Meow. Meow." Then he assumed an air of puffed up sleepiness behind the wires.

Cash poured Guinness out of the tap. "Here you go, Sean."

"That bird never does that laughing gag for me," Sean said.

"Maybe he knows something about you that we don't," some salty dog said down the bar from me. "Like he knows you don't got no sense of humor."

"Drink your beer, Fred," Cash told the scrawny man.

Fred shook his shoulders laughing, leaving him coughing up phlegm into a cocktail napkin.

After Fred gained some control, Sean asked, "Where's your oxygen, old man?"

"Baa. Left it at home." Fred turned up his mug of beer.

"What meanness have you gotten into today, Sean?" Cash said.

"Down in Crackavania again," Sean said after a long gulp of Guinness. "Target rich. Chasing crack heads. Chased one four blocks all the way into the Pimpbrook Apartments. When one of the guys finally tackled one of them, he liked to have broke the creep's arm. The guy stuffed the crack in his mouth and tried to swallow it. Then he started foaming like a dog with rabies." Sean looked at the old man. "Kind of like you, Fred."

The telephone rang, rang, rang. Cash answered it.

"Aw. In my day," Fred said, "we would have just shot the bastard in the leg. If we missed and he got hit in the back, well, it was the stupid idiot's own fault for running. We didn't this chasing after people if we could help it. When you told people to stop they damn well we weren't messing around, that was their one warning, then we'd shoot. Wasn't any of this chasing bullshit."

"There wasn't civil rights lawsuits in your day, either."

Cash hung up the phone. "Fred. That was your daughter. She said supper is ready, and time to come home."

"All right. So what did you end up doing with the perp?" Fred said.

"I tased him four freakin' times," Sean said.

"Tased him? Back in my day he'd of been dead," Fred said.

"Of course," Sean said.

Fred stood and dropped a dollar on the bar. Within his white forearm hairs was a tattoo of a smiling well proportioned nude woman riding a WWII era airplane.

Sean slugged the Guinness and wiped his mouth with the back of his hand. "Whatchyou pouting about, Cash?"

"He lost a lot of money on that damn gambling boat last night," Fred said.

Cash dipped glasses in the sink water under the bar. "I tell you, those games are rigged. I'm done with that boat. Y'all need to send some undercover people into there and infiltrate that place. It's corrupt. It done it to me again."

"I told you," Sean said. "You're just throwing good money after bad."

"That was the worst thing they ever did around here was bring in that gambling boat," Fred said. "Nothing good comes from gambling operations. Just more vice."

"I'll have another," Sean said.

"Well, I'll see y'all later," Fred said. We watched him swagger out the door.

"Bye-Bye. Come back. Be careful," the bird said.

"You think he's okay to drive?" I said.

"Oh, he's all right." Cash said. "Sober as a Pentacostal preacher." Cash wiped a glass dry.

"Been called into jury duty?" Sean said.

"Pardon?" I said.

He pointed. "Jury duty. You got jury duty coming up?"

I waved the summons and half laughed. "Yeah."

He reached for the summons. "Can I see it?"

I handed it to him.

"The jurors we got in this county got the IQ of Billy goats. Watch too much C.S.I. on TV and think you can get a fingerprint off a human hair. Hell, in this county they won't convict a jaywalker without forensic evidence." Sean took a swig of his Guinness and wiped his mouth with a cocktail napkin. "So, you been getting drunk on Scotch hoping this jury summons will just go away, is that it?"

"Well . . ."

"You think if you just ignore it, it'll just evaporate into thin air?"

"No, no, that's not what I was thinking. I--"

"Sure you were." He laughed and slapped me on the shoulder. "We put enough whiskey in our guts and hope things will just magically disappear. Drink a little more and we start getting forgetful, start disremembering things, recreating memories. Ain't that right Cash?"

Cash stacked glasses on a shelf behind the bar. "Hey, I'm in the business of selling drinks. The reason why a customer wants a drink is none of my business. I'm just glad they come in to my bar. I got bills just like everybody else."

"Yeah." Sean fluttered his fingers. "Ignore the bad things and they'll just fly away."

"I'm supposed to report tomorrow." A mosquito flew round my face. I swatted at it and almost knocked over my drink.

"If you're driving, you got no business in your condition."

"Ah, I feel fine," I said. "I don't live too far from here."

"Yeah. I hear that all the time." Sean pointed to his mouth. "Your speech is a little slurred." He blinked and pointed at his eyes. "And your eyes look red around the edges. If a cop stops you between here and home, I don't think you'll pass the field sobriety test. You'll end up spending a day in jail. You want to tell the clerk the reason you missed jury duty was because you got a DUI? The chief judge won't like that at all."

"I'll be fine."

He told me to get off the stool and stand.

I rolled my eyes to Cash and took another sip of my Scotch. "You're not serious."

Cash cleared his throat, snickered, and grabbed the TV remote to find the Braves game. That's when I saw the police badge float slowly into my vision and remain there. Sean took off his jacket. There was the holstered pistol on his belt.

"Okay. Now, I want you to stand and spread your arms at your side."

I complied.

"Now close your eyes. Touch your nose with the tip of you finger."

I performed.

"Now open your eyes."

"How'd I do?"

"We're almost done. Where are you from?"

I told him, "But my mother's French."

"You speak it?"

"Yeah. I lived in Paris until I was fifteen."

"You don't have that kind of accent."

"Well . . . "

"Can you speak any?"

"What?"

"French. French, man. You know." He enunciated slowly, "Can you speak any French?"

"Yeah."

"Well, say something. Prove it."

"Ah . . .ah . . . My damn mind's gone blank."

"I'm sure it has."

There was some excitement on the TV. Sean took hold of my chin and held up a little flashlight and shined it in my eyes. "What in the world are you saying?" he asked.

"I'm doing the play-by-play."

"What?"

I pointed at the TV. "To the Braves game."

He turned his head and watched the game. "Do it some more." I could have been discussing the nature of mid-east politics or how I might grab is gun for all he knew.

"Now, look. I want you to keep your head still and follow this little light with your eyes. Don't move your head, all right? Just your eyes, okay?" He moved the light up and down and sideways.

"For the last test, the very last test. You're doing well . . ."

What did well mean – I was passing or failing? He cleared away some stools so there'd be some room to walk on the black painted concrete floor.

"Now, this is what I want you to do. I want you to walk like you're walking a tight rope, okay?"

So, I tight roped like a performer in the circus. He told me to stop, and I hollered, "Ta-da-a-a-a," and began singing the circus song.

"Now stand with your feet together--"

"Hey, I thought you said that was my very, very last test."

"It is. This is a subpart of the last test."

"Goddamn," I said under my breath.

"Now, stand with your feet together. I want you to lift your leg at the hip, like this, okay?"

"I've performed a bar trick touching my nose with my finger with my eyes closed. I've done baseball play-by-play in French – I'd like you to find somebody else in this town who can do that. I've tight roped like your very own circus performer. And now you want me to do a ballet move? Are you an art critic or a cop?"

He glared at me, legs apart, arms cross.

I bowed. "To regale you with my grace and sobriety, I will perform a battement." Ten years of ballet in Paris as a child. Like the typing classes she made me take in high school. They kept coming in handy. I put my heels together, back straight, head and chin held in correct position, my arms and hands likewise. A deep breath for dramatic effect. Then I slowly raised my right leg.

My foot barely aloft, excruciating pain like hot metal jolted up my left ankle, knee, hip, spine, and all at once, spots filled my vision, a hum and beeping, all I heard when I toppled. I took out a line of stools.

Sean pulled me up and sat me on a chair where my feet could touch the floor. "Put your head between your knees, Baryshnikov." Cash came round and righted the overturned stools.

After a time, I sat up. "Can I drink the rest of my Scotch now?"

"Yeah, but you have to promise me you're going to call a taxi to get you home," Sean said.

"I promise."

"I'll make sure the knucklehead gets a taxi home," Cash said.

I took two long sips of Scotch. "Since you know my name, what did you say yours was again?"

"Locke. Sean Locke."

"Locke. Locke. Lock 'em up Locke. Seems you were destined for your line of work. People tell you that all the time, huh?"

"Gets old, Tommy."

"Who tells you?"

Locke shrugged. "Mostly drunks who think they're clever."

Cash took our glasses and swiped the bar with a towel. "You guys want another?"

"Not for me," Locke said. He put on his jacket and lifted his foot on a stool's foot rest. From his front jean pocket he pulled a money clip of cash. He walked over and tapped on BoBo's cage. "Laugh BoBo."

From somewhere deep, Bobo roared, "No."

He stepped back. "Damn."

Shouts came from the baseball game on the television. One of the Braves circled the bases. "Home run," Bobo said.

"That damn bird. Why is he like that to me?" Locke said.

"You shouldn't aggravate him," Cash said.

Cash slid Locke a clear plastic baggie and Locke palmed Cash some folded bills. Cash pocketed the money, and then raised his head to the baseball game.

Locke dropped the baggie in a brown paper bag, rolled it up, and slid the bag down his back waistband. "See ya, Tommy. Be safe."

I nodded and waved weakly.

"Bye-bye," Bobo said.

The door slapped shut.

"Moron," Bobo said.

"I called my boys," Cash said. "They're coming over to get you and drive your car home." He slipped a baggie of pot to me under a napkin. "I know you're going through some rough times. You're a good customer, Tommy. I don't like seeing you down every day."

My hands shook. I put it in my coat pocket, thought about smoking it. Then I pulled the bag out of my pocket, pushed it slowly to Cash inside the napkin. "Thanks all the same. I guess I'll stick to the Scotch."

Cash scooped up the bag. "Get yourself home. Get some rest."

"Yeah, I need it. Thanks."

Cash's boys came in the bar. One gave his dad a rolled up brown bag. Cash walked to the back room. A few seconds later, he was back prompting Bobo to ask one of his sons, "Boy, did you work today?"

"Yes, I worked today, you dumb bird."

"Give me your money."

The boy reached into his jean pocket. He put a dime in BoBo's beak. BoBo side-stepped across his perch and dropped the coin in a tobacco can on the cage floor piled with pennies, nickels, and other dimes. When the coin splashed, Bo-Bo shrieked and flapped his wings, creating a downwash that churned seeds and feathers out of his cage.

A clerk carrying a clipboard ushered us into the courtroom, a dark paneled room with no windows. Hung over, muscles and joints stiff and sore, the good air conditioning helped keep the nausea in check. The hard wooden pews we were herded into must have been to remind us that one's duty as a citizen was the austere demands hardship brought. I could find no comfortable position. Eventually my legs were numb and I could not feel my feet.

Our names were called and the judge made his introductions. After our oath, twelve of us were impaneled in the jury box which allowed the lawyers to probe. The prosecutor was interested in if we'd had had bad experiences with police officers, if we were distrustful of the criminal justice system, whether we felt police officers would lie on the witness stand to gain a conviction, whether a prosecutor would do anything at trial to gain a conviction, whether the state would falsify or conceal evidence, and if any of us had a loved one in jail or in prison presently. He told us that this was a gang related execution style shooting concerning a turf war among drug sellers and wanted to know if any of us had a problem with the State seeking the death penalty. A few of us, including me raised our hands.

"You don't think you could vote for the death penalty, sir?" the prosecutor asked.

"I don't think I could," I said.

"Do you have a philosophical opposition to capital punishment?"

"Not in all cases."

"Can you expand on your answer?"

"My opposition is based on economics and politics. I think it's usually sought to seek political points despite the fact that it drains the budgets of the local governments."

"So you don't think the death penalty is appropriate in this case where two people were shot execution style?"

"I think it would be cheaper to house people in prison for life."

"You are in the Navy, sir?"

"Yes, sir."

"Did you serve recently in Iraq, Afghanistan?"

"Yes, sir."

"How do you feel about the war there?"

"I'm a sailor. I follow orders. I'm not a politician or a policymaker."

"Surely you have an opinion about the war. Do you think we need to have troops there? Do you think we're bankrupting our nation--"

"You're getting off track," the judge said. "Move along."

"Commander, how do feel about illegal narcotics?"

"Don't use them. They're not good for you. They fry your brain, destroy your life."

"Do you think they should be legalized?"

"Marijuana should. Why not? It's no worse than alcohol."

The defense attorney, a tall, slim, long-legged woman in her late thirties, looked at her legal pad on the lectern, then gazed at me, and smiled. She asked if I believed the criminal justice system was stacked against people on the fringes of society such as the poor and minorities. I smell her lavish perfume from where I was sitting in the second row of the jury box.

"It can be. Yes."

"It says here on the questionnaire that you are a Commander. You must have taken on great responsibility and achieved success in the matters you were tasked to rise to such rank."

"I'd like to think I did my job and I achieved my rank on my own merit, ma'am."

"In your experience as a Navy officer, you have had command over men and women sailors, is that correct?"

"Yes, ma'am."

She poured a cup of water and took slow sips at her table before returning to the lectern. She wore a fashionable dark grey skirt and jacket with pin stripes, a white pressed cotton blouse unbuttoned enough to appreciate her cleavage. Nothing belied her confidence and comfort in the courtroom.

"Do you think innocent people are routinely convicted?"

"In this country? Not routinely. Does it happen? Yes. But routinely? No."

"Why do you think it happens?"

I adjusted in my seat. "Well, I guess it happens when defense lawyers don't do their job, witnesses lie or testify mistakenly, incorrectly--"

"Oh you think witnesses lie on the stand even though they swear to tell the truth?"

"Sure I think they lie."

She stepped from the lectern and paced in front of the jury box. Her black heels accentuated her long hard legs. Her skirt hugged her hips. "Why do you think witnesses, under oath, might not tell the truth, Commander?"

"For all different motivations. I mean I'm not a psychologist, but I would say self preservation, carelessness, to carry out a vendetta, power, any number of reasons, malicious or otherwise."

"Even under the penalty of perjury?"

"Yes."

"What other reasons do you think people are convicted wrongly?"

"Well the evidence is not accurate such as DNA, evidence is withheld like you hear about, or witnesses testify untruthfully or incorrectly, or the jurors just don't do their jobs honestly, conscientiously."

"Will you be a conscientious juror in this case, and consider the evidence fairly and objectively and wait to make your decision after you've heard all the evidence?"

"I will try."

She crossed her arms across her breasts. They were wonderful. "Would you punish the defendant if he did not testify?"

It would be nice to have dinner with wine and good conversation with this woman. "Like I said earlier, I'd like to hear his side of things."

"Right. But would you punish him for exercising his constitutional right to remain silent?"

"I guess I couldn't because it's the law."

"That's the law. You're not supposed to punish him for not taking the stand at his trial and exercising his right to remain silent. Do you understand?"

"Yes."

"So what you are saying is you would not punish him for exercising his right to remain silent? That's just what you said. Right?"

"Well, I guess that's right."

"That's right. It's the law."

"I'd follow the law." She turned on the ball of her shoes. My focus narrowed to her undulating ass.

"You follow the rules, don't you Commander?"

She bent over the table at the hip with her ass to me reaching for something.

"I'm sorry?"

She turned her head. "You follow rules."

"Yes, yes."

She sashayed back in front of the jury box and smiled. Her hands were empty. Her perfume was of a flower garden to lie down in and inhale. I tried to keep a respectful eye contact, but couldn't help staring at her cleavage when she would lean on the front rail. "Thank you, Commander, for your service." And she walked seductively back to her chair.

The prosecutor bolted up. He asked a question.

"Yes, sir," I said.

He looked over to defense counsel. "Yes, what?"

"I'm sorry?"

"I'll repeat my question. I just want to know if you can be fair to both sides, or do you come into this case with some kind of reason that you might be partial to one side or the other?"

"*I* can be fair."

"We just want to know how you feel. What you think. There is no right or wrong answers. This isn't a test."

"Well, I guess I do have this question, and that is can the *State* be fair to the defendant?"

"What do you mean by that?"

"I'm just saying, is it going to be a fair trial?" I pointed to the lanky medium skinned kid with hair twists, dressed awkwardly in black slacks and a white ill-fitted shirt and loosely knotted blue tie. "I don't think the defendant is going to have a fair trial."

The prosecutor made a note. "So you *can't* be fair to the State. Is that what I'm hearing you say?"

I leaned forward in my seat. "*I* can be fair. I'm not saying *I'm not* going to be fair. What I said, sir, is I don't think the *defendant's* going to get a fair trial from the *State*."

"And why is that? Can you be clearer in your explanation?"

"It's the way the thing is set up."

"The thing? What is the thing?" The prosecutor held both sides of the lectern and leaned one ear toward me. "The way what is set up? Is it the courtroom, the system, the rules, the people who run the system? Do you mind being more specific?"

"I think that the people who are seeking a conviction have an interest in getting a conviction, not in making sure the trial is fair. The system is flawed because of the people who run it and participate in it."

"Let me ask you," the prosecutor said. "People make up the system, so you think they are corrupt, or they are fallible, make mistakes – is that what you're saying?"

"I believe that the police especially have an interest in achieving a conviction. I think sometimes some will lie or cheat to get a conviction, not all the time, but some of the time, enough to make us mistrust them, or at least me--"

"Are you aware that you as a juror are to weigh their credibility like any other witness?"

"--I think crime labs cheat sometimes to get convictions, too, and that scientific tests are performed incorrectly, or are flawed. It gives me a lot of concern--"

"Crime lab people's credibility are weighed, too."

"--People come into court and identify the wrong person. Poor people get bad lawyers. Too many people are getting wrongly convicted. And if a defendant in a death penalty gets wrongly convicted and put to death it's too late if it's later found out he didn't do it."

"It's an imperfect system. But it's the best we've got. We're a country of laws. And we must hold people accountable who break the law. Do you agree?"

"Sure. But I wanted to express my concerns."

The prosecutor wiped his nose with a handkerchief, folded it, and replaced it inside his suit's coat pocket. "Sorry. I'm suffering from a cold."

"That's all right."

"Have you ever been wrongly accused of a crime?"

"No, but I have had cousins who have. A cousin is in prison right now because the judge made him go to trial with a lawyer who never came to talk to him before trial and never talked to witnesses and never filed any motions. An uncle is on death row."

"Your uncle?"

"For a double murder."

"Do you think he was unfairly treated?"

"Yes, from what I've heard. I was in Iraq at the time."

"Do you think he was too harshly punished?"

"Yes, very. That was the only time he has ever been arrested for anything. He's a good man. He just married a sorry woman. She had even been in prison before for drugs. She was sleeping with another man who got her using crack cocaine again. When my uncle tried to rescue her, get her away from that man and take her home, the man and my uncle's wife attacked him and my uncle had no choice but to defend himself. In the process he killed the two."

"I see," said the prosecutor. "Where was he prosecuted?"

"Down in Mobile."

"Alabama? So you think he should have been acquitted? Should have been found not guilty?"

"He was defending his life against these crack heads. He was trying to save his wife. He didn't go in there with a weapon. He's a peaceful kind-hearted, God fearing man. The best Christian man I've ever known."

"That's what you heard," the prosecutor said.

"That's my understanding of what happened," I said. "He certainly was not guilty of murder."

"Let me ask you this. Have *you* ever had a bad experience with a police officer?"

"I've been stopped a few times when I was younger. I was in visiting my grandparents. I was stopped for no reason other than being a black male out at dark."

"Were you treated badly?"

"I'd say rudely. It made me nervous because I didn't know what the cops were after. You never know what the police are going to do. You hear stories from friends, uncles, cousins. The police have all the power on the streets. We have none. When I was stopped, because I acted *nervous*, the police officer thought I was guilty of something. So he called for backup. A second officer came with a dog. It was two against me with a German shepherd. It was dark. On the side of a road that didn't get much traffic. Not a main road, not many cars. I was sixteen and hadn't been driving by myself that long. I was spending a few weeks with my grandparents. This was north of Mobile. On this evening I was returning from my uncle's house after a Fourth of July cookout. It was a scary experience. They kept me there for what seemed hours; left me handcuffed sitting on the side of the road while they searched my car – the interior, the trunk, under the hood. Eventually, I was put in the back of a patrol car. One officer kept asking me if I had any secret compartments in my car and where I'd come from and where I was going. I let them search the car so a dog wouldn't go in there and tear it up. They tore the car up anyway looking for secret compartments. Then without a word they un-cuffed me, gave me back my driver's license, and let me go. No apology for damaging the car or anything. They did over $2000 worth of damage. It was my grandmother's car – an old Buick. When my grandparents sought reimbursement for damages, the police told them to sue."

"Does that experience still bother you?" the prosecutor said.

"Sometimes."

"Do you distrust law enforcement because of your bad experience?"

"Not all."

"Because there will be police officers, investigators, and crime lab workers testifying in this trial?"

"I understand."

"Will you evaluate their credibility like other witness?"

"Sure."

She led with her legs getting out of her chair and moved unhurriedly across the room, smiling. "I just want to follow-up on some of the questions the prosecutor asked. So your opinion about the fairness of whether this trial can be fair to my client, the defendant, is from your experience, is that what you said?"

"Yes."

"What do you think we attorneys are looking for in a juror?"

"A juror that's going to think your way, vote your way. Isn't that what you want me to be?"

The prosecutor objected to the answer as nonresponsive, as responding with a question.

"Sustained. Let me stop things for a moment," the judge said. "What we're trying to determine is whether or not you can listen to the evidence in this case and make a decision based upon the evidence you hear in the courtroom, whether you're going to be fair to both sides. Those are the questions. And so--"

"Yes, sir, I'll be fair to both--"

"Let me finish, all right? But it is very important for you to answer the questions, the actual questions that are asked by all the lawyers in this case. We actually have to hear the explanations. Okay?"

She continued. "So, Commander, you don't think the State can be fair to my client, the Defendant?"

"I think the State wants to convict. They are advocates and have their perspective and want to win, not lose."

"So you're not saying the system is unfair. You're just saying it's an adversary system. Is that what I'm hearing you say?"

"Well. I guess that's a better way of saying it."

"The system is imperfect, would you accept that."

"Yes, I guess I will have to accept that. Nothing is perfect."

"And if you are chosen to sit on this jury, you will be fair and impartial to both sides in this case, won't you?"

"Yes."

On my escape out of the courthouse, I ran into Locke. He was dressed in a black suit, black shirt, maroon and silver tie, and black leather shoes. But for his badge clipped onto his belt, he didn't look like a cop to me. He grabbed me round the shoulders and hugged me like we were old chums. "Tommy," he boomed. "Where are you getting away to?"

"I got struck and excused for the week."

"Whatever it takes, man. They don't want a smart guy like you, anyway."

"I was so distracted by defense counsel. She was really putting it out there--"

"Oh, you got the Harmony Lutz treatment. All they need to do is give her a pole."

"Maybe it was only me--"

"She's dating some producer. Maybe she'll get her own show and we'll be shed of her." He glanced at his watch.

"She certainly seemed--"

"I got to get upstairs and testify, brother." He unhanked me and pealed off laughing. "Don't get drunk and drown out there." He took the stairs two at a time.

On the sidewalk, a man that reminded me of my granddaddy. It was his strong knobby hands holding his cigarette. I asked him for the time. He looked hard at my Bulova diver's watch.

"It's gone out on me," I lied.

He stretched and twisted the gold band on his. "Ford gave me this un when I retired. Thirty years."

"Detroit?"

"Atlanta." He tapped the crystal with his fingernail and put it up to my face. "It's a Timex. Never give me no trouble." He brought out his reading glasses. "Say's it is quarter past eleven."

"Can I bum a cigarette off you?"

"All I got is filterless."

"I can handle 'em."

He offered me his pack of Pall Malls. I tapped one out and lit it with his silver Zippo with the Ford emblem on it.

"What do you drive, young man?"

"It's not a Ford."

"One of them Jap jobs?"

"German."

"I've always owned a Ford, myself. Always a truck. Trade 'em every two years."

Our discussion drifted to the generic issue of the weather and then a discussion of his children. He had put two children through medical school. But there was the youngest.

"I always wanted him to find a steady job like I had. Find a job in the government or go in the service and make a career of it, do his thirty years, have a good retirement, be set for his old age. There ain't nothing I can do for the boy. They're just going to have to lock him up to keep him away from that crack. He done about killed his momma with worry. All he does is steal from us. Come at me with a gun the other day, say he was going to shoot me and his momma. The boy was out of his mind. He got caught last year yanking out copper from a power box behind a strip mall."

We took pulls on our cigarettes and blew. He wanted to know about my children. I told him about my daughters, the oldest who was the ballet dancer and pianist, and the four-year-old, the youngest who loved to draw and paint, daddy's pride and joy. And the boys, athletic and smart who people always complimented on their manners: "Ma'am and Sir."

He smiled, said he wished all parents brought up their children in the old fashion ways like that. Said it gave him a lot of joy to hear that.

I felt guilty for lying, thanked him for the cigarette. We shook hands and said our goodbyes.

At the street side door to the parking deck, a man was darning the pocket of a brightly printed shirt. He wore a homemade hat made of palmetto prawns, khaki shorts, a colorful shirt with palm trees, and sandals. He leaned in a worn folding chair, legs crossed at the ankles, peering through a pair of half moon drug store reading glasses. Rolled next to him was a grocery store cart heaped with what seemed to be all his belongings. Stuck in the cart was a hand painted placard advertising, *Tourist Information.*

"Good morning, sir. Can I help direct you around?" He had one of those Chamber of Commerce tourist maps folded in his shirt pocket, creased and stained, probably grubbed out of a dumpster.

"No, thanks."

"Well, can I bother you with the time?"

I looked down at my watch and told him.

He looked up at the sky. "She's right on."

I took a baring. "You follow the sun or something?"

"No, sir." He pointed.

I turned and squinted.

"I follow the bank clock across the street there." A Marine Corps. bicep tattoo slipped out from under his shirt sleeve.

"The Corps?"

"Yes, sir. 1975 to 2003."

"Navy," I said. Low key. "Helicopter pilot."

"I saw your academy ring, sir. Retired?"

"They'd like me to be. They'll have their damn way soon enough."

"What do you fly, sir?"

"Sea Dragon, mostly. I did some Harrier flying earlier, but the Sea Dragon."

"Goddamndest ride was one time off the deck of a carrier in a hellacious storm in one of those damn things. Half of my men were puking, thinking we'd be dead before we got where we were going. Goddamnedest ride."

"You retired?"

"Yes sir. Gunny Sergeant, sir. Last bit I was going through those god forsaken mountains trying to find old Ben." He darned his shirt. "I got a boy in the Army. He's done one tour already with them Afghanistan people. He re-deploys in a few weeks. They got them stretched thin over there."

"That's what I read."

"Me and my old lady split up. She couldn't take me staying home all day and not working." The needle went in and out, in and out. "She thought that if I just worked I'd get to feeling better. 'Buck up, Stew,' she'd say. 'Get out and get you a job. Go out to Walmart and be a greeter.' Hell, I'm not going to be a damn greeter."

"You're preaching to the choir."

"I get shot up and my ex-wife gets most of my monthly retirement check. I've been clean and sober for 38 months, and two days. AA's been the best thing for me.

Go just about every day. I go to the V.A. hospital, but you know how that is, sir."

I nodded. "I'm divorced. Most of my money goes to child support."

He locked his eyes onto me as if he was challenging me to divulge some deep hurt or secret he intuited. He waited. I almost did unburden myself.

"I've got to be going, Gunny" I said. "I'll leave you with the clock and the tourist."

"I buy all my clothes at the thrift stores. Got these shirts for a dollar a piece." He pinch his khaki shorts. "These shorts are brand new. I got them for three dollars. That's the only places I go now. You can find new clothes or almost new clothes that folks just give away. All you got to do is take your time and have a good eye. I go to mass at noon. Then go to AA. Leading a simple life with no credit cards, no damn TV, just being outside, enjoying what life I got left." He smiled and pushed himself to his feet. We shook hands and he held mine firmly. "Hey, sir, if you don't have anything to do in the evenings, we meet at the Legion at around seven. We drink coffee and visit for a while, play cards or dominos."

"Thanks. I usually spend a couple of hours over at Cash's bar after work. It's on the way home."

"He a friend of yours, sir?"

"I guess you could say I'm one of his regular customers."

"Oh, I see, sir." He eased himself into his chair and went to darning his shirt.

"I like the place because it's quiet – not one of those loud sports bars. I have a few and just sit and visit. I'm divorced. You know how it is going home, an old dismal place with just four walls."

"I understand, sir. I just wanted to say that you hear things."

"What do you mean?"

"You need to be careful about Cash's place."

"I don't understand?"

"What I'm hearing is that there's an undercover investigation."

"By the cops?"

"About cops using steroids."

"What about Cash?"

He tied the thread and bit it. "He's apparently their dealer."

"Are they going to shut the place down?"

"Pretty soon," he said. "That's what I hear, anyways. Pretty good sources."

I stood there for a while watching the traffic and him start darning another shirt. "Well Gunny, it was nice meeting you. Thanks."

"Sure thing, sir."

I took a few steps.

"Come on by the Legion. You're welcome any time."

I could barely fold myself into the driver's seat of my car. When I got home, I took a couple of pain pills, three Xanax, my anti-depressants, something to help me sleep, and a large Scotch. The pizza I ordered was delivered about an half hour later. The last thing I remember was sitting down with it on the couch. It was dark when I awoke. My face was in the middle of cheese and tomato sauce. I was confused. Ifell back to sleep in the floor and awoke the next day. I guess it's a wonder I didn't die to only be discovered days later due to the smell of my decomposing body.

I fished the rest of the week with some buddies. We hired a guide and caught our limit each day. On Thursday evening, out eating and drinking to celebrate with the crew, I met an energetic woman about ten years younger than me. She had long straight blonde hair. That was what first attracted me, and her smooth white skin. Her name was Sydney. She was from Boston, and a huge hockey fan, terribly allergic to mosquitoes and gnats and chiggers, and loved deep sea fishing. Now she was a professor at one of the colleges in town teaching French and French literature.

We ate steamed shrimp and raw oysters, and drank beer.

"Do you know what a freebie five is?" she asked, shoveling cocktail sauce with a large shrimp, bending her head back on her long stem neck, and leading the shrimp into her mouth with her tongue. "Mmmm."

I grinned and stared, followed the shrimp as it slipped slowly down her throat. She gazed back. "A what?" I asked.

"A freebie five? It's something I heard my students talking about over beers a few nights ago. The rule is if you could have sex with five women in the world, past or present, who would it be? Girls have four guys and one girl. They have to have one girl. Guys – straight guys have their pick of five women, past or present."

"Never heard of it."

"Who would be on your list?"

I swallowed an oyster on a cracker. "Christ. I've no idea. What about you?"

"I have a few, but I haven't had enough to drink yet. What do you think of tattoos? Women with tramp stamps on their backs?"

"Do you have one?"

"No. Do you?"

"A Chinese dragon on the back of my left shoulder. I got it in Hong Kong one night I got really drunk with some buddies while on shore leave."

"Maybe you'll show me later?" She was pleasantly buzzed resting her chin on her laced fingers, then teasing me, licking cocktail sauce off her finger. "So has anyone popped into your head who'd be on your freebie five?"

"I don't know."

She dipped another shrimp in the cocktail sauce. "Me too."

I leaned in and smiled. "How about you?"

She licked her fingers and we laughed.

After looking around the place for a time, she cut her eyes at me, threw back her head and grabbed my hand. "Let's dance, Tommy. I need to move."

She was a great dancer – paired with me, when she improvised, and when she teased me exotically in her short silver dress that hugged her curves.

"You're a one woman man, aren't you Tommy?"

I shrugged.

"What about you?"

She didn't answer.

Wearing spiked heels, she matched my height. It was easy wrapping my arms round her small waist, resting my hands over the curve of her hips, or pressing her bare back to tighten my hold, to feel her breasts through my sweaty shirt.

Back at our table we sat pressed against each other and ordered fresh drinks.

"I bet Gatsby is your favorite character in literature."

I looked at the bottom of my glass. "Actually *The Count of Monte Cristo.*"

She blew a stream of smoke over her shoulder. "Of course." She tapped the ash into the ashtray. "A hopeless sentimentalist."

Our drinks arrived. I reached over and held her hands. She raised her chin, leaned back and shook her hair when I complimented her in French. We kissed.

"Your accent is Parisian, no?" she said in French.

"I was born south of there. I lived in Paris until I was a teenager."

We took a walk along the river as the bars and restaurants closed in the quarter. She drove us to her home.

I awoke naked, perfectly fitted against her naked back, my arm draped over her shoulder, her hand weaved in mine. I dozed back to sleep.

The bedroom was full of the aroma of rich coffee, frying bacon, and eggs. I lay under the cotton sheets realizing how much I missed the feel and scent of a woman. The French doors opened to the morning breeze. From the living room stereo, a woman sang, breathy French ye-ye style. Sydney padded over the boards, wearing a long peasant gown, carrying a tray of coffee.

"*Bon jour. Ça va ?*" She set the tray down on the nightstand and kissed me gently.

"*Très bien. Merci, merci. J'ai faim.*"

She whirled in a slow dance to the singing. The moment was too good to seem real.

"Do you dream in French or English?" Sydney asked in French, taking in the sun and the outside air.

"I haven't thought of that. I guess English," I said. We continued to converse in French.

"That's a shame."

"You?" I asked.

"English. I used to dream in French for a little while I was in school there. It made my dreams . . . different. Less . . . I don't know, I can't describe it. I keep wishing that they will come back."

"My mother is a painter," I said. "We were always going to museums."

"I miss them, too. Also, getting on the train, going to Italy – Florence, Rome, Milan, Venice. I miss Venice, especially."

With my mouth full, I said, "*Il tuo corpo è bellissimo. Voglio fare l'amore con te.*"

She bent with laughter.

"*Sei incredibile. Sei stupenda. Ti adora.*" I held out my arms. It was an operatic performance despite the French accompaniment. "*Mi fai eccitare. Sono pazzo di te--*"

"Stop it, stop it, you crazy--"

*"Voglio farlo sulla lavatrice, nell' ascensore, in macchina--"*

"Enough, enough."

I set the breakfast on the dresser table beside the bed. When she returned from the bathroom, we continued the conversation in French. She said, "I haven't been to Paris in a long time. I loved the holidays there. Christmas and New Years – all the lights."

I leaned on my elbow. "We should go. Become expatriates."

She laughed and fell to me on the bed. "I can't go back. Too many bad memories left there."

After a time, I told her of my daughter and my career, or the downfall of it. In embarrassing drips I let fall the account of my divorce, about Nigel, my son's Australian soccer coach and now his stepfather, after he and my wife's affair while I was on sea duty.

"They are a better match," I said."

"What do you mean?"

"They make a better appearance together than we did."

"Do you have any pictures?"

I showed her my wallet photos. I even had a photo of my wife with my son during one of our vacations snow skiing.

"The biracial marriage bothered her?"

"She never said anything. She said I was away so much, with Phoebe, our daughter, never concerned for her. Then Nigel and she started talking after my son's practices and games. The divorce papers – they were unexpected. That was four years ago. Now my kids live in Australia."

"When was the last time you saw them?"

"Two years ago."

Sydney started cleaning out my wallet while we conversed. "How do you get it to close? Do you throw anything away? I would hate to see what your apartment looks like?"

Chuckling, I said, "It's surprising bare. I keep everything is in there. When I get home everything pops out of my wallet – my bed, lamp, table, chair. Then when I leave, I snap my finger and they jump back in my wallet. I'm very mobile. When I retire I'm going to buy my clothes at the Goodwill and put all my belongings in a grocery cart and sit outside all day with a tourist map, take my meals at the Legion or at the Church."

"Where would you live?"

"I haven't thought it out that far. Maybe I could get a job where I could live upstairs or behind the store or shop."

In unloading my wallet, she came by the sealed locket of baby's hair. "Who does this belong to?" she whispered.

"It's my daughter's baby hair. You're the only person in the world besides me who knows about it being there."

We listened to the rain for a long while before Sydney began talking. She shared the suicide of a lover, an abortion, two miscarried babies, and the guilt and pain she wrestled with every day that not even psychotherapy or a box full of pills could suppress.

She led me to explore those long sinewy dancer's lines, long past when a warm Sarah Vaughan CD was finished and the coffee and food on the tray had turned cold.

We lay entangled among her pillows as an afternoon thunderstorm blew in from the ocean and darkened the afternoon sky, wrapping the rest of the day in a thick drizzle and fog. Before finally rising from the bed, she kissed me lightly and said, in English, as if breaking the spell, "You know this is all we will have, darling." And I did, and was surprised I didn't feel terrible about it.

Sydney's two orange cats sat on the windowsill, and a light rain fell as we shared Thai takeout and the Sunday newspaper and cigarettes. The Mission Accomplished photograph was on the front page, in color, accompanying other articles about the war. Sydney read the article over the glass kitchen tabletop. She took a long drag on her cigarette then mashed it out in the ashtray.

"That carrier landing and speech was ridiculous," she said. "All for TV. Did anybody get that it's a rainbow the President walked through." She took a sip of milky sweetened coffee and pointed to the photograph. "Look. Yellow, blue, red, green, purple. Get it? Don't ask, don't tell? It looks like he's walking through a homecoming court, carrying that helmet under his arm, wearing the flight suit. Like I don't know when I'm being manipulated."

I read the sports page and spoke through the page. "I was there--"

"What?"

"I didn't have anything to do with that. I just stood where they told me. The president's people were there."

"You're full of it," she said in Italian – a beautiful language, and appropriate for emoting disgust. "You were on the deck of this ship when Bush went gallivanting in his flight suit like Tom Cruise?"

I sat up and pointed to the photo. I'd been cropped out. "I was standing right here next to this guy. I'm out of the picture," I said.

"I don't believe you," she said.

I shrugged and put my head behind the sports page again. I told her all she had to do was go to Cash's bar and look on the wall behind the bar.

She stabbed the newspaper photo with her index fingernail. "This photo makes you guys look like a bunch of stooges."

I glared at her around the paper. "I dare you to tell my carrier crew that to their faces. It was a privilege that the president came aboard our ship. You have to understand that at that time we thought we – the U.S. military – had done something good and right in Iraq by getting rid of Saddam. So yes, we were proud. I was proud. We didn't learn about all the other stuff until later. Most of those people on board ship were a great bunch of men and women. Anyway, I thought you didn't believe I was there."

She huffed, folded out of the chair and walked over to the bookshelf and retrieved a photo album. "You wouldn't believe I was here, either." She opened the album and flipped through the pages slowly – photos of musicians and singers, a rock band. She pointed. "That's me."

I strained to make out her features. The woman singing with two others under bright lights had long flowing blonde hair. "That's you?"

"That was back in the early nineties. I was on tour with Pink Floyd. We all wore a lot of stage makeup. But, yes, that's me."

I stared at the photographs.

"You see, in this picture that's Nick and David and Richard. And that's me and Nick, and that's me and Richard, and that's us messing around before a concert." She scrambled on her knees to her CD shelf, put a CD in the player, and brought back a CD case and opened it. "See. That's me there."

"How did you make the band?"

"It's a round-about story. I went to the Berklee Music School in Boston. I got a gig singing with these guys in the evening. One night, some guy, a manager came through and heard us play and heard me singing and asked if I'd be interested in singing backup with the band on tour in America because one of the backup singers had gotten sick or something, I can't remember. Of course I said yes. David liked me and invited me to continue touring with the band in Europe, too."

I flipped through the pages of her photo album.

"You still don't believe me, do you?"

"I didn't say that."

"That CD is a composite of our live performances on that tour."

"You just did that one tour?"

"Just that one tour. America followed by Europe. It was the most incredible experience of my life. Then I went back to school."

"I haven't heard much of Pink Floyd's music."

"What do you listen to?"

"Other stuff . . . just not Pink Floyd."

"I can't believe you've never heard of Pink Floyd. Back then I had no ties to anything or anyone. I just grabbed my passport, packed a few things in a backpack and picked up my ticket at the counter and met the band in Los Angeles. I rehearsed with them for a few days and then . . . See here's a picture of me and David. She wore a short flashy silver dress, and heals that accentuated her long muscular legs. Her eyes were heavily mascaraed, her eyelids colored, her lips painted, her face perfect. She was glamorous. It would have been almost impossible to unmask that woman from that photo alone. David was in jeans and black t-shirt with a guitar strapped over his shoulder. He signed the photograph: 'To Sydney, my darling, Sweets, Much Love, David'"

"David?"

"David Gilmour."

We listened, she singing along. Her voice could reach down soulfully and bend and mourn, sustain a note without a quiver, sparkle in the high range.

"You're skeptical," she said. "You don't believe me."

"No, no. I believe you, I believe you. Here you are in this photo with . . ."

"David." She sprang over to the bookshelf and brought down a jewelry box and rolled a joint. Her hands shook. "No you don't."

"You're very remarkable, Sydney. People don't come into contact with remarkable people just every day."

She lit the joint and we smoked it together, laying in the floor, propped on large throw pillows, listening as she sang, as I had never heard anyone sing.

"I've never been in a room and heard anyone sing like you do."

"It's a professional voice."

"Do you continue to sing professionally?

She didn't answer.

"You know, do any backup work, or sing solo, or studio work?"

"Sure. That's what paid for undergrad and grad school. Made good money. Traveled all over the world. I lived in Europe."

"What happened?"

"I've already told you most of it. James was the love of my life. We lived in Venice, Paris, Lyon, Florence and then Amsterdam. He was an architecture student from London when I met him in Rome. I supported us singing. He was a dazzling painter. That's what they said about him. He used such bright colors and strident brush strokes. I traveled a good bit. What I didn't realize was that he had become terrible addicted to heroin while we were living in Venice. We had a wonderful place there. I loved Venice. I was gone for a month. But I had to get him away from that crowd. That's why I moved us to Amsterdam. I spoke to him on the phone every day except for the last week. I couldn't get in touch with him. I called some of our friends. None of them had seen him around our usual hang-outs. It wasn't unusual for James to hole-up in his studio when his work was flowing intensely. When I arrived home, he wasn't downstairs in our living quarters. I called out to him. I walked upstairs to the studio. I called out to him again. He was hanging . . . In the floor were syringes . . . He didn't leave a note. There were no finished or unfinished paintings in the studio. It was bare. No paint, no brushes, nothing. Everything was gone except his heroin stuff and syringes. I was two months pregnant. A month later, I lost the baby. It was my second miscarriage. I packed up, had the miscarriage in London while I was staying with James's family. I wasn't singing. I couldn't. I felt burned out, exhausted. A couple of months after the miscarriage I got a studio job in London. I guess it was too immediate. I didn't see a therapist. I should have. I went to Paris. That's where I got my graduate degree in French literature. I doing some singing to make some extra money, but emotionally I was flat."

After a while, she asked, "Do you miss your daughter and son?"

"Very much."

"Nobody knows where I am – any relatives of mine, I mean."

"Why is that?"

"My parents are dead," she said. "All I've got left are a couple of older sisters. They are like sour aunts. They could care less, anyway. They've always hated my lifestyle. I haven't spoken to them in years. They think I'm nuts. That's why I cut them off."

She stood and put some papers in the trashcan and dishes in the sink. "You really believe you are inessential, an inessential cog?"

"No. My primary role right now is I'm a paycheck."

Her fingers were long and statuesque; her hands attached to narrow wrists that flowed up long arms. "You don't know how lucky you are."

"I've got a divorce decree in a box in the trunk of my car to remind me. That's what I'm supposed to do. I've always done what I'm supposed to do, you know, follow orders." I held the joint nub with the forceps and inhaled.

"We get caught in one of those currents that pull us out to sea, and we forget how to swim out of it, or give up and let the current pull us out to sea to drown." She pressed her fingers against her temples and massaged them.

Her knees buckled. She caught herself with her elbows on the kitchen counter before crashing head first onto the kitchen counter and the floor.

I yelled her name as I sprung across the room.

She pushed herself to her feet. I guided her to the small downstairs bathroom. She retched and coughed. I stood helpless nearby the closed door. I asked if she was alright. There was more retching and coughing. The toilet flushed, the water ran in the sink, coughing, gargling, then the water turned off. She stumbled from the bathroom, a wet hand towel to her face, and guided herself by the banister upstairs.

It was quiet for a time. She returned downstairs, padded barefoot over the carpeted floor, and nestled herself into an overstuffed denim chair with a worn afghan over her shoulders. She turned off the lamp next to her chair. "Would you mind turning off the kitchen light, Tommy? It's killing my head."

It was dim in the room – the only light coming from the outside. I settled into the deep stuffing of the chair across from her and listened to the drip, drip of the rain. I almost was asleep when I heard her humming soothingly. She rocked with her knees drawn, her arms wrapped around them.

"I'm ridiculous – an over sensitive ridiculous mess. I can't believe I'm crumbling like this in front of a man I barely know." She raised her face. "I took some medicine, so forgive me if I seem loopy. Loo-oooopy. Loopy." She laughed over her shoulder and waved her hands over her head. "Aren't I ridiculous, darling? You should walk out, now. Run while you have a chance. Run, run, run, run . . ." Tears streamed down her cheeks. "Lock the door and throw away the key."

"It will blow over," I said. One of those trite phrases I hated. I couldn't believe I said it. I wish I could have taken it back.

"I guess. Would you mind getting me a ginger ale out of the fridge? And a few Saltine crackers? It's one of those homely Southern remedies that one of my students taught me. It seems to work."

I fixed the glass of ice and ginger ale and walked it to her. She ate a few crackers quietly and took a few gentile sips.

"Will you stay with me a little while longer, Tommy?"

"Sure. Whatever you need."

She took a few more sips of ginger ale, wiped the corner of her mouth with her finger, gave me the glass, sat back, and closed her eyes. I watched her until I let my eyelids close, too. Later, I heard her singing softly. It grew sweeter, clearer. "Daisy chains and boutonnieres, glass slippers and four leaf clovers, white gloved teas, curtsies, daffodils, and lavender . . . daisy chains and boutonnieres . . . daffodils and lavender." And she sang. Mournfully. Gazing out the window.

I waited until I felt she was well asleep curled on the living room couch wrapped in a quilt. A cat at her feet, the other stretched on the windowsill. Then I gathered my clothes upstairs. Medicine bottles lay strewn on her bed. Pills for pain, sleep, anxiety, depression, bipolar disorder, some I didn't recognize. The thing was Sydney was not the name on the pill bottles. I sat on her bed with the pill bottles in my lap, thinking about this stage name, her persona, thinking about the change I witnessed, and about the burden the persona placed on the real identity.

The cab horn blew outside. I jerked awake.

I locked the door; closed it silently; bent my head to the misty rain; scuffed down the oyster shell pathway; ducked into the back seat of the taxi.

Bo-Bo slept under his cover. Cash delivered beers to a table of eight Marines who'd ridden in on motorcycles. The Braves were losing to the Dodgers out west. It was the next day. The clouds had blown through.

Cash set a bottle of Scotch before me. I poured half a glass, let the whiskey slide down in a long settling gulp. I poured another. I took it the same way.

I motioned Cash with a quick tilt of my head. In the dim corridor leading to the bathrooms, I warned him about the undercover operation. He nodded and walked stoically into the back room.

I drove off feeling the warmth of the Scotch, wondering whether tipping Cash off was doing him any good.

At my apartment door were two white tattooed, earringed, drug investigators. I only knew they were police because they were wearing badges around their necks. One had a shaved head and goatee, the other long hair pulled back in a pony tail. Both wore jeans and biker shirts. Goatee wore black boots, Pony-tail high-end sneakers. They wanted to know if I could answer some questions about Officer Sean Locke and Cash. I didn't have anything to hide. I didn't have anything incriminating that I was going to spill – to speculate about stuff under napkins I never saw or smelled or used myself. When the scrawny goatee one asked if they could come into my apartment, it was the Fourth of July, I was sixteen, handcuffed on the side of the road. It was two against one.

# THE FIRE CEREMONY

I was lost in the trees trying to find Uncle Doc's place. Driving around, sweat through with the windows rolled down because the air conditioner quit. I thought about the song lines that Australian aboriginals use to navigate from one point to another without the use of a map. I imagined myself walking on broken glass barefoot in a barren wilderness with an aborigine on my back; his arms choking me around the throat, his knees squeezing into my ribs, his feet jamming into the pockets of my britches; him wearing only a loincloth, white paint on his face and arms, orange paint covering the rest of his body, and him giggling and wheezing into my ear as I stumble in the heat and humidity, making it hard to keep my grip on the old man, him readjusting and squeezing and gripping me harder, me the mule, him the navigator, no map, only the Aborigine's song lines and my trust that he delivers me to the place *he* knows I seek.

By an accident of fate or dumb luck, I finally found the place at the end of a dusty red clay road along a creek that required crossing over a rustic plank bridge. The house, surrounded by white oaks and pines, azalea bushes, dogwood trees, abundant tall windows that could absorb light, and a red tin roof.

I got out of my pick-up truck and was greeted by an arthritic red hound with white hair round his mouth, wagging his tail listlessly. The dog barked once and sniffed the air before he hiked a rear leg and made his mark on my truck's front left tire. I put on a dry t-shirt. The dog sniffed my boots and hand. I patted his head. Then he walked with me down the hill past the well house, the vegetable garden, toward a barn and corral. Two mules and a horse stood in the corral eating hay. There was a pasture beyond, and a wall of pines surrounded it. Poss and Uncle Doc, my boss, were waiting for me in the farthest corner of the pasture. A tractor trail leading into the wood snaked out behind them.

Poss grinned and wiped his forehead with the back of his enormous hand. "We was wondering if you were gonna show."

"Sorry," I said. "I couldn't get my bearings."

"Didn't you bring any beer?" Uncle Doc asked.

I already felt embarrassed and guilty for being an hour late. "I had every intention, but then I got lost, and I knew I was holding up the show . . ."

"That's all right, son. We got plenty," Uncle Doc said. "We better hit it before it gets too dark to see." He handed me a pair of leather gloves and we set to collecting wood.

A thick layer of pine straw carpeted the floor of the woods. The scent of pine mixed with honeysuckle was pleasantly thick. Uncle Doc drove his tractor between the trees. Poss and I walked behind the trailer – Poss loading three limbs for every one of mine. It did not take long for the heat and humidity to make our sweat soak through our ball caps, clothes, and gloves.

We could barely see the trailer by the time we had it heaped full. Poss and I held onto the trailer as Uncle Doc

guided us out of the woods to the fire site at the edge of the
pasture.

The old hound, Boozer, was waiting for us. Poss
grabbed a Dr. Pepper out of the cooler and plopped down
beside the dog. Boozer rolled over on his back. Poss
rubbed his belly. Uncle Doc went to work molding the
wood carefully into a pyre, then stuck a piece of cloth
soaked in diesel fuel in the middle and lit it.

It was a while before Poss's stomach pangs and
Uncle Doc's bladder jarred them awake. Uncle Doc stood
slowly, worked the stiffness out of his back and the
numbness out of his right leg, and then drifted behind a
tree. Poss struggled to identify points of light in the sky
that he'd heard talked about on a public television program.

With a fourteen-year-old being tried as an adult for
murder of his younger brother approaching the next week,
Uncle Doc had invited me out to his home for a fire
ceremony he called it, which would cleanse me and give
me some magical momentum so I'd be ready to pick a jury,
or some such bullshit that went through one ear and out the
other. It was a case that I could win. You never had to
worry about the loser cases. It was the ones you had a
viable defense and you could or should win that terrified
you.

Uncle Doc hobbled from behind the tree, zipping up
his britches, the dog sniffing and limping behind him. He
went to the coolers and retrieved three wire clothes hangers
and a packet of hotdog wieners. After untwisting and
straightening the hangers, we threaded a couple of wieners,
squat by the fire, and watched the wieners char and blister
over the flames.

Poss let out a long belch. "Whoo-wee! Ain't nothing like a weenie roast."

"Michael," Uncle Doc said, "have I ever told you about Lamar?"

I bit into my hotdog and shook my head.

"Back in1967, right after I had gotten my driver's license, I remember the Methodist Ladies Auxiliary Club in Pine Log thought it the Christian thing to do to buy my cousin Lamar a new bicycle. I think it was Homecoming Sunday or some to-do, the Ladies had a special ceremony, they called it a "Holy Bicycle Ceremony" in the church parking lot to bestow the bicycle on Lamar. The ladies were so full of the Spirit, so eager to have people see they were generous Christian women with love in their hearts.

"Now Lamar was a frail little fella. His head tilted to one side. He had hearing aids in both ears. He wore these real thick glasses that made his eyes look like black half dollars. We all loved him and petted him, but the boy liked to sneak off with anybody's bicycle and ride all over the country. One time he went missing for almost a day. I think it was my sister and her boyfriend found finally found him off in Cartersville, thirty miles away.

"After people filled themselves from the pot luck at the church, they gathered for this Holy Bicycle Ceremony. It was the middle of September and felt like the hinges of Hell. The Reverend began the ceremony with a long prayer. Then the choir led everyone in 'What a Friend We Have In Jesus,' Lamar's favorite song.

"The President of the Ladies Auxiliary, Mrs. Wright, presented a bicycle to Lamar. Lamar's momma cried, she was so appreciative toward the good Christian ladies of the Auxiliary.

"Lamar jumped on the new sleek red bicycle and thumbed the bell as he rode round and round and round the church parking lot.

"After a time, he needed to get off so the ceremony could be wrapped up. Nobody, not even Lamar's momma, could get Lamar off that red bicycle. Mrs. Wright, giggling, finally threatened to take the bicycle away if he did not mind his momma. That worked. Except, when Lamar tried to stop, he couldn't. He didn't know how to use the bicycle's new fangled hand brakes. Nobody had stopped to think to show Lamar how to use them. Everybody started hollering, 'Use the hand brakes. Squeeze the lever on the handlebar. Sque-e-e-e-eze. Squeeze the lever. The lever, the lever, the lever, lever, lever, lever. Sque-e-e-e-eze.' Lamar's hearing aids were whistling. He kept spinning the foot pedals in reverse as the choir sang with their backs to the action, *What a friend we have in Jesus, All our sins and grief to bear! What a pri-vi-lege to carry, Ev-'rything to God in prayer!* I started running after him, but he was going too fast. Lamar's momma told the choir to stop singing.

"I yelled for Lamar to jump. It was a helpless thing to watch. He finally spread his legs from the pedals like wings. When he reached the road, that's when he really got going. There he was, legs sticking out, hanging on for dear life, face twisted up, his eyes bugging through them useless glasses and those dag gum hearing aids whistling."

Uncle Doc took a long swig of beer and stood.

"I was sucking in air and shouting stop over and over. I'd start running then stop, run then stop. It was heartbreaking. I started bawling."

Uncle Doc pretended he was riding a bike. "As his momentum carried him faster down the hill he turned over his shoulder and yelled, 'How nyou snop nis Gnobnamn ning?'

"Then, BLAM! Lamar and bicycle crashed into the rock and concrete railroad underpass.

"It was the first time I ever cussed in front of grownups. People that had known me since I was born, who had fed me, taken me into their homes, babysat me, whose kids I'd played with and gone to school with. I cussed at them all for being ignorant and old and slow, and at God for leading them astray and being a mean son-of-a-bitch for making Lamar retarded and helpless and making him have to wear them thick glasses and those useless hearing aid, and that damn bicycle, that goddamn bicycle. I gave Him the finger and wondered if He was getting His jollies over some helpless boy He had born this way. Then I ran down to the bottom of the hill.

"Lamar bounced off that underpass like a ball. It was a damn miracle. God looks after drunks and children. Lamar survived with only broken glasses. It was that damn bicycle that saved him. It weighed and was built like a dag gum Cadillac. It took a chunk out of the concrete underpass.

"I beat everybody down to him. I was holding him and talking to him when somebody gathered him up and the ambulance was called and came and took him to the hospital over in Calhoun.

"I took that bicycle and threw it up against that underpass and kept throwing it up against that underpass, cussing, picking it up, taking a step back and heaving it again at that overpass until my arms could not lift its frame, because that's all that it was when I got through with it. Then my daddy put it in the back of his truck and I slung it over the fence at the steel recycling yard."

Uncle Doc refreshed his beer and drank near all of it. Then he began singing "Victory in Jesus." Poss joined in with an overpowering bass when Uncle Doc got to the refrain. I followed the best I could. When we played that song out Poss announced it was time for dessert. Uncle Doc pulled out a box of Suzy-Qs, two pieces of chocolate cake with whipped cream in the middle – Poss's favorite, he said.

"What's the lesson of that story?" Uncle Doc said.

"I don't know," I said. I felt like I had been sliced opened and was carved out and left hollow and then filled with guilt. I had plenty of guilt built up in me to share with everybody. At dinner, a week before coming to Uncle Docs, with the kids corralled to table, we crossed ourselves and all joined hands, and my five-year-old volunteered to say Grace. "We miss Pepper. We love Pepper. God, take care of Pepper." His three-year-old brother repeated the prayer. My wife and I stared at each other. I shook my head. It had been the same blessing every meal for the last three months since we gave Pepper (a black Labrador Retriever puppy) away to the County Animal Control Department, hoping and praying that we were not sending him to his euthanized death. I said my own silent prayer for Pepper, too. What kind of role model was I being to my children? I felt I had no choice giving Pepper away. He was tearing up the carpet, barking at all hours, playing too hard with the children, taking up too much room in our small apartment. I couldn't go to the bathroom or to the kitchen to get juice for one of the kids in the middle of the night without risking waking Pepper and then having to spend the next hour calming him and then not being able to get back to sleep and then being sleep deprived and not rested for my new job where I needed all my energy. The neighbors would complain. We'd be evicted. We wouldn't get our security deposit back, and I'd have to pay for the damage to the apartment – I didn't have any disposable income to fix what the dog was damaging moment by moment. The dog was also growing like kudzu. Soon he wouldn't be able to fit in his travel crate/bed. He was becoming a big active dog that needed room to run and romp and roam. He was growing out of our small apartment where the three kids were sleeping in one room, one child "camping out" on the floor to sleep. Pepper needed people to allow him to be a dog. He needed a family who would love him, play with him, spend time with him. My wife was a saint, but she was reaching her limit, too, working from home and simultaneously taking care of the children. We were beyond claustrophobic. Something had to give. Pepper had to go.

I met my wife at the Animal Shelter. She carried Pepper in his crate with his stuffed toy dog that was his Momma dog and his bed cushion and his toys. Pepper had no idea that we were going to abandon him there with all those big dogs barking and all the loud noises coming from trucks that had traumatized him when he was abandoned on the side of the road as a five-week-old pup before we were given him by a neighbor who thought the kids needed him. My five-year-old insisted on coming with his mother to say goodbye to Pepper and to see for himself where Pepper was going. I cried. My wife cried. She told the worker that Pepper had had all his shots. She told the worker about Pepper's toys and his need for his Momma dog. The man toted the crate with Pepper inside. We turned around with our guilt and our disappointment in ourselves and drove off.

"The lesson is stop and think before you go and show off being a do-gooder. I still have terrible guilt about the whole thing. But it taught me to distrust do-gooders. People that smile all the time and just want to offer a helping hand." Uncle Doc belched faintly. "They made me a party to their stupid little ceremony and it still hurts me to this day. At Lamar's funeral, somebody wanted to laugh about it. I cut them off real quick and told them it wasn't funny at all. Lamar was taken advantage of by us. He was just an innocent little being we all were responsible for and that day we failed him. They didn't like me saying that. I didn't care." Uncle Doc opened another beer and took a long swig.

Poss wiped his mouth with his shirt tail. "Michael, I was a preacher until I baptized this young lady named Twinkie."

"Oh Lord," Uncle Doc said shaking his head as he sat against a tree.

"There we was," Poss said, "standing in the baptistery pool, the church was packed, the congregation beholding us." Poss stood. "I placed one hand over her head and said, the usual. "Sister, based upon your profession of faith I baptize you in the name of the Father, of the Son, and of the Holy Ghost.' I held Twinkie's hand and put my other hand behind her back like this. I made sure my feet were under me good like this. Twinkie held her nose. I guided her down real slow, as careful as I could. And you see, I'm not a little man, but I was worried I wasn't strong enough to control her. I knew if I leveraged her and got her balanced with my legs and my arm, everything would turn out fine. I really didn't anticipate her slipping out of my arms, but that's what she did. She slipped out of my arms and plopped down and sank like lead. I tried to pull her up by her robe, but I couldn't budge her. She got stuck, jammed somehow. I still to this day can't figure how. My first mistake was I started to panic. I started to panic when my fishing waders started filling with water. Fifteen, maybe thirty seconds or even a minute went by. It felt like a long time. It probably wasn't any time at all. She was under water and I was water logged trying to get her unstuck, praying, 'Lord, don't let Sister Twinkie drown.' Then she started kicking and twisting her body."

Uncle Doc snickered. I tried not to laugh, too.

"Doc, you know this isn't funny."

"I know. I'm not laughing at her. I'm laughing at you . . . telling it."

Poss looked at me. "I ain't telling you this to make you laugh. It's not a funny story at all."

I drank a few sips of beer to recover my composure.

Poss said, "She got one of her chunky legs caught over the top of the observation glass on the front of the baptistery. Then her arms were flailing and splashing the water. I squatted to get some leverage to get her vertical, but she'd slip every time I tried to get a grip on her. Water was sloshing and going into the choir loft. A couple of deacons ran up. One of them unhooked the leg. The other deacon tried to get in the pool with us but there just wasn't any room to manage. All of a sudden, and I mean miraculously, for it had to be the hand of Jesus Himself reached down and plucked her out. Twinkie came out of the water gasping for air, screaming and snorting and hollering with her hands over her head, 'Sweet Jesus God!' Then she grabbed me by the neck and let loose a stream of cuss words like she was speaking in tongues. The head deacon reached out to grab my hand and had me almost pulled out, but then Twinkie grabbed me by the wader suspenders and jerked me back. My feet came out from under me. I remember she had long curled-in fingernails like claws. I get the shivers every time I think of those things. She pushed me under the water and held me there and coughed and cussed me, calling me every name no church should hear. She'd pull me up, let me struggle to get a breath, and then push me under again, and again, and again. Three deacons and two other big men finally restrained her. I had gashes all over my face and neck and knots on my head where she banged it against the baptistery wall.

"I knew her mother and remember her when she was growing up. She was always over weight. The kids in the neighborhood picked on her. Her brother was a big boy and went on to play football in college in Alabama until his grades got so bad. Anyway, Twinkie got tired of being picked on and instead of withdrawing she got mean. I was real glad when she asked me to baptize her. She said she was a changed person after spending a year in prison beating up two girls and tearing up one of the girl's car with a tire iron. I knew it was going to be a real challenge. When I let her slip and couldn't get her up, her short fuse sparked, and she came up fighting, her natural reaction to everything. After thinking about it, I didn't blame her. I shouldn't have been surprised by her reaction. It was my fault, after all.

"But the thing that put the candles on the cake was Flutie Billue, the music director. He jumped up real quick in his raspberry loafers and led the congregation in what else? 'Love Lifted Me.'" Poss started singing.

*I was sinking deep in sin,*
*Far from the peaceful shore,*
*Very deeply stained within,*
*Sinking to rise no more;*
*But the Master of the sea*
*Heard my despairing cry,*
*From the waters lifted me,*
*Now safe am I,*
*Love lifted me!*
*Love lifted me!*
*When nothing else could help,*
*Love lifted me!*
*Love lifted me!*
*Love lifted me!*
*When nothing else could help,*
*Love lifted me!*

"I heard later that the congregation did not join in the singing. I was so embarrassed and demoralized and guilt stricken, I didn't have the heart to get back in the pulpit after that."

Uncle Doc held his hand out toward Poss. "Behold the man."

"Did you ever talk to her after that?" I asked.

"I went by her mother's house a few days later. Her mother babysat me when my mother went to work. She was just a girl then – before she had her own kids. I apologized. They were quick to forgive. I couldn't believe it. The biggest question she had was whether the baptism was legal. I had forgotten all about the baptism as I was so caught up in myself – my embarrassment and self pity in how this whole ordeal had made me rethink whether I should stay in the ministry. I gave Twinkie the signed baptism certificate I'd brought with me. That was the last time I saw them."

I sat taking in the balm of the fire and the shrill rhythmic drone of the bugs. For some reason I remembered something I usually worked hard to suppress: the awful memory of my cousin who was killed accidentally by a shotgun when he was eleven and I ten. His eight-year-old brother never got over the trauma of being in the same room when the gun went off. Nor could he deal with the guilt of living. Life unraveled for him after that, being alive and playing with his brother one second, seeing him dead in a pool of blood the next. His nightmares haunted him until he died at thirty-two after a long illness. I could imagine the screams and terror moans of my helpless aunt and uncle who ran into the room after hearing the shot. Overcome with a shiver, I thought about how much I hated guns and how my greatest fear was of my own children's death in such a sudden inexplicable way and how or whether I'd be able to survive it. My dad – whom I only saw every other weekend and on particular afternoons during the week after my parents' recent divorce – had the unenviable task of breaking the news to me and my younger brother that Sunday afternoon in February, just like he had seventeen months earlier when he told us about our bigger than life Granddaddy dying in a car wreck. Life was a dangerous and scary place for me after my cousin died. It was as if the devil cut out my childhood light with the dull rusty steak knife we used to cut weeds with, and pointing the blade down at me, threatening that I was next, soon, soon, very soon. It became hard to sleep, as it still is. I withdrew and a new feeling – melancholy or the blues people called it – disturbed me more and more, as I was terribly afraid of when unnatural death would visit me, too.

After a time, Uncle Doc added more wood to the fire. Outside the fire circle, lightening bugs hovered and illumined. Poss caught one in his hands. He watched the bug glow for a moment, then opened his cupped palms and the lightening bug floated away. Then he began singing,

*Old Uncle Doc is a sorry ole soul,*
*Washed his face in a toilet hole,*
*Brushed his teeth with a wagon wheel,*
*Died with a tooth-ache in his heel.*

Uncle Doc kicked Poss on the bottom of his shoe.

Dr. Pepper spilled down Poss's shirt. "Look what you done."

"I love you plumb down to the bone, Poss," Uncle Doc said, "And even the bone."

"Well, now I know you're drunk."

Earlier in the day I had an initial visit with a client.

Heavy steel doors snapped unlocked and sounded like a hammer driving a railroad spike into my skull. When they slammed shut, the sound reverberated. It was a terminal sound – of mortality, a closing in, all former identity dissolved.

A chubby, unmotivated fellow with a crew cut, who stressed every seam of his brown and orange jailer's uniform, escorted me. His knee-knocked trudge made me think he must've played the tuba in high school. He sweated and puffed down the hall, thighs rubbing, while some soul kicked and hollered behind some other heavy steel door.

He locked me into a six-foot-by-six-foot windowless interview room – a cold space of off-white painted cinderblocked walls and linoleum floor, with two white plastic chairs: one for me and one for a large, loosely breasted woman wearing orange surgical scrubs, shackled at the ankle and wrist, wheezing and curling her bottom lip. I sat across from her and asked her name. She leaned, exposing a good bit of her large cleavage, and turned one ear toward me.

"Are you Polly? Polly Pomeroy?"

She smiled toothless. "Yes. Everything be beautiful." Her eyes widened and narrowed, widened and narrowed. She looked behind her shoulder and mumbled. She did this for a while, talking to some hallucination, a person I guess, pointing to it and then me, and nodding.

"Ma'am."

She held up a hand as if I was interrupting.

A few seconds later, she swatted at something and then faced me and giggled behind her hand.

"How are you doing?" I said.

"Fine. Fine. I got no man. Live by myself in my trailer with my beautiful dogs." She looked behind her and mumbled, then looked at me, and pointed, and looked behind her again and mumbled. After a pause, she spun serenely to meet me.

"You having a conversation with someone?" I said.

"My people. Keeping me informed about my beautiful dogs."

"Do you mind telling me who they are?"

"Why my Momma and Daddy. They keep me informed about my beautiful dogs."

"They exchange messages to you from the outside?"

"From wherever I need them to. They are very sincere and conscientious."

"Can you give me your Mom and Dad's name and address and telephone number so I can contact them?"

"Didn't you know that my parents were dead? You see when you make it to heaven or to the other side, however you want to look at, you can communicate with those on earth." She talked with her hands. "Those on earth have to be open to receive their communications." She took on a British accent. "I have that skill. I always have. People call me schizophrenic. But I assure you I am *not* schizophrenic. Ha. Ha. Ha. Ha. Ha. I definitely do not show any symptoms of that disorder. It's not in my brain chemistry." She leaned, sniffed me, and narrowed her eyes. "M-m-m-m. You smell like cookies."

I was beyond my script, the initial questionnaire my office used to take down information from new clients. "Is there anyone in this room besides you and I?"

She returned to her original voice. "When I being good."

"Well, do you see them now?"

She crossed her arms over her breasts, pressed her chin against her chest, and cut her eyes up at me, grinning. "No-o-o-o. I'm thinking naughty thoughts, now." She sniffed. "Y-u-u-m-m. You is beautiful and just good enough to eat."

I pushed my chair back. "Do you know where you are?"

"Oh, yeah!"

"Where are you?"

She held up an index finger. "First. You got a cigarette and a Coca-Cola for a beautiful sexy lady?"

"You can't smoke in here."

"Oh, that silly policy. That's just blown up political correctness." She opened her legs and rubbed her crotch. "Ask for me. Tell Mr. Hal I'll give him some of this if he will. It's all wet and warm for him. Just tell him. He knows where momma lives."

"I'll see . . ."

"Ask about getting me a bond, too. Tell Mr. Hal I'd like to be able to be released on Monday, Thursday, and Saturday afternoons so I can sit on Miss Mable's porch. On Sundays I'll go to Calvary Holiness. And if I don't make it there I'll stay here and go to the church service for the inmates." She swiped at something behind her shoulder, then leaned forward and summoned me with her index finger. "I got something to tell you. You know, I'm a queen. . . Well, maybe not a queen. But, I'm a daughter of a queen. So that makes me a princess."

"I'm eighth Cherokee myself. Now look, I'm from the public defender's office, and have come to talk to you about what happened at the grocery store the other day."

"Yeah, you be a good *looking* defender." She rocked and whistled. "I be all by myself. Got no man. I got big beautiful titties, don't I?" She smiled over her shoulder and talked and cackled. Then she grabbed my tie and fondled it. In a different voice, "Where'd you get this *beautiful* tie? Oh, and these vibrant colors." She turned the tie over and examined the tag. "Not from Brooks Brothers?"

I plucked my tie from her plump fingers. "Do you know who I am?"

"You is from the good looking defender's office, that's who you is. And you come to see me about my *beautiful* dogs." Her eyes narrowed and she leaned closer to me. "You can come around *any* time."

I pushed my chair against the wall. "Tell me what happened at the grocery store."

"I had parents once. They were *beautiful*. They sang and danced and played music all day. Then they decided to go to heaven and leave me. I was only a child then. I couldn't stop them. I don't know what I did. Didn't they know that by going to heaven they couldn't' come back? That's when I developed the skill of communicating with them in heaven. Don't you think that a rational thing to do when your parents decide to do such an irrational thing?"

"Do you remember what happened at the grocery store?"

"Yes," she said in a singing voice. "Polly went to get some Coca-Cola and cigarettes and some Vienna sausages and mustard, dog food for her *beautiful* dogs." She rubbed my tie smooth as if it were a flower. In her British accent, she said, "You are a charming man. Has any woman ever told you that? Polly is very disturb, you know. Poor, Polly. She is . . . very sensual. Yes, she is, I would say. Be careful with her. She's not like me. I'm very up front and honest. She, on the other hand, is very manipulative. She acts, how would you describe it, primitive, but she's knows exactly what's going on. I have observed her over many years and have determined that she suffers from a low level of the necessary minerals found in your common chocolate chip cookie. I have shared my theory with any number of her mental health professionals but they say, 'Patricia, we believe we are more qualified to diagnose Polly . . . and *your* disorder.' *My* disorder? Can you believe such malpractice? Why I'm perfectly sane. Don't you think I have a beautiful voice? That my diction is exact and my tone is resonant? Like my parents, I am also a trained singer. I think I could have sang in the Metropolitan if Polly would not have interfered."

"The police report says you were exposing your breasts at the grocery store."

Still very British. "Now, I thought you to be a more . . . *enlightened* man. Do you believe everything in a police report? Why are you asking me? I'm sure that it's all pure fabrication."

"The police report is based on statements given by four witnesses who saw this happen."

She rocked and touched her nose with her bottom lip.

"The witnesses all say that you pulled up your shirt and brassiere and showed everybody at the grocery store your breasts. That's why you're in jail."

She mussed her hair and scratched her arms. Her eyes darted at the ceiling, the floor, my eyes, the floor, and my tie.

A different voice said, "*Polly did not. Polly was shopping for chicken breasts and looking for sharp dressed men!*" She popped to her feet, chains clanging, waving her index finger back and forth. "No, no. Uh-uh. Uh-uh." Round that small space she shuffled, shackles clanging, flip-flops flip-flopping, wheezing and chanting. "Polly was shopping for chicken breasts and looking for sharp dressed men. Sharp dressed men. Sharp dressed men. Sharp dressed men. Sharp dressed men, yeah-yeah-yeah. Sharp dressed men, yeah-yeah-yeah. Sharp dressed men, yeah-yeah-yeah . . ."

I reached behind me and pushed the buzzer next to the steel door.

Polly chanted and hobbled. "Sharp dressed men, yeah-yeah-yeah."

I pushed the buzzer.

Time passed and I heard somebody coming, but it was nobody for us. I buzzed and banged and kicked the door and hollered for help. This went on for ten, "I got to go pee," fifteen, "I got to go real bad" flip-flop, flip-flop, twenty, "Mmm-mmm, mmm-mmm, pee-pee, pee-pee," flip-flop, flip-flop, clink-clink, round the room, bent over, hands gripped between her legs. "Sharp dressed men, sharp dressed men," at a whisper now. Round and round and round, flip-flop, flip-flop, flip-flop. And I kicked, demanding to be let out louder, holding down the buzzer, thirty, forty, forty-five minutes . . . becoming hoarse, anticipating Polly to make water anytime. An hour. An hour fifteen.

Keys jingled outside, talking over a walkie-talkie. A key jiggled in the lock, the door opened, and before me was bovine jailer, red-cheeked, sweating, and out of breath, blowing his tuba. "Y'all finished?"

I stared at him a few beats. You stupid useless bastard, I thought.

"Polly's got to go pee, right now. And then make sure she gets her meds."

He shrugged. He blew.

Polly swooshed by me, shackles clinking, flip-flopping. She brushed my arm lightly with her hand, puckered her lips and kissed the inches between us. "Love ya babe."

Poss slouched behind his Dr. Pepper can. Uncle Doc spit into the fire and rubbed his mouth coarsely. "Polly has never tried to kiss me. She ever tried to kiss you?"

Poss shook his head.

Uncle Doc said. "Poss and me have been dealing with poor Polly and her multiple personalities for years. As long as she's taking her medicine, she's right pleasant. But then she gets to thinking she's cured and doesn't need her medicine and starts unraveling and ends up like she did at the grocery store. Hell, she witched my well here at the house."

"She can talk fire out, too," Poss said.

"What?" I asked.

"I burned my hand one day. She was at the office, took hold of my hand, and talked the fire out," Poss said.

"How'd she do that?" I asked.

"She says some bible verse or something," Uncle Doc said before spitting into the fire. "I'm sorry I sent you to deal with her. I thought she could use a different face. I didn't want another scene like the last time I went."

Poss said, "He's going to have to deal with her some time or other anyway."

Uncle Doc said, "She's really not that bad. You just have to know how to communicate with her and be able to adjust and think on your feet."

Poss said. "Didn't she go up north to college to be a singer?"

"That what her family tells me."

"Patricia's personality wasn't lying to me about that?" I chuckled at myself, picked up my beer-can off the dirt and finished it off. Then I limped behind an oak. Standing there waiting to make water, I wondered what direction I was standing. I looked at the sky but knew nothing of navigating by the stars. I was one lost useless what? I couldn't fill in the blank.

When I returned from behind the tree, Uncle Doc pulled out a long wooden pipe and stuffed it with tobacco. He said, "This don't look like much but we pretend it's our sacred pipe. And this I'm stuffing it with isn't anything illegal. We're not that bold around here. It's just Captain

Black. Not my favorite. Sometimes I'll stop by the tobacco store in town and buy a nice blend."

Poss retrieved a jelly jar of clear liquid from the now empty cooler. "Son, this is some of the finest moonshine whiskey this side of Talladega Prison."

Uncle Doc winked at me.

I peered around us into the void beyond the firelight. "I want to tell y'all something more about Polly. She was holding her head as she was walking out into the hall and kept saying in a totally different voice, 'Baby, I hear the bells. I hear the bells. Lawd, Lawd, I hear the death bells. Who dyin'? Somebody dyin.' What the hell does that mean?"

"She hears the death bells," Uncle Doc said.

"The what?"

"Death bells." Poss said. "She sometimes goes a little gooney when they go off in her head. You'll see her walking the street banging her head with her hand. Sometimes she'll bang her head against walls and such. There'll be blood everywhere and the ambulance will have to come and take her to the hospital to get her stitched up. They might keep her for a few days, too, in the psych ward, get her stable, let her go.

"Poor old Polly," Uncle Doc said. "Don't know if it's a gift or a curse. I got a call this morning from her niece. She said that Polly's auntie died. Wanted to know if I could do something about persuading the Sheriff to let her go to the funeral. Until they get her meds evened out she's not going anywhere. They're going to make her do about sixty days of D.A. time and then the bastard will let her go. Dogs will be gone. Trailer will be gone. Social workers will have to find her another place to live. They'll have to help her get her S.S.I. check coming regular again. She'll eventually start believing she's a demigod or something and stop taking her meds. Then she'll be right back. D.A. doesn't give a shit that we go through this mess about every six months. Social Services calls me, the family calls me, I tell them to call the D.A., and the D.A. tells them to call me. Why me? I haven't got a dime's worth of power. We're right back to where we are now."

Uncle Doc tamped the tobacco into the pipe. "But, yep, Polly hears death bells likes she witches wells and puts out fire."

Poss retrieved a couple of styrofoam cups from the cooler and poured some of the moonshine in the cups. I peeked into mine. Poss and Uncle Doc raised their cups. Poss said, "Well, don't let it sit in them cups too long 'cause it's liable to eat a hole plum through 'em." We all whipped our heads back and took quick swigs. Poss walloped me on the back. "Breathe through it. Don't that feel good?"

We sat there for a time and watched the flames. Uncle Doc lit the pipe and puffed off it. He passed the pipe to Poss who drew a couple of puffs before passing it to me. I was going to pass the pipe back to Uncle Doc, but he poured himself another cup of moonshine and got up and started dancing around the fire and chanting. He took a drink of the moonshine, swished it around his mouth, spit it into the fire, and jumped back. A flame swooshed up and out and I smelled burnt hair. Then Uncle Doc spun around on one leg. Poss caught him by the arm and sat him down before he stumbled into the fire. Poss poured more moonshine for himself and Uncle Doc. Both turned their cups up in a shot.

I smoked the pipe and sipped another cup that Poss poured and watched Poss and Uncle Doc dance and sing arm in arm round the fire. I felt as if I were spinning and floating off the ground. I pulled the cooler next to me and drummed it. Our chanting erupted low as if from below ground and grew to great supplications with our heads raised to the stars like wolves. "He-e-e-e-y ya-a-ah, hey yah yah ah yah ha-a-a-e-y. He-e-e-e-y ya-a-ah, hey yah yah ah yah ha-a-a-e-y."

Everything got louder and less in focus. Whiskey, fire, chanting, smoking, spitting, drumming, singing, sweating, howling.

Instead of holding the rusted steak knife over me, the Devil was laughing at us from the flames, or maybe he was laughing at the painted aboriginal man dancing in the shadows.

After a time we all got quiet and reflective again, watching the blaze, hearing the wood pop and hiss.

I followed the aimless smoke realizing how directionless I was, how guilt interfered with my compass and could paralyze me if I stopped long enough and thought about it.

# THE PROBATIONER

1.

The grass ditches along the highway between Rydal and Fairmount were groomed and clean while Perry Elrod was on probation for driving drunk, second offense.

"Well, judge, can I at least have a work permit to drive to and from work?" Perry asked. He had bonded out of jail after his mandatory 48 hours. He adjusted his weight on his steel-toed Redwing boots. His jeans were worn to flecks of holes but clean, as was his plaid shirt his sister had ironed for him. The bailiff had reminded him to take his cap off that had his employer's emblem on it, which he wrung in his hands. His daughter drove him to court today. She and her screaming two-year-old had been waiting in the hallway for three hours. Like his ex-wife, there was going to be hell to pay. He could expect one less person to ask for a ride.

"Since you were almost four times over the legal limit when you were caught this time," the judge said, "I find you are a risk to the community. Request for a work permit is denied."

"Judge, I got a four wheeler . . ."

"You can't drive a four wheeler . . . even during deer and turkey season. I know you hunt, don't you?"

"Yes, sir. We have a club--"

"You're going to have to walk to your stand or get a ride then."

"That include one of them golf carts?"

"Yes, sir. The statute covers that as well."

Perry had a John Deere riding mower his brother unloaded in his back yard one day and told him to park in his shop for a year to let cool down.

"What about a riding lawn mower, Judge?"

"That's a vehicle."

"A lawnmower?"

"Before we keep going down the list," the judge said, "that includes a go-cart, and a tractor, too, Mr. Elrod. Any motorized thing with wheels, a seat, and a steering wheel are off limits during your probation, do you understand?"

"I guess."

"You've got to pay a fine and perform the community service that I've already covered. Your probation officer will go over that with you again so there's no misunderstanding. I don't want to send you back to jail."

"Your Honor, when am I going to have time to do all the community service because it's going to take all the overtime I can get just to pay all the fines and fees?"

"Now Mr. Elrod, that's not my problem." The judge popped a hand full of peanuts in his mouth. "You should of thought of that when you was liquoring yourself up and getting behind the wheel of your truck."

Perry tapped his cap on his knee. "I reckon so."

The judge popped another hand full of nuts in his mouth. "If you want to get around you might consider a bicycle. Improve your health. Throw them cigarettes away. Start eating better and getting more sleep."

"Judge, I'll get run over sure enough riding a bike on the highway or kill over with a heart attack."

"Best way to get in shape, clean out your system, stop drinking, stop smoking, eat more fruits and nuts and vegetables. Quit eating them convenience store burritos. The exercise will do you good." Another hand full of nuts tossed in his mouth. "You'll thank me for it." He looked down his robe and brushed crumbs away. "Give yourself two weeks to get use to it and then your body will be in sync with your new regimen.

"Has anybody on probation ever done that, Judge? Completed their probation that way, and thanked you for it?"

"No, but you can be my model probationer. That's what I want you to be, my model probationer. I want to be able to show you off. Make you my poster child. Big photographs of me and you smiling. I don't want to send you to jail for disappointing me. All right? That a deal?"

"I'll try," Perry said.

The judge pointed. "Good. Now, have a seat over on that bench over there. A probation officer will talk to you before you leave."

"Your Honor, can I get an appointment to see her later, because I need to get to work?"

The Judge looked over his glasses and chewed. "What's more important, Mr. Elrod? The Court's business or your job?"

Perry didn't answer. He looked at the judge blankly.

"Have a seat over there," the judge said.

"Yes, sir."

2.

Cartersville was under a tornado watch. Perry had his first appointment with his probation officer, Ms. Irene Demond. A greenish gray sky, rain falling like gravel. Leaves, pine needles, trash blowing into little vortex. Tree limbs falling across the road.

Perry walked into the Guardian Probation office as the tornado siren started blowing. Nobody was in the front waiting room or at the reception desk, only a bell with the handwritten instruction to ring for service.

A slim woman with hair streaked blonde, wearing navy slacks, a silk blouse, and heels hitting the floor hard, came to the front room. She looked Perry up and down. He was soaked, head to toe. Her left eye twitched, the corner of her mouth went into a spasm, her neck cocked.

The pointed to the wall clock. She huff. "Mr. Elrod, you are four minutes late. If you're not going to take your probation seriously, then I'm not going to waste my time with you."

"There's a tornado watch--"

"I don't care if there's a forty day flood, a nuclear holocaust, an earthquake, or if it's the Second Coming. When you have an appointment with me, you show up on time."

"Yes, ma'am."

"Probation is a privilege, not a right."

"Yes, ma'am. I'm sorry, ma'am. I tried as hard as I could to get here--"

"I don't want to hear any excuses. The next time you're late, I'll place you in handcuffs and put you in jail overnight. Do you understand me?"

"Oh, yes, ma'am. But the weather is real bad out there," Perry said. "That's the siren going off. I really think we need to take cover. Tornado--"

"Come on back to my office. And take off your hat."

He shook his hat off and rubbed the bottom of his shoes on the threshold floor mat. The soles squeaked on the hall tile as he lumbered behind Ms. Demond's clacking heels.

3.

Perry and his uncle, Grady Moss, worked together at the truck bed assembly plant in Rydal. Grady tried to keep his tattooed and pierced son, Dennis, occupied with a small engine repair shop in Fairmount, fixing lawnmowers and chain saws, rather than burgling or crawling under cars cutting out catalytic converters. But like father like son. The Sheriff considered Grady a recidivist thief. When things went missing in the county, the first place to look was at Grady Moss's. Grady had learned over the years to filter what he stole through people that didn't know him or didn't know anything about where the stolen thing came from. That way it protected the person and him. With this system, Grady had been able to shake arrest for going over twenty-five years.

Fog stuck to the top of the hills, a misty rain fell. Grady had the wood stove heating the shop, a pot of coffee brewed fresh.

"That boy had everything going for him," Grady said.

Lloyd Matthews was the postal carrier. His mail jeep was parked out front. He sat in his uniform eating a Vienna sausage sandwiches with white bread and mayonnaise. "I heard he made a perfect score on that college exam."

Dennis was in the back with the radio blaring sharpening a chain saw.

Grady turned his head. "Turn that shit down."

Dennis turned the radio off and walked up to the group with the file in his hand. His hair was still buzzed prison style. Silver studs punctured his ears and nose.

"He had it all going for him," Lloyd said. "You should have seen all the schools that sent him mail. They came from everywhere. Stacks. Schools I never heard of."

Dennis stood there in his camouflage shorts that bagged below his knees, a black t-shirt with a skull and a devil air brushed on the front, and black Converse high top sneakers. "I'm walking to the store and buy me a pack of cigarettes and something to eat." He wiped his black greasy hands on an oily rag. Grady handed him some money. He pulled a black stocking cap on his head. The men watched him shuffle out the door, stooped shouldered.

"His momma is a Thurmond, isn't she?" Perry said.

"His daddy works for Mohawk," Lloyd said. "His momma used to work for the bloomer mill here. He's their only child."

Ralph, a survivor of Omaha Beach, the Bulge, and prostate cancer, stood stooped and bow legged in his bib overalls. He earned extra money cutting fire wood. Perry gave Ralph his chair and sat on a stool and poured Ralph a cup of coffee. "Hot and black, like I like it," Ralph said.

Grady said, "Yeah, that boy went up there—"

"Where is Princeton?" Ralph asked.

"New Jersey," Grady said.

Ralph nodded. "New Jersey."

"That's right," Lloyd said.

"Isn't he still up there in one of them mental hospitals?" Ralph said.

"That's what we're talking about," Grady said.

Ralph put his mouth to his cup. "Didn't he try to kill some woman?"

"They found him insane," Lloyd said.

"Insane. What's that mean when somebody does something like that?" Ralph asked.

"He's got to stay in a mental hospital for as long as they say he has to," Lloyd said.

"I guess that could be forever," Ralph said.

Grady said. "Take that guy that shot Reagan . . ."

"Well what's that lanky character there coming in the door?" Ralph said offering up his hand.

Woodrow stomped, shook Ralph's hand, squeezed Lloyd's shoulders. "What's this? The meeting of the bootleggers of Gordon County, I see." He went round shaking hands.

"Get you a cup of coffee," Grady said.

He held up the pot. "Y'all are almost out."

"What are you doing, Woodrow?" Ralph asked.

"We put a new water pump and alternator in my truck. I'm on my way to Calhoun to buy two new tires to put on the back."

Grady dumped coffee grounds into the garbage can. "You still got that girl living with you?"

"Which one?" Woodrow said.

Ralph guffawed. "Which one?"

"The one that used to work down here at the clinic," Grady said.

"Oh. Her old man came back."

"What about that girl at the plant that you were all hot about," Grady said. "I saw y'all at the fair. Real nice girl. Too nice for you."

"Lord, no. She didn't turn out nice at all. The first night she spent at my trailer, we had just finish having sex – and I'm telling you that girl knows what she's doing – her little girl woke up crying. Her momma went in there and tore that little thing up. It wasn't that baby's fault. She wasn't but three. She didn't know where she was. She was scared. And her momma went in there without a stitch on and just started beating her. I couldn't take that baby crying and screaming. It turned my stomach. When she came back in bed I told her to get her ass dressed and I took her and that baby home. That was the end of that. Any woman that would treat her baby like that, I didn't want no part of."

Dennis walked in with a cigarette dangling from his mouth and a handful of burritos. He cleared a spot on an oily work bench, sat on a stool under a bulb and crammed a burrito in his mouth, cleaning cheese from his mouth with an oily rag.

"Woodrow," Dennis said, "Tonya came by last week selling your chain saw."

"So that's what happened to it."

"I'm telling you she's trouble," Dennis said. "She'll steal you blind."

"Is she the one that worked at the nudie bar?" Lloyd said.

"How did you know?" Woodrow said.

"It's on my mail route," Lloyd said.

"When did you start going inside to deliver mail?" asked Woodrow. "Don't they have a mailbox outside?"

"You better watch her," Dennis said. "She'll have your ass put in jail before you can blink. She put two boys I know in jail for doing nothing but leaving the seat up."

"That crazy bitch said some Mexicans stole it," Woodrow said.

"I figured it was yours," Dennis said.

"What did you do with it?"

"It's out back."

"How much did you give her?"

"She wanted forty, I gave her thirty."

"Hell, it was worth more than that," Woodrow said.

"You want it back?" Dennis said.

Woodrow thought for a moment. "I don't know. It doesn't run worth a damn. Naw."

"That Tonya was a Resaca Beach Calendar Girl, isn't that right Woodrow?" Lloyd said.

"Remember when Marla Maples was the Resaca Beach Calendar Girl" Lloyd said. "She still married to what's his name?"

"He's moved on to another wife," Grady said.

"Hey Dennis," Grady hollered back, "Ralph needs his chain sharpened on his saw."

Dennis walked to the back of the shop.

"How long is it going to take for you to finish that chain?" Ralph asked.

"Give me ten minutes and I'll be done," Dennis said.

Perry faced Grady. "I came in here to see if you had some kind of thing to get me to and from work that won't violate my probation."

"What are you talking about?" Lloyd said, fingering a Vienna sausage.

"I got put on probation. DUI," Perry said.

"Again?" Ralph said.

"How long?" Grady asked.

"Twelve months."

"You mean, like a bicycle?" Ralph said.

"No," Perry said. "Not a damn bicycle. Can you see me peddling a damn bicycle on the highway between here and the plant?"

"You'd probably get run over," Woodrow said.

"What about a motorized bicycle?" Lloyd said. "I was at the Cassville store and started hearing this buzzing noise. I thought it was one of them ultra-light airplanes, so I was looking up in the sky, looking all over the place for that thing. Then here came this kid on one of them scooters with handle bars with a weed eater engine he had rigged up to it. You could have walked or jogged faster than the thing was going. But that was the dog-gonedest thing, and here I was looking up in the sky looking for a little airplane."

"That would be too much like a motorcycle and that would be a violation," Grady said.

"Yeah," Woodrow said. "He's right."

"You know all about that, don't you?" Grady said.

"I've done my time for DUI," Woodrow said.

"Yeah, there's all kinds of big trucks on the highway between here and there. They about blow my jeep off the road every day," Lloyd said.

"Judge said I couldn't use no lawnmower, or a four wheeler, or a golf cart," Perry said.

"Hey wouldn't that be something if we rigged a chainsaw engine to a bicycle?" Dennis said walking into the conversation with a file and a work rag in his hand. "Man, that'd be funny as hell once you got that thing going. Try braking that thing. You'd have to carry an anchor as an emergency brake. Just throw it over your shoulder."

The men ignored Dennis.

"Well, that leaves footing it or getting rides," Grady said. "How far is it? Ten, twelve miles?"

"Eight miles," Lloyd said.

"Judge said I couldn't use nothing with wheels a motor a seat and a steering wheel," Perry said. "So y'all got any ideas?"

"I cain't think of nothing," Ralph said.

Lloyd stood and stretched. "Me neither. You got me stumped on that one. Well I got to get back on my route before somebody starts calling."

"Yeah, I got to get on to Calhoun and get those tires," Woodrow said.

Grady returned with fresh water in the coffee pot and poured in the machine. He turned it on to brew.

"Perry. I don't know any way round your problem, right now. Give me a little time to think about it. There's got to be a way."

"There is a way, Dad." Dennis stood holding Ralph's chain saw and the file.

"Aren't you finished with my chain saw?" Ralph said.

"I just got started on it," Dennis said.

"How long will it take you?"

"What have you got to do out in this weather?" Dennis asked.

Ralph said, "That gal of Woodrow's is a Santie Claus woman. That Tonya."

"Yes, we all know." Grady said. "What you got on your mind, boy?"

"There's a way to get around Perry's probation."

"You ain't going to get Perry in trouble with one of your crazy ideas, are you?" Grady said.

"Do you remember that lawnmower you had me use last summer before I was sent away?"

"Remind me," Grady said.

"It was that one that I had to stand on that little platform and steer with the two handles. It was self-propelled. I think it would get around the rule."

"I don't know. You're still riding it." Perry said.

Dennis pulled back a finger to mark each point. "It doesn't have a seat. It doesn't have a steering wheel. You're standing on a little platform disconnected from the cutter. You're not sitting. It's not like a riding lawnmower. It's like standing on a self-propelled walking lawnmower. It has a way that you can convert it into a walking mower, too. If somebody comes round like your probation officer, just hop down and start walking."

"That might work, Perry," Grady said.

"You still got that thing around?" Perry asked.

"Which shed is it in? The hot or cold one? Grady asked.

"It's in the cold storage shed," Dennis said.

"Can we get to it pretty easy?" Perry asked.

"Yeah," Dennis said.

"How long has it been since it ran?" Perry asked

"About a year," Grady said.

"How fast can it move?" Perry asked.

"It would get you to work in about an hour, maybe less. I'll see if I can make some modifications," Dennis said.

"That's better than nothing." Perry asked.

"Just think about how you'd be beautifying the highway," Grady snickered.

Ralph laughed. "You might pick up a side business with them cans and bottles."

"Dennis, y'all go over there and put it on the trailer and bring it back here and we'll tune it up and get it going," Grady said.

"What about my chain?" Ralph said.

"Give me five minutes," Dennis said.


4.


It took fifty minutes and half a tank of gas to make a one-way trip on the mower, sometimes longer depending on the amount of debris in the grass, notably carcasses that

had to be cut around or kicked out of the way. One swath
of the blade covered forty inches. Perry cut one side of the
road coming to work and the other side going home – the
direction to and from work was based on the side the
mower threw the cuttings. It took two weeks to make a
complete sweep of the grass on both sides of the highway.
He and Grady and Dennis had rigged headlights and back
lights so people could see him on the early mornings going
to work, and the evenings going home. Plus, he wore a
yellow fluorescent vest. He wore his plant ear plugs and
safety glasses, too.

The first month he was ready to quit every day – the
tractor-trailer trucks blowing by, honking, and the cars not
giving way. He didn't have the benefit of orange warning
signs: Mowers Ahead. He didn't have the luxury of an
orange truck escort. All it would take was somebody
clipping him. He would be dead in an instant. A body in
pieces spread out all over the place. Blood and gore. He
cussed himself for getting himself in this predicament.

But as spring drew closer to summer and the days
grew longer, he didn't have to contend with the early
morning darkness. The regular drivers grew used to his
presence and a comradeship formed. They slowed and
drove into the other lane for him. They would wave and he
would wave and they smiled and the highway shoulder had
never looked better, the kudzu did not creep onto the road,
and the Johnson grass did not suffocate the drainage ditch
when the rain poured down.

A reporter from the newspaper in Ashville passed
Perry, and curious, stopped and started talking to him one
afternoon. The story from the interview ran the following

Sunday. In following weeks other reporters from newspapers in Rome, Cartersville, Calhoun, Chattanooga, wanted to interview Perry. Grady told him he didn't need to worry about working in exchange for using the mower and buying the gas. Grady was going to sponsor him and put a homemade sign advertising his lawn care and tree service business on the front of the mower. TV news crews from Atlanta followed Perry cutting the grass down the highway, before the setting sun. The story ran during all the evening time slots, during the morning slots the next day, and that noon. It syndicated on CNN and the video went viral on the Internet. People started sending in money. Within days, Perry had his fines and fees paid off. Additional money coming in was put into an account to pay for the lawnmower's gas and maintenance costs. A few weeks later, the miles of mowing everyday took its toll on the old mower. With the money, Grady and Perry bought a new mower with lights. What lights they didn't have and needed, Dennis rigged. Grady bought a new more colorful sign advertising his lawn and tree businesses. Grady was getting calls daily for work from Rome to Chattanooga to Gainesville. He quit his job at the truck assembly plant. In time for the Fourth of July, Dennis had thousands of postcards made of Perry riding the new mower wearing an American flag shirt with an American flag waving from the mower. Dennis had come up with the slogan, "Everyday, From Fairmount to Rydal, Freedom Rings!" The photo included Perry's signature. Perry rode on Fourth of July floats in Marietta and Atlanta. They had him sitting on a black Harley-Davidson motorcycle in Atlanta between two girls in bikinis. He said they smelled like coconut oil and giggled. Dennis and people from Fairmount who had never been to Atlanta walked beside the float giving away hundreds of Perry's signed post cards. Weeks following he was throwing out the honorary baseballs at major and minor league games. One of his biggest thrills was sitting in the owner's box on the field at an Atlanta Braves game. He met and was photographed with some of his favorite players of the past and present. He received a ball signed by all the players, the coaches, and manager. He rode his mower round the outside of the field before the game, hopped off, and he threw the honorary ball. In the seventh inning, he led the sold out crowd in "Take Me Out to the Ball Game". They treated him, he said, like royalty.

5.

"Look, Perry," Grady said, "we can't risk you out there in the rain tomorrow." Dennis and Lloyd had come along with Grady. The three showed up unannounced. They awoke Perry from his nap.

Perry rubbed his eyes and searched among a table of empty packs for a cigarette. "How am I going to get to work, then?"

"We sold lottery tickets for two dollars, three for five, and picked a lucky winner from one of your fans," Grady said. "The winner is giving you a ride."

Grady didn't wear his navy overalls anymore. He bought the crew new uniforms. These were paid with the donated money. They had a khaki scheme right off the catalogue cover from the uniform distributor. Their shirts had their business name embroidered on their right breast and their first names embroidered on their left. They also had new tan boots. Included with the new look was the latest cell phones with email, texting, and Internet access. The phones fit into holders clipped onto their new brown belts. Grady prevented Dennis from wearing the studs in his ears and nose. He also had to wear his shirt sleeves rolled down to cover his violent looking tattoos.

"They're called the 'Rainy Day Drivers'," Dennis said.

"How many tickets did you sell?" Perry asked.

"Over a thousand. I still don't have the exact tally yet." Dennis said.

"What did y'all do with the money?"

"It goes directly and immediately into the account we set up down at the bank," Grady said. "It goes to maintaining the lawnmower and paying for gas. With the price of gas, it doesn't take too long to go through some money. Of course there's administrative fees and all we pay to Sissie."

"I don't think it looks good for me to be seen being given a ride to work and home by some stranger who won me in a lottery."

"Perry, we're supposed to have thunder storms tomorrow," Grady said. "You don't have any business out there in that weather."

Lloyd adjusted his glasses. "Yeah, it wouldn't be prudent,"

"It wouldn't be what?" Perry said.

Lloyd hiked up his britches.

Perry shook his head. "I guess I'll have to agree. Who won me?"

"Mrs. Carmichael," Dennis said.

"Our old school teacher?" Perry asked.

"She bought twenty tickets," Dennis said. "She's president of the Fairmount Garden Club. You get to ride in her immaculate Mercury Marquis."

"She's tickled as can be," Grady said, "You don't want to disappoint her, do you?"

"I see this as a great marketing opportunity," Dennis said.

"Is that something that they taught at Alto?" Perry said.

"That boy reads all the time," Grady said. "You should see the books stacked in his room."

Perry pulled on his cigarette and smashed it out in the ashtray. "All right. But, no more of this lottery business, all right?"

"We've already had two more drawings," Grady said. "I'm telling you it's good for the community. We're making sure the winners are retired people."

"You're messing with the results?"

"One's a veteran of D-Day. He's just proud as can be to give you a ride. The other is Mrs. Scott. You remember Mrs. Scott?"

"I almost married her daughter. When I got back from Vietnam I found out she had left out of here and become a stewardess with Eastern. And all that time she was writing me letters like she was waiting on me and couldn't wait to get married. Just stringing me along. What else do you boys got up your sleeves?"

"Just some more benefit rides like to a Civil War re-enactment site in the spring," Dennis said. "It's just up the road in Resaca. We've also been talking to the NASCAR people."

"My God. Don't y'all think this thing may have gotten out of control?"

"We've been doing a lot of good I think," Dennis said, nodding at Grady.

Grady nodded. "Why don't I brew up us some coffee. You want me to scramble you up some eggs?" Grady sidled into the kitchen. He peeked into the fridge. "Forget the eggs. Coffee, too. Son, we've got to get you some groceries." Grady looked at Dennis. "Call Sissie and have her go to Calhoun and fill Perry's refrigerator and cabinets with some groceries. She's been here, she should know what he needs."

Dennis pulled out his phone. "I'll text her." He walked down the hall of the trailer.

"You probably need toilet paper and stuff like that, too, don't you son?" Grady said.

"Yeah, I'm about down to using those newspapers you left for me to read."

"We'll send Sissie out here," Grady said. "She's got the checkbook. You tell her what you need." Grady walked through the trailer. "I told that girl to come over here twice a week and clean."

"I've been wondering who's been in here," Perry said. "This place hadn't been vacuumed and dusted in months. I think it looks great. Like it has had the woman's touch. I'm terrible at keeping house. I'll go hungry before I'll fix myself something to eat."

Grady stuck his head in the hall bathroom. "She said it took her three weeks to get this place to a point where she'd allow her kids inside."

"It wasn't too good I moved in."

"And you allow yourself to live in such filth?"

"It was all I could afford. I've just learned to ignore it as best I can."

"You still having trouble with the bugs since I had the pest control people spray?"

"I hadn't noticed any in a while."

"You can tell nobody's cooked in this kitchen. It's spotless."

"Like I said, I don't cook. I barely have the gumption to make coffee."

"Son, you can't live off cigarettes."

"You know, I need to be out there in all kinds of weather—" Perry said.

"—Sure, sure," Dennis said. "To keep it real. We got to keep it authentic."

"Keeping it real, keeping it real," Grady said.

"That's real important, Dad."

"I can't be seen to be hiding from people," Perry said.

"Sure," Dennis said. "We need to be transparent."

"Y'all remember, it's me that's on probation. I got to go to AA today."

"Well . . ." Grady said.

Dennis said, "I'm even thinking about a ride across Georgia for the soldiers—"

"Y'all are not listening to me." Perry said.

"We can get a couple of Hummers," Dennis said. "Wouldn't that be cool to have a couple of them to escort you down the highway? Think of the media coverage I could get us. Think of the donations."

Perry took a step toward the bathroom. "Hold on. I'm doing this because I'm on probation. I'm not trying to save the world here."

"This thing has gotten bigger than any of us could have imagined," Dennis said. "You've become an icon, a national figure. You represent the little man over the big man. They can't revoke your probation now. You've done too much, now. With the money we've taken in . . . ."

"What are you talking about?" Perry asked.

"Hey, Dad," Dennis said. "I've got an idea how we can protect Perry."

Perry walked into the bathroom and peed with the door open.

"How's that?" Grady said.

"We can do like those people who ride their bicycles across country. We'll follow Perry with a motor home, or like Junior's red monster truck. That way we can protect Perry from traffic and can advertise out businesses."

"I like it. Yeah, I like it a lot," Grady said.

Perry flushed the toilet and stood facing the hall zipping his jeans. "All thanks to Perry."

He brushed his teeth and shaved. Yawning to his bedroom, he armed into a plaid shirt, pulled on a pair of white socks, combed his thick hair, and stomped into his steel toed boots.

"Who's going to take me to my AA meeting?"

"Dennis," Grady said. "You sit in there with him. You need it, too."


6.


He preferred the morning commute. If there were no carcasses, it was the simple meditation of dew, the sunrise, the birds flitting about, the scents of the vegetation. He'd almost been able to block out vehicle sounds, the air blasts after a car or truck passed, and exhaust.

Since the press coverage, sometimes people stopped on the side of the road and waved or photographed him as he went by. He didn't like to stop on the way to work. But on this morning, a young family unloaded out of a rusty minivan with Indiana plates. Five children, the oldest twelve, the youngest not yet walking held by her mother. The father, an excited little bearded man waved Perry down while videotaping him approaching. Perry stopped, and turned down the engine.

"How are you doing, Mr. Elrod?" the man asked.

"Fine, fine. How are you folks?"

"We saw the story about you on the news. My wife and I wanted to come down here and meet you. We admire what you're doing." The man waved his wife over. Perry turned off the engine.

"This is my wife Karen. I'm Keith. And these are out children." The children hid around their mother's legs except for the two oldest who squinted at Perry. "The two oldest are Luke and Paul. Then there is Lucy and Emma. And the baby is Katlin."

"Hey, kids. Nice to meet you ma'am."

"It's very nice to meet you," the mother said.

"How about a family picture?" Perry said.

"Do you mind?" the mother said.

"No, ma'am."

Perry and the mother and children grouped together round Perry's lawnmower. "Say pickles," the father said. Then Perry took a photo of the family.

Perry started the lawnmower, waved and moved along the roadside grass. He didn't see the pickup come up from behind and slow, or the four helmeted and goggled people standing in the bed bring out small rifles. He put his arm over his head and fell off the mower into the water filled ditch. He heard yelling and screaming as he lay in the ditch, being shot repeatedly. The yelling stopped and there was screeching tires. After a moment, he pushed himself up. People called to him from the road. He looked up. He could not open his eyes. "Don't move, I've called 911." He was led crawling out of the ditch. The Indiana mother, a nurse, turned him on his back in the grass and laid him on a blanket. "Don't open your eyes, Mr. Elrod. You've got paint all over your face."

"Did somebody get the tag on that truck? Did anybody see what happened?"

"Has anybody got any bottled water? I need some water to wash his eyes out."

7.

"Well, Mr. Elrod, you've made the news again."

Perry's eyes were gauzed over.

"You were supposed to come see me today. Then I saw the news and here you are. They say that you are going to be up and walking in no time. You don't need to worry about your probation until you're out of the hospital."

The back of his hand felt her badge clipped to her belt, her holstered semiautomatic pistol. There was something he needed to ask. It was the lawnmower. He knew she was going to get onto him about it, whether it was legal to drive it.

"Don't say anything, Mr. Elrod. Lay back down. We'll talk later. I'm glad you're all right. That was some attack you survived." She patted his arm. "The meanness of people . . . It surprises me every day." She still held his arm. "Well, I just wanted to come see you. Get your rest. Mind your doctors. That's the most important thing. Take care. Good-bye."

8.

"We're going to have to get you a mower with a seat," Grady said.

"Y'all know I can't do that," Perry said.

He'd been out of work three weeks. The gauze had been removed from his eyes. He wore large sunglasses. It was difficult to stand for any longer than fifteen minutes. Concrete floors were torture. He wore an elastic brace to support his lower back and his still tender ribs. A walking cane to lean on helped to hobble around. The doctor told him he shouldn't go back to work for ten weeks.

The medical bills were mounting. Dennis put the news of Perry's attack on their website and facebook page. Grady set up a fund, and donations streamed in to pay Perry's medical bills, child support, trailer rent, utilities, groceries, and anything else.

"She's gotten wise to the lawnmower," Perry said. "I don't care how much good we've been doing. I think she gone put me in jail."

"Naw she ain't. We'll go to the newspapers. Hell, son, people will storm her office doors if she does. You're like Robin Hood."

"Robin Hood. I like that," Lloyd said.

"It'll create a huge civil rights movement behind you," Dennis said. "People won't stand for it."

"There ain't no way I can stand on a lawnmower between Fairmount and Rydal, anymore. Not the way I'm beat up."

Grady had a lawnmower catalogue. "We're working on something."

"I consulted with a lawyer the other day," Dennis said.

"Who was that?" Grady said.

"Friedman."

"Your lawyer," Grady said. "Did you get your thing straightened out?"

"He thinks he can get my charges dismissed. Those prosecutors just hate to see him coming."

"What did he say about Perry?"

"He said as long as Perry uses the lawnmower to *cut the grass* it can't be considered an instrument of transportation. That would be like him cutting his grass

around his trailer or working for a landscaper. He said he
represented a fellow once before like that and got him off."

"But that wasn't what the judge told me when he
sentenced me," Perry said. "Did you tell him I was riding
the lawnmower on the side of the road – using it to get to
and from work?"

"It doesn't matter. You're cutting the grass. That's
the difference. You're not just riding it back and forth."

"But you told him?"

"Yeah, yeah, I told him. It doesn't matter, he said.
We're a go."

9.

While he was out of work, Ms. Demond had him
work the desk at the animal control office to complete his
forty hours of community service. Grady drove him. He
showed up fifteen minutes early every day.

It wore on his mind to take the donated money to
pay his bills. He went back to work three weeks before the
doctor cleared him. His supervisor found him something in
the warehouse where he could sit a good part of the day.
Grady and the Rainy Day Drivers got him to and from
work. Getting to work on the lawnmower was physically
impossible. He couldn't stand and balance and hold the
handlebars and take all the jarring and shaking.

Grady ordered a new lawnmower like the old one,
including a seat on the platform. Dennis modified it with
extra shock absorbers. It took Perry another month to
recover enough until he could ride it. Grady and Dennis
escorted him in the morning and afternoon. The commutes

took longer because he drove slower over the ruts and holes and humps.

Benefit rides started again: one to raise money for a little girl with leukemia; another for wives of soldiers fighting in Iraq and Afghanistan; for the County Sheriff's Department and Fire Department to purchase new equipment; and for the highway beautifier's movement for Mothers Against Drunk Drivers.

On the last day of the month, on his way back from work, Ms. Demond drove alongside Perry and waved. She pulled her car off to the side of the road and took some photographs of Perry as he drove up on the lawnmower. He didn't pose as he usually did for tourists.

"The ditch grass looks great," she said.

He took off his cap and wiped his forehead and face.

"That a new lawnmower?"

"Yes, ma'am."

"How are the ribs and back?"

"Sore. But I grit and bear it. I wear this brace. It's hot, but I wouldn't be able to make it without it."

"Going to physical therapy?"

"I was. It didn't seem to help."

"I was noticing your lawnmower. It's got a seat. You're sitting on it."

"I tried the old one, but it was too rough on my body."

"You know I let the old one slide. I still think it was a violation of your probation, but then you became this celebrity . . . You should have been having somebody give you a ride."

She handed him a paper.

"What's this?"

"It's a show cause warrant. It says that you are to appear next week for a hearing to show cause why you should not be arrested for violating you probation. If it's shown that you violated your probation for this riding lawnmower, then I'm going to ask that the remainder of your probation be terminated."

Perry read over the paper.

"Make sure you appear on time or a warrant will be issued for your failure to appear and you'll be put in jail without a hearing." She got in her state car and drove away.

10.

The judge found that Perry's new lawnmower was a motorized vehicle and that by riding it along the state highways of Georgia he violated his probation.

Ms. Demond requested that the balance of his probation be terminated. Perry's lawyer asked the judge take into consideration all the mitigating facts. He argued that Perry was actually cutting the grass just like any landscaping employee as the sign read on the lawnmower. He was not merely riding it along the side of the road. He asked the court to continue Perry on probation.

"That's a state road and we have state employees paid by the taxpayers to cut the grass on the side of all state roadways." The judge then terminated Perry's probation. He noted that Perry's first lawnmower technically may have been a motorized vehicle, but he was not asked to rule on that issue. He commended Perry on his resourcefulness, using the lawnmower for benefiting the county as well as himself. He noted his community outreach beyond the court ordered community service. "Many people received a great deal of assistance from your benefit rides, not to mention the county's Fire and Sheriff's Department. I commend you for that." The judge then ordered that the balance of Perry's probation be terminated but suspended.

"You may go, Mr. Elrod," the judge said.

Perry stood stunned. He turned to Mr. Friedman. "What's that mean?"

The lawyer attorney faced him, shook his hand, smiled. "You're done. No more probation."

Ms. Demond walked passed him, shaking her head, smiling.

Everyone was smiling – Grady, Lloyd, Dennis. They all shook hands. The reporters interviewed him, got his reaction.

11.

Until the end of the twelfth month the Department of Motor Vehicles wouldn't give him back his driver's license. He still had to drive his lawnmower to and from work. There were benefit rides almost every weekend, signing autographs, smiling with strangers for photographs, talking with reporters, making speeches against drunk driving.

When he got his license back, he paid cash for a used red Chevy pickup with an air conditioner. Months later, losing the lawnmower was like a man losing his blindness. He lost his specialness.

On the way home from work on a hot day, the air conditioner cooling him, there were orange Department of Transportation signs on the road warning *Mowers Ahead.* He slowed, moved into the other lane, giving room for the mowers. Then he eased back into the northbound lane, building speed. Home was not too far in the distance.

# THE HOLDING ROOM

He could not control his shaking. His hands and feet were numb. Waiting on his dad to come get him, he laid his head on the table and concentrated against his burning need to pee.

The windowless cinderblock room was bleached in fluorescent light. There was space for a flimsy aluminum table with a faux wood top and three thinly padded chairs that scuffed the gray Formica tile. It was in this room, in the detective section of the local police department, fourteen-year-old Jeremy Jackson found himself, isolated at 9:45 p.m. on November 4th with frigid air blowing from the ceiling vent.

The detectives' chatter and laughter bobbed through the holding room door.

"Who's going to interview the kid?"

"Nobody. He's not talking."

"I can get him to cooperate," hollered a different voice.

"We're not doing anything."

"You want me to check on him -- see if he needs anything? He's been in there for a while."

"His old man's FBI. Nobody's going in there."

After some time things quieted except for the air sluicing through the vent. His nose ran. His sneezes were eruptions: rough and deep. He used his shirt; wiped his hands on his shorts.

The door opened. His father entered with a detective.

He sat up.

"Let us know if you need anything, Agent Jackson," the detective said.

His father thanked the detective as he closed the door without a noise.

"You're shaking," his father said.

Jeremy nodded, balled up and rocking.

His father took off his suit jacket and wrapped it around Jeremy's bony shoulders.

"I need to go to the bathroom," Jeremy said, barely audible.

"Have you talked to anybody?"

"No, sir. I did what you said."

His father pulled a chair next to him. "Did they say why you're here?"

"Not really."

"A store was robbed and the clerk behind the counter was shot."

Jeremy stopped rocking. "Was he killed . . . Was he shot bad?"

"I don't know. There was a video camera, but there wasn't a tape in the machine." His father surveyed the room. "I don't know why these people don't make sure their equipment is working properly." He bent close to Jeremy's ear. "Were you out with any friends two nights ago?"

"No, sir. I was home studying for tests."

"If you know anything about this thing that could help the investigators catch who's involved, tell me so we can go home."

"How can I when I was home?"

"Keep your voice down." His father looked under the table, both their chairs.

"I don't know anything, dad."

His father studied the drop ceiling tiles, especially in each corner of the room.

Jeremy hunched over and wrapped his dad's jacket tighter around him up to his eyes.

His father sat next to him again. Almost whispering, his father said, "Well they think you know something. They think you were involved."

Jeremy shook his head. "No way."

"They showed me a scarf they recovered outside the store." His father thumbed the indentation formed by his missing wedding ring. It had taken him a long time to decide what a widower was supposed to do about his ring; what was appropriate, if there were any rules. He wore it for over two years. One week his hand swelled and the ring cut painfully into his finger. During the night the swelling went down and the ring slipped off without a tug. "I bought the scarf for her for . . . France . . . a long time ago . . . before you were born. It doesn't matter . . ."

Jeremy's sobs came as a sudden torrent. He tried to hide it by putting his face into his armpit. But there was no way to withhold the sobs. His father swept his arms over him like a large bird laying its wings over its young for protective cover.

Jeremy cleaned his nose and eyes with the handkerchief his father retrieved from his inside jacket pocket. Jeremy stared at the wall opposite. In a boy's unchanged voice, he slowly told his father the details of what happened.

His father was quiet for what seemed a whole day. Then he said, "What did you do with my gun?"

Just as softly and exhaustedly paced, Jeremy replied, "I took out the clip, buried it in a dumpster, behind the grocery store, next door."

"And the bullets, son?"

"I dropped them all, all of them, down a storm drain, down the street from our house, during the storm, last night."

"There was a storm?"

"You were asleep. I snuck out real quick . . ."

"You turned off the alarm system and . . . I didn't wake up? . . . You've done this before?"

Jeremy looked past his father's face.

"This night? Of the robbery?"

His father's chin quivered. He'd never seen his father cry except at the funerals.

"The man is in the ICU, at the hospital. It looks like he's going to pull through and be okay."

"I, I never pointed it. I didn't want to shoot. I just wanted to get out quick as I could."

"It doesn't matter, son."

"I pointed at the ceiling."

"It doesn't matter. You were robbing his store." His father glanced at the vent. "They do keep it very cold in this room. You know why? It's to keep people uncomfortable. That's what they want – to keep people very uncomfortable. They use all kind of tricks and tactics to get people to talk themselves into jail – whatever is needed to get confessions. That makes the investigation."

His father stood on his chair and ran his fingers over the vent.

"What are you doing?"

"Make sure they're not listening in on us."

"I wish Mom was here."

Since the accident, his father had turned into a white haired skeleton that rambled around the house most nights smoking on the back deck, one cigarette after another, drinking vodka mixed with cranberry juice until he collapsed with a pillow on the living room floor – the only place he said he could comfortably sleep since the accident. They had stopped going to the grief counselor; stopped going to mass. Jeremy tried to think of things to do – take in a movie or a sports game, or an afternoon of bowling, nine holes of golf, or a weekend camping and fishing. His dad took no interest in anything, claiming he hadn't recovered enough from his injuries to allow him to enjoy those things anymore.

"I want to go home," Jeremy said.

His father kissed him on the forehead and stood. "I love you very much, Jeremy. Very much."

"I really need to go to the restroom."

"I'll take care of it."

His father left the room.

Two detectives – one squat, the other with the face like a goat's – burst into the room. His father stood at the threshold. The goat-face detective sidled behind his chair, stood him, and brought his arms behind his back.

Jeremy's throat seized and tears welled in the corner of his eyes.

Goat-face jumped back.

"What's happened?" the squat detective said.

"He's peed himself." The handcuff made a metallic clicking sound as it tightened round Jeremy's wrist.

"Dad. What's going on?"

The squat one screened Jeremy from his father. "We're placing you under arrest."

Goat-face palmed Jeremy's shoulder and looped the handcuff chain with the fingers of his other hand and pushed him out of the room, past his father.

"Dad, aren't we going home?"

"They had to be told. It was the best thing . . ."

"I thought we were going home?"

"We're going to get this straightened out, son."

The goat pushed him down the hall almost at a jog.

"It's all going to work out," his dad shouted. "It's all . . . Yes . . . You'll be home soon . . . soon, soon."

Made in the USA
Charleston, SC
01 June 2012